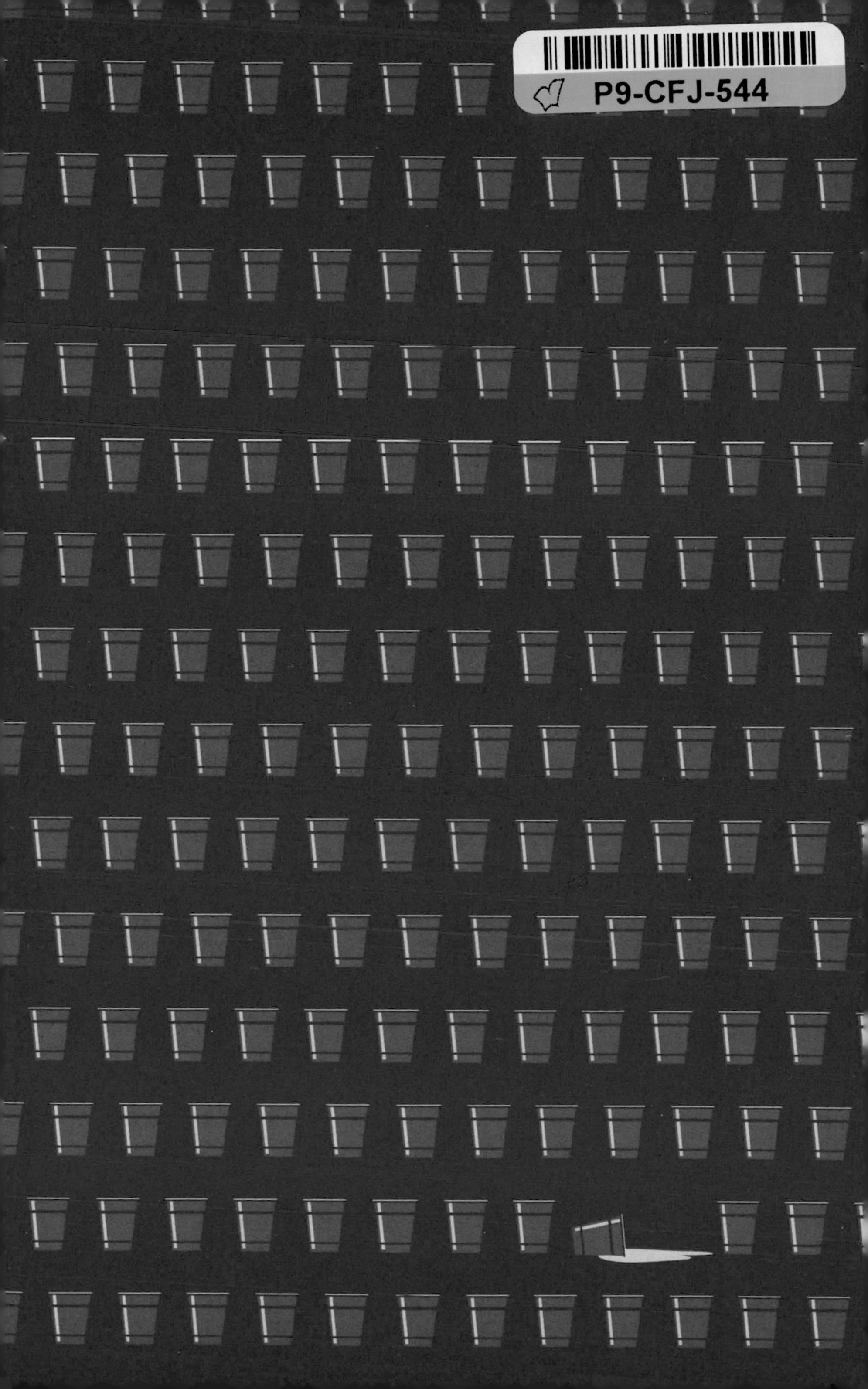

FRESH

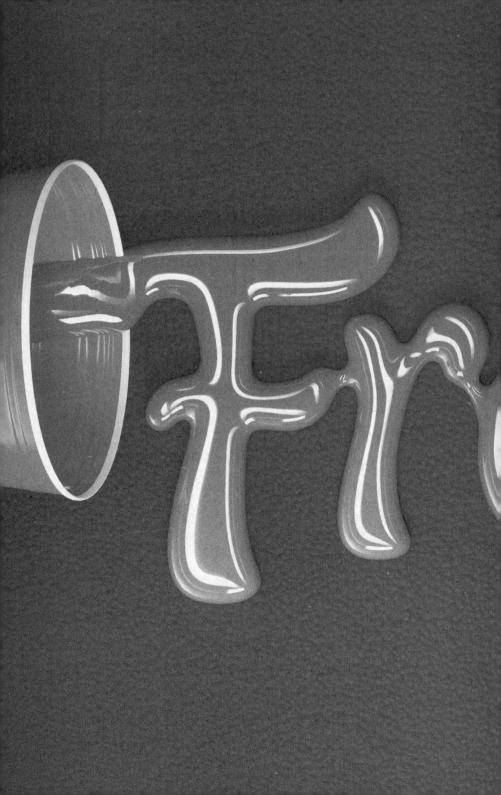

**MARGOT
WOOD**

AMULET BOOKS · NEW YORK

Cataloging-in-Publication Data has been applied for and may be obtained from the Library of Congress.

ISBN 978-1-4197-4813-4

Text copyright © 2021 Margot Wood
Book design by Hana Anouk Nakamura

Published in 2021 by Amulet Books, an imprint of ABRAMS.

Printed and bound in U.S.A.
10 9 8 7 6 5 4 3 2 1

Amulet Books are available at special discounts when purchased in quantity for premiums and promotions as well as fundraising or educational use. Special editions can also be created to specification. For details, contact specialsales@abramsbooks.com or the address below.

Amulet Books® is a registered trademark of Harry N. Abrams, Inc.

ABRAMS The Art of Books
195 Broadway, New York, NY 10007
abramsbooks.com

Dedicated to all my mistakes.
I wouldn't be here without you!

CHAPTER 1

ELLIOT MCHUGH, BEAUTIFUL, CHARMING, AND UPPER middle class, with a mediocre wardrobe and a hyperactive disposition, seemed to unite some of the best blessings of existence; and she had lived nearly nineteen years in the world with very little to distress or vex her.

Whoa, whoa, whoa. Let's back that shit up right here. It's super weird to be talking about myself in the third person, isn't it? It makes me sound like I'm some sort of omnipotent narrator of my own life, which is partially true, because technically this is my book, but I don't think I could write this whole thing from a third-person POV. Don't get me wrong, I'm vain but I'm not third-person-narrating-my-own-life vain. Here's how this is gonna go. I'm gonna tell you a story—probably a semi-unflattering one—and most of it will take place up here.[1] So, let's just go ahead and start this thing all over, shall we?

---

1 But sometimes I'll be down here. What can I say? I'm a girl with a healthy footnote fetish.

CHAPTER 1

HEY, HI, HELLO THERE. MY NAME IS ELLIOT MCHUGH, I'm eighteen years old and hail from Cincinnati; I'm a Leo, a (mostly) chaotic-good extrovert, a freshman at Emerson College in Boston, and I have no idea what the hell I am doing right now.

You know those epic battle scenes in fantasy movies when hundreds of dudes are fighting and it's total chaos and the young, inexperienced main dude is in the middle of it all, looking like he's about to shit his pants because he's just trying to figure out what the hell is going on while also, you know, not getting killed? That's a lot like what the first day of college feels like. I mean, that's what I *think* it feels like. I obviously have no experience fighting in fantasy battles, but the terrified look on those characters' faces is roughly the same as the one I am currently sporting, so I can only imagine that my current emotions parallel theirs.

Here I am, in the bright, marbled lobby of my new dorm, the Little Building, nestled on a pile of black trash bags filled with my crap while I wait for my dad to park the car and help me move in. The lobby right now is eerily similar to an airport on Christmas Eve when a snowstorm has just canceled all the flights. Stressed-out parents are arguing with purple shirt–wearing, moving-day volunteers over who gets to have the next empty moving bin; visibly nervous students run in all directions, towing swollen suitcases with wobbly wheels behind them as they try to avoid tripping over loose Bed Bath & Beyond bags; and small siblings loiter in everyone's way as they scan the crowds for the families they've been separated from.

It's hard to tell if everyone knows what they're doing or if they're just pretending to know and they're actually just as confused as I am. There's a girl five feet to my right, sitting alone on top of a red duffel bag, crying. I would go to her but I don't think I'm qualified to console anyone as I am dangerously close to crying myself and that's not a thing I do very often.[2] I am two seconds away from asking a purple shirt to help me when my dad finally strolls into the lobby. He slips out of the way of a luggage cart and casually leaps over a row of suitcases.

"What took you so long?" I ask as I struggle to stand from my trash pile. He extends a hand and pulls me up, and I notice

---

2 At least not in public.

this goofy, triumphant grin on his face—a look I am, unfortunately, very familiar with. "Seriously?" I deadpan. "You've been playing Ping-Pong all this time?"

His grin widens as he starts gesturing wildly with his hands. "They have a brand-new table in the dorm down the street, I think it's called Piano Row? Have you been there yet? Anyways, I was walking by and saw a table in the lobby and no one was using it so I got this other dad to play and I totally smoked his ass. It was great." I honestly do not know how my dad got through college, let alone medical school, because he is the most ADHD adult I have ever met. He's more easily distracted than I am. Under normal circumstances, having the Fun Dad is pretty fucking great, but moving into my first dorm room is not a normal circumstance. He looks at my bags on the floor and the frenzy around us and says, "So is this where you'll be sleeping or do you have an actual room in this building?" He bounces on the balls of his feet, itchy to do *something*.

"I'm on the third floor, room 311," I tell him, and I wonder how we'll get there. For a brief moment, I think about snagging one of the big luggage carts, but considering I saw two adults nearly come to blows over one five minutes ago and the line for the elevator is nine miles long, I think it's best to do this by hand. "If you want to stay here and guard my shit, I can do this in about four trips," I say, kicking one of my lumpy garbage bags.

"What are you talking about? We can do this in one trip," he says confidently.

I narrow my eyes at him. "There is *no* way we'll be able to carry all these—" I start to say but the words die on my tongue as I watch my dad squat down and easily lift three bags and sling them over his shoulder.

"Will you be able to manage?" he teases, watching me mimic his squatting technique beside the remaining bag.

"Yes," I scoff. "*Of course* I can."

"First one up the stairs wins!" he shouts and then takes off ahead of me.

I try to lift the last garbage bag but it's heavy as balls, so I drag it behind me as I follow him up to the stairwell, the bag knocking against my heels with every step. It takes me a week to climb two flights of stairs because a) I'm out of shape and b) my bag ripped open somewhere along the way, leaving a trail of thongs and socks in my wake, but eventually I reach the top and step out onto the third floor—my new home.

Annnnnd, holy shit my new home is LOUD. The halls are clotted with a menagerie of families either hugging, crying, or fighting over the proper way to build IKEA LACK tables. There are empty cardboard boxes, open suitcases, and half-built furniture scattered everywhere. A person wearing a vampire cape sits in the middle of the hall playing on a Nintendo Switch. The soundtrack to *Hamilton* blasts out of one room and Black Sabbath booms out another, a roll of toilet paper whizzes by my head, and someone in a *Scream* mask sprints down the hall in one direction while a girl vlogging on her phone with a selfie stick passes by us going in the other direction.

Dad and I pick our way through the gauntlet until we find my room, #311, all the way at the other end. Dad walks right in, the weighted door closing behind him, but I don't follow, not yet. This feels like a Pivotal Life Moment®—a rare and particular subtype of moment that seems more significant than other, regular moments—and I have two choices here, so let's make this an interactive reading experience, shall we?

THE
ELLIOT MCHUGH INTERACTIVE
EXPERIENCE!

OPTION A: Should I embrace this Pivotal Life Moment®, stare at my reflection in the shiny metal door handle, and do the Disney princess thing where time slows down, music swells, and I ruminate on the fact that once I walk through this door, I leave my past behind and step into my future?

OPTION B: Or should I just open the damn door already and walk through?

If you selected option A, please proceed to the next footnote.[3] If you selected option B, please proceed to the next sentence.

For most things in life, I like to set the bar real low, that way I am never disappointed—it's my patent-pending method of living and it works in nearly every situation, including this one.

This room is, essentially, a ten-by-fourteen-foot box of blah. I am very glad I did not succumb to the expectations of what a college dorm room should look like based on what Hollywood (and the Emerson catalog) have tried to sell me, because otherwise this big reveal would have been a major bummer. Everything is painted this bright, kinda yellowish, kinda off-white color: the walls, the floor, the ceiling. It's a fluorescent-lit beige shoebox and the monotony of it is only interrupted by one window facing a brick wall four feet away, a collection of unnaturally shiny wood furniture, and two twin bed frames with blue vinyl mattresses bunked in the corner. It's quaint, in an insane asylum kind of way.

The first thing I do upon entering my room is climb inside the ugly wooden wardrobe and close the mirrored door behind me. It smells like mothballs and wet feet but that's beside the

----

3 It's strange to go from one day living at home with my family like I have for the past eighteen years to the next day living in a strange building with strange people, sharing a strange room with a stranger. I've spent the past three months, the past year really, preparing for this moment, but nothing can truly prepare you for the first time you leave home—you just have to do it. And as I stand here, outside my room, pondering my life in the middle of a crowded hall, a large man carrying heavy boxes that obscure his view accidentally knocks me over and in the commotion he drops the boxes on my face and I am crushed to death. End of story. Proceed to acknowledgments.

point, which is if it's big enough to hold me, it's big enough to hold all my shit and I won't have to make a last-minute online purchase for more storage. I know I was supposed to spend the summer planning for this day, but, well, I kinda put it off and since my mom was in charge of moving my older sister, Izzy, to medical school last year, it was my dad's turn this time around, and let's just say he spent more time planning weird excursions to pepper our Cincinnati-to-Boston road trip than he did making sure I got everything I needed. "Meh, we'll figure it out when we get there," he said as we hit the road three days ago, and that's why I have only four bags full of unfolded clothes and an unopened bedding set my mother bought in bulk from Costco five years ago when my little sister, Remy, was going through her sleep-pee stage.

Satisfied with the size of my new wardrobe, I step out of it and politely announce, "After careful research, I am comfortable declaring that there is no passage to Narnia in there."

"That's because it's *Narnia business*," Dad says and starts laughing at his own awful joke. "Do you get it? *Narn-ia business*, like none of ya—"

"Yes, Dad, I get it," I groan.

He glances around the room and sits on the bottom bunk bed, bouncing a little to test the mattress. "So what do you think? Should we keep 'em bunked?" I shake my head no because bunked beds give me middle-school summer camp vibes, so we work together to lift the top bunk off and arrange it against the opposite wall. "You're lucky your mother stayed home," he says as we maneuver the bed I have chosen into place. "Last year when we dropped Isabella off at Columbia, your mother tried to sage the room while Remy rifled through Izzy's clothes and put a pair of underwear on her head just as Izzy's roommate showed up."[4]

I would say I really wish my mom and sisters were here to move me in but that would be a lie. The truth is, I am relieved to be doling out my goodbyes in installments. As much as I like to pretend they all annoy me, it would be too painful to say goodbye to my whole family at once—it's easier on my heart this way.

I look around the room, unsure of what to do next. Since I didn't bring anything to decorate with, I decide to unpack first. I tear open my designer trash sacks and dump all my belongings on top of the rock-hard mattress with a mysterious stain in the center that I'm just going to pretend isn't there. A week ago, my mother suggested I organize my clothes by type and label them in those vacuum-seal ziplock bags. Naturally, I chose to ignore her, and now I deeply regret that decision because I can already see I did *not* bring enough underwear and also seem to have forgotten a winter coat, but whatever, that's a problem future Elliot will deal with in a few months when it gets cold.[5]

---

4   And now the image of my little forest sprite of a sister running around with a hot pink thong on her head is forever burned in your memory. Sorry about that.

5   Or in, like, a week when I discover Boston is frigid nine months of the year.

"What's that?" Dad asks, as I stare at my clothes mountain, willing it to put itself away. He points to a lump hiding beneath my unopened comforter. I reach under it and pull out a gift I didn't notice before but immediately know is a present from Remy by the glittery unicorn wrapping paper that has now unintentionally glitter-bombed all my clothes. I unwrap the box and find a purple box of dryer sheets inside with a note attached to the front. I can't help but smile as I read the note my little sister left for me:

> Hey Big Sis,
>
> You're a college student now! That's so cool! I wish I was in college too because then I wouldn't have to be away from you. We could be roomies again, like when I was little! I wanted to write you a letter and hide it in your bag so when you got to school you would find it and then you wouldn't feel alone. I got you some new dryer sheets from this limited edition scent collection. I had to use my allowance to buy it so you better use it, Smelliot. Don't forget to put one inside your pillowcase so your dreams smell nice. Okay, that's it. Love you, kthxbye!
>
> ~ Remy ~
>
> PS: I'm taking your room now that you're at college. Mom said I could.

It almost hurts, smiling this much. I'm not at all surprised to find dryer sheets hidden in my duffel bag. It's sweet that my little sister loves me enough to give me a whole box instead of just one sheet. Remy has been obsessed with dryer sheets ever since she was four years old and Mom found her playing inside the dryer one afternoon. Since then, Remy has had this semi-unhealthy infatuation with them. She likes to put them in everyone's dresser drawers, purses, and backpacks. She's even taped the sheets to the front of every fan and air conditioner in our house and car.

"Whoa, Remy gave you an *entire* box of dryer sheets?" Dad looks shocked when he sees the box.

"I know, I never thought I'd live to see the day."

"She's going to miss you, you know," Dad says in a surprising display of tenderness.

"I know," I tell him. "I'd miss me too, I'm awesome." I take a few sheets and use them to line my dresser drawers so my clothes will smell like Lavender Dreams™—a vast improvement over the dresser's previous rich bouquet of stale armpits and mothballs. I finish lining the bottom drawer just as I catch my dad checking his watch, and it sends a wave of panic through my system.

His spidey-senses must be tingling or my face is betraying my emotions because he takes one look at me and says, "Don't worry, I'm not going anywhere." He takes a seat on the unmade bed and starts rifling through my stuff. "Where are all the road trip snacks, or did we eat all of them?"

I toss him the snack bag. He reaches in and pulls out a box of Cheez-Its while I go back to prolonging his departure by taking my sweet fucking time putting my clothes away in the dresser. With one hand he's eating Cheez-Its and with the other he starts throwing articles of clothing at me from across the room, forcing me to put them away faster—a ritual for us ever since he taught me how to do laundry when I was a little kid and *fuuuuuck*, this memory is making me feel very anxious again. This would be easier if he weren't here, if he had just dumped me on the curb, called out a line like, "Don't screw up!" and taken off. I hate this, I hate the buildup. I'd rather just get it over with and rip the Band-Aid off. He checks his watch again and *fuck fuck fuck*. I'm acutely aware that we have only minutes, maybe half an hour left before he leaves and I know he's not leaving forever. I'll see him in a few months when I go home for winter break, but I can't stop counting the seconds as they tick by, wishing I could make them last longer. I have waited so long for this day, the day when I would be officially free to start my new life as a college student, a life without parents and curfews and a forced daily serving of vegetables, but now that it's here, now that the time has arrived for me to say goodbye to him, to my family, to that old life . . . it feels like I'm not even remotely ready for this.

Fuuuuuuuuuuuuuck.

My dad tosses me the last pair of socks and I shove it in the back of the dresser. I look around for some other excuse to stall him, to keep him here as long as I can, but I'm short on ideas—and time. He stands, brushing orange crumbs off his lap, and pulls his car keys out of his back pocket.

I have a lump in my throat, my heart is beating so fast my limbs are vibrating, and I am scared. I have this urge to kick and scream, cry and beg my dad to stay and never leave like I did when I was a little girl and had trouble with separation anxiety. But at the same time, I really just want him to get the fuck out of here already.

I deeply dislike this. TOO MANY FEELINGS.

I pace around the room and decide the best thing to do right now is to avoid emotions and wash my new sheets. I should have done this before I got here—everyone knows you should wash new sheets before using them for the first time. Yes, this is exactly the best moment to do some laundry. I start ripping open the bedding set when Dad comes over and drops a heavy hand on my shoulder to still me. I look up at him, fully prepared to laugh at whatever dad joke he's about to crack, but *oh shit*.

He looks . . . somber.

He's being serious.

He is *never* serious.

Last year, we were dining out as his favorite restaurant when an elderly gentleman at the table next to us started choking on a piece of overcooked meat and even as my dad was giving the guy an emergency tracheostomy right there, in the middle of the Outback Steakhouse dining room, he was cracking jokes with the old dude's family and making casual conversation with the terrified waitstaff. The *only* time I have ever seen him look this way was when I was thirteen and he told me my grandfather, Pappy, had died. So yeah, this look he is giving me right now? It's scaring the shit out of me. It means I can't hide from this. I can't just rip the bandage off and get it over with. I have to give my dad a proper goodbye. I know I will regret it if I don't. I take a deep breath, turn into his big chest, and hold onto him.

"Dad, please don't go," I choke out. He wraps an arm around me and squeezes tight.

"It's scary, but you'll be okay. I'll always be here." He kisses the top of my head and for once I don't try to squirm away. "Elliot, this time in your life, what you're about to do . . . it's exciting! You should be excited! Your life is one long story and this is only the next chapter. You know the knights who go off and slay dragons in those fantasy books I used to read to you as a kid? It's your turn now. You are about to embark on a big adventure, and it's going to be hard and some parts will be scary but you gotta make the most out of it. Go slay some dragons, my girl."

And now I am laughing and crying and he's laughing and crying and we're both laughing and crying in a strange little dorm room in a strange little building in a strange city that I will hopefully, someday, come to think of as my home. Dad pulls away enough to wipe away some tears that have formed in the corners of his eyes. I give him one more tight hug.

"Make good choices, Elliot," he says as he gives me one last kiss on top of my head. "You will always be my most favorite middlest daughter."

"I'm your *only* middlest daughter," I say back and he laughs as I finally let him go.

He stretches, all his bones cracking in unison, and just as he is about to leave, he turns back and gives me a wink and that's it. He pulls the door closed behind him and he's gone.

My dad is gone.

I am on my own.

I start to panic: My face burns and my eyes swell up with tears again. I pace back and forth, rapidly shaking my hands as I try to steady the rising ache in my chest. *Fuck it.* I quit trying to hold it all back and finally let go. I let go of the fear and doubt and sadness that's been building inside me and for a full minute I scream and cry into the pillow I brought from home so no one can hear me.[6]

And once it's out, I instantly feel better.

A good cry can do that.

I dry my eyes with a dryer sheet—because I forgot to bring tissues and that is all I have—and it reminds me that a good way to keep yourself from getting stuck is to just keep going. I need something to do—I need to give my hands a task other than nervously running my greasy Cheez-It fingers through my road-trip hair. I look around my barren room and realize I am sitting on top of the answer. This ugly-ass mattress wrapped in swishy, waterproof vinyl needs to be covered and

---

6   I try to do most of my crying into pillows as I am not a polite crier. My cries come out in thick sobs and spastic bursts, my face reddens, my lips swell, and snot drips out of my nose.

yes, that's right, that's what I had already decided I was gonna do before: laundry.

I may not have fully prepared to leave home, I may not have brought enough underwear, I may have forgotten a winter coat, and I may have just now remembered that I left my toiletry kit in my dad's car, but the one thing I know for certain I did *not* forget is laundry supplies. You see, laundry is a deeply soothing ritual for me and it's the only chore I take great pride in.[7] I dump all the snacks out of their tote bag and fill it with the box of dryer sheets from Remy and the box of fancy, handmade detergent I can only buy from a shop online. I open my door and carefully peek out into the hall. It's still chaos, but I see no sign of my dad secretly hiding somewhere waiting to jump out and scare the crap out of me like he usually does, so I sling the tote over my shoulder, wipe away any remaining traces of tears, grab my new bedding, and set off down the hall until I find the laundry room. It's a small, narrow room with only two washers, two dryers, and a three-column vending machine offering just one option for detergent, fabric softener, and dryer sheets each. I get my new linens going in the wash and leave my tote bag full of laundry supplies on the windowsill with my name and room number written on the front for when I'll be back in half an hour to transfer everything to the dryer.

---

7   For the record, I don't really care what happens to my clothes after they've been washed and dried. They can be wadded up in the back of my closet for all I care. It's the ritual I love.

And you know what? Avoiding your feelings by unhealthily distracting yourself with menial chores always works. By the time I get back to my room, I am still missing my dad like crazy . . . *but* . . . that sadness is starting to fade while another feeling emerges. And it's the kind of feeling I am much more comfortable with: exhilaration. One hundred percent pure, unprocessed, free-range joy. As soon as I get back in my room, I close the door behind me, jump on top of that hateful mattress, and start pumping my arms up and down and running really, really, really fast in place.

HOLY SHIT, YOU GUYS.

I AM IN COLLEGE!!!!!!!!!!!!!!

WHEEEEEEEEEEEE!!!!!!!!!

MWAHAHAHAHA!!!!!!!

I cannot believe I am actually fucking doing this!

OMGGGGGGGGGG!!!!!!

So, gentle reader, are you ready to join me on this adventure? Because I am 1,000 percent ready to slay the shit outta some dragons. I cannot fucking wait to end this literal chapter and begin my new metaphorical one, because right now I feel like maybe, just *maybe*, I can do this. But before I can do, whatever *this* is, I must first get off this bed and make myself presentable because someone is knocking at my door.

Which can mean only one thing.

My roommate is here.

And it's time to put my carefully laid plan into action.

CHAPTER 2

WELL, THIS IS AWKWARD.

I had this whole plan, you know, for winning over my new roommate. It's been dubbed Project Friendship® by my little sister and we worked on this plan all summer. After roughly 120 hours of hard work, Remy and I got the Project Friendship plan from a *this is just embarrassing* place to a *this is so embarrassing it has circled around and is now totally endearing* place with an (untested) guaranteed success rate. There's even a whole choreographed dance number in the middle with expertly timed confetti poppers at the end, but the entire plan rests on my roommate entering our room alone, not surrounded by her entire extended family.

There's, like, ten of them of varying ages, and they have either a thick Russian-sounding accent or a thick Boston-sounding accent and they're all talking over one another in a competition for who can be the loudest relative ever. They squeeze through the doorway as a group, and each is carrying either a big box or a big bag or a big glass container full of food, so I have to hug the wall just to avoid getting trampled. They don't see me standing there beside my bed, looking like a Popsicle stick with two googly eyes. I can't even see my roommate yet, she's gotta be somewhere in the middle of this mosh pit.

"Are you sure this is the right room?" An older relative asks. "This doesn't look like the right room."

"Lucy, honey, did you get enough to eat? Did anyone see if they had potatoes on the menu in the dining hall?"

"Where's the furniture and her mini fridge? Ari, what did you do with the IKEA furniture? Did you bring it up?"

"Are you sure she's rooming with a girl? *Elliot* doesn't sound like a girl."[8]

"Where's the *pahhhk*? I thought this building overlooked the Boston Common?"

There are so many loud voices that those are the only sentences I can make out. I stay frozen against the white wall, absolutely still, hoping I'm pale enough to blend in and remain unnoticed, but a woman who looks in no way old enough to be an eighteen-year-old's mother spots me in the corner.

"Look, there's someone already here!" She points directly at me. "Are you Elliot, my daughter's new roommate?"

Everyone turns and looks at me expectantly.

I look at them.

They look at me.

....

8 Goddammit.

I look at them.

They look at me.

"Yes?" I say.

"ELLIOT!" They yell in unison and rush over, smothering me in one oversize group hug. I am completely swarmed by a tangle of limbs and voices and it's strikingly similar to getting attacked by a horde of zombies but with 21 percent less carnage.[9] At this point, it's unclear if they are hugging me or hugging one another, but suddenly, from somewhere in the hall, I hear a girl's voice come in hot above all the others.

"Okay, everybody out!" she orders them, and to my complete surprise, her family obeys. No McHugh has ever listened to any other McHugh and we're only five people. This girl just said one sentence and all nine thousand listened. I haven't even met this girl and already I am impressed. The family sets her stuff down on her mattress and files out of the room one by one, each taking turns to say goodbye to my roommate who still remains out of frame in the hall.

"Bye, honey," one says.

"See yah latah, kid," says another.

"Don't forget, I put the tabouli in the fridge," says the cute old lady who definitely has to be a grandma.

"I'll swing by on Tuesday with your winter gear," I hear Lucy's mom say in the hall. And then . . . I hear a throat being cleared and footsteps as she comes around the corner and into

---

9 Again, I have no way of verifying this statistic.

our room, and I finally get to lay eyes on my new roommate, Lucy Garabedian. And now it's just me, my new roommate—and the deafening awkward silence between us. She's pretty—tall and curvy with light beige skin and long, silky brown hair with full bangs that stop at her thick eyebrows. Her makeup is minimal but bold, just mascara and a matte red lip. I look at her and smile and hope she'll be the one to break the ice, but she just smiles back and fidgets with the rings on her fingers. I have no idea what to say to her since my original plan was ruined the moment her family barged through the door so . . . I panic and improvise. I rummage through the pile of snacks on my bed, grab the box of Cheez-Its, and hold it out to her.

"Cheez-Its in exchange for friendship?" I ask. I have no idea why I chose to go this route for our first introduction but it's too late now. I'm going with it.

She looks confused. "What?"

I shake the box and repeat the question. "Would you care for a Cheez-It in exchange for friendship?"

She shoves her hands into the pockets of the oversize cardigan she's wearing over her plaid dress and leans against the doorway. "Sure," she says, hesitant at first, but then more confidently adds, "but before I can accept your offer, what are the terms of this friendship?"

"What do you mean?" I ask.

"Well, you just requested my hand in friendship without providing any sort of context. I cannot enter any agreements without knowing which level on the friendship scale we will be."

I pop a single Cheez-It into my mouth as I think over my response. "Okay, how about this, you get to choose one of the following friendship types: 1) Will Hold the Elevator Door Open but Not Say Anything Once We're Inside kind, 2) Goes Out in Groups but Never Just the Two of Us type, or 3) Holding Each Other's Hair When We're Puking level."

"And what is the time limit on the friendship warranty?" she fires back and damn, this girl is quick.

"The options include first semester only, all of freshman year, or a lifetime-guarantee friendship."

She tucks a strand of hair behind her ear as she thinks about it. "Okay," she says. "I'll take Holding Each Other's Hair When We're Puking level of friendship with a lifetime guarantee. Once you're my friend, there's no turning back."

I hold the box out for her to take and she eyes it carefully, arching one of those thick, caterpillar eyebrows for a moment. And then, she stuffs her hand into the box of Cheez-Its and shoves a fistful of salty orange squares in her mouth, forever sealing our friendship fates together. I run to my dresser and grab the secret stash of confetti poppers I brought for the grand finale of my original plan and explode them in celebration.[10]

---

10 You should always have a pack of these on you. You never know when you're going to need a little spontaneous confetti in your life.

As the last piece of confetti falls to the ground, Lucy turns to leave. "Hey! Where are you going?" I call out to her. "I thought we were friends?"

"We are!" she says as she continues her way out the door. "I just have to get the rest of my stuff from the hall."

"MORE STUFF?!?" I look around at the assortment of boxes, containers full of food, suitcases, and various pieces of furniture taking up nearly every inch of our tiny room, including a big thing on wheels in the back by our brick window. "Is—is that—did you bring a *tea cart*?" I call out to her.

"Yup! It's a gift from my high school bestie!" She reenters the room, lugging two huge floral-print duffel bags behind her. "I firmly believe in afternoon tea and soon you will too."

"I can't believe how quickly your whole family goodbye went," I say as I help her heave the duffel bags onto her mattress. "I thought for sure there would have been more tears."

Lucy laughs but waves me off. "We live in Watertown, just outside Boston. My mom's bed and breakfast is, like, fifteen minutes away. My whole family lives here." Lucy rests her manicured hands on her hips and catches her breath as she looks around the room, taking in all its pathetic glory. There's not much to look at, but that doesn't appear to bother her.

"Should we set up the room? Make it look nice?" she asks.

"For sure, but fair warning, I am very unqualified to decorate. I do not live the tidy life. I live the slug life."

"Don't worry," Lucy snorts. "I'll take care of it! You can help by entertaining."

"*That* I can do!"

I do offer to help her unpack, at least, because I am an extremely nice person who wants to get to know her new roommate.[11] We spend the next hour arranging and rearranging the furniture, putting away her endless supply of floral dresses and brightly colored yoga wear, and organizing her eclectic collection of vintage mugs and loose leaf teas onto her tea cart—or I should say, Lucy spent the last hour doing all that. I was helpful for all of five minutes before I got distracted unpacking her fun jewelry collection, and now I've been lounging on my bed ever since, draped in all her jewels while I observe Lucy in her natural habitat, mesmerized at how someone can be so fastidious for so long. I watch as she meticulously decorates her side of the room: placing each object in a designated spot, moving a throw pillow here, hanging a framed photo there, making tiny, minuscule adjustments until everything is just to her liking. She tells me about how she has about ten thousand cousins, aunties, and uncles who all live within five minutes of one another, how she spent all summer splitting her time between working at her mom's B&B and waitressing at her uncle's restaurant.

And I tell her about my sisters. How my older sister, Izzy, a.k.a. The Golden Child, is a level-five pain in my ass and a second-year medical student at Columbia University in New York City and my little sister, Remy, is twelve and wants to

---

11 And because I kinda sorta love snooping through other people's shit.

be a pink jumping pony when she grows up. And after we've exchanged the SparkNotes version of each other's familial and personal backstories, the conversation drifts to the reason why we're here in the first place.

College.

Education.

School.

LEARNING.

"So what's your major?" Lucy asks as we start in on her last two unopened boxes. I rip the tape off one and discover it is completely full of tangled strands of tiny white fairy string lights.

"I, uh, haven't declared a major yet," I tell her and brace for more questions about my lack of an academic focus.

"Do you at least have an *idea* of what you'd like to major in?"

"Nope," I say. I turn over the box and dump the knotted mass onto the floor.

"That's cool, I'm sure you'll figure it out." Her words say one thing but her eyes are screaming a different truth. I choose to ignore this and shift the focus back onto her.

"What about you?" I ask as I try to detangle a bundle of lights. "What's your major?"

"I'm double majoring in public relations and marketing."

I lower my light wad and look up at her. "For real? I haven't decided on *one* major and you're already going for *two*? Damn, lady."

"I have to, I took out a ton of loans to be here! But we'll see how long I last juggling two majors at once."

"Are you one of those people that already knows what you want to do for the rest of your life?"

"Of course not, that'd be ridiculous," she says, and I breathe out a little sigh of relief. But then she adds, "I do have my five- and ten-year plans mapped out—I want to go into business with my mom, expand her B&B business into a chain all throughout New England."

"Well, shit. That's so—ambitious," I say, feeling a little inadequate, but, as I've learned from years of practice, if I ignore this feeling, it will eventually go away.

I manage to work two strands of lights free and hand them to her. She drags her desk chair over to our window and drapes the strands across the top, instantly improving our sorry excuse for a view. Then she steps off the chair and takes a few steps back, looking at her work like she's analyzing a painting for AP Art History.

"Do you think that's too many lights?" she asks.[12]

"I once read on the back of a Snapple cap that there is no such thing as too many fairy lights."

Lucy clasps her hands together and beams. She drops down, reaches under her bed, and magically produces four more boxes of lights. She holds them up for me, her face lit up.

---

12 Lol, as if I have any clue about how to make a dorm room look pretty.

"What if we cover the entire ceiling with them too? Or would that be too much? Maybe that's too much."

I stop her before she can talk herself out of it. "No, no, I like it. It'll be like we're sleeping in a planetarium. It'll be so Instagrammable."

Lucy looks skeptical. "Are you on Instagram? I couldn't find your account."

"Ohhhh, I'm on Instagram, but I don't post, I prefer to lurk." I give her a wink and she makes a face at me.

"That is so creepy! Do you use *any* social media at all?"

"Nah, I'm old-school. I prefer to air my grievances out of a window instead of on Twitter."

Together, Lucy and I finish untangling the rest of the lights and line our ceiling with rows and rows of the delicate, twinkling orbs. When we're done, we stand in the corner of the room and assess our work. I don't know how she did it. An hour ago our room looked like a panic room that ran out of funding, but now . . . now our room is what dreams are made of. At least, her side of the room is. Our ceiling and walls now glitter and sparkle, and every surface is color coordinated in soft pastels and creams. Her bed has more pillows than I have friends, and her floral down comforter is the kind you want to fall onto in slow motion. I pull out my phone and text a picture to my little sister.

And when she's done surveying her side of the room, Lucy glances over and frowns at my bed, which is still just the blue vinyl mattress. "Where are your sheets?" she asks and *ahhhhh shit*, I completely forgot I left my sheets in the wash over an hour ago.

"Be right back!" I say as I moonwalk out the door. My ass starts vibrating and it's my little sister calling me. "Hey, Remy, good timing, I'm about to do some laundry," I say into the phone as I walk down the long hall toward the laundry room. This is something my little sister and I have been doing for years: laundry and sisterly bonding. "Did you get the pic I sent you?"

"OHMYGOD," Remy screams so loud I have to hold the phone away from my ear. "YOUR ROOM LOOKS SO AWESOME!" And then, at a lower decibel, she adds, "It's giving me tons of ideas for how I'm gonna redecorate your room at home."

"What do you mean *redecorate*? I've only been gone for three days. What'd you do with all my Angelina Jolie collages?"

"Don't worry, I put them all in the basement storage room."

"So you've put my personal hero next to the cat's shit box."

"According to this show I saw on Netflix, you should get rid of anything that doesn't spark joy," she says firmly.

"*Excuse me?*" I scoff. "Late nineties and early aughts Angelina Jolie ab-so-lutely sparks joy. Have you ever seen her in *Gia*? Actually, no, you're too young for that. Watch *Tomb Raider* or better yet, watch *Maleficent*."[13]

....

13 The first time I snuck onto my parents' HBO Go account to watch that movie, *Gia*, was the first time I realized I was capable of experiencing intense sexual feelings for women. So you could say Angelina sparks joy . . . in my pants. (Sorry! I can never resist a good "in my pants" joke.)

"Don't you ever watch movies from this decade? You know, everyone hates it when you make outdated references." I can picture her now, standing in the laundry room in our house, her small hands on her hips, her blond curls shaking as she cuts me down like only a twelve-year-old can. "What are you doing right now, why is there so much noise?"

"Sorry, I'm trying to get to the laundry room to transfer my sheets to the dryer but to get there I have to pass through a gauntlet of people still moving in. There's a lot of shit going on right now," I say as I sidestep someone recording a dance routine on their phone.

"Don't say *shit*," Remy scolds. "Are you using the dryer sheets I gave you?"

"I'm about to, I left all my supplies in the laundry room."

"Aren't you worried about someone taking your stuff?" Remy asks.

"Nah, I wrote my name and room number on all my supplies so people will know it's mine." When she doesn't acknowledge my innovative solution right away, I begin to worry. "Why? Should I have not left it all in there? Do you think someone's going to steal my stuff?"

"How would I know?!? I'm only in sixth grade!" I pick up the pace because Remy's got me all panicky and come to a skidding halt when I get to the laundry room. I peer in through the glass window in the door.

"Shit."

"Don't say *shit*!" Remy says again but I've stopped listening.

"Listen, Remy, I gotta go." I try to sound as normal as possible. "Talk next week?"

"What? Why? What's going on?" she asks eagerly. She's so good at sensing the changes in my tone. I could never lie to her—she'd know instantly.

"You were right. Someone is in here," I whisper into the phone. "And she's using my detergent."

"Oooooooooh! Go kick her butt, Elliot! You should totally—" I don't hear the rest of what Remy says because I hang up on her and push open the door to the laundry room. I clear my throat to get the person's attention. Whoever this person is, she is way too dressed up for laundry. She's wearing a long, sheer, floral-print duster thing over white overalls and four-inch-heeled black combat boots.

"Hey! That's my detergent," I firmly announce to the thief's back. She still hasn't turned around, even now as I yell at her. I wave my arms in the air, trying to get her attention. "Excuse me? Hello? I'm talking to you! That's *my* detergent you're using. You can't do that."

"Anything left in public spaces is fair game," she says over her shoulder. *Who the fuck does she think she is?* On any given day, I like to radiate calm, chill vibes, but if someone is openly rude to me, it's the quickest way for me to go from zero to rage. I cross my arms in front of my chest, tilt my chin up, and rip into her.

"Hey. *Asshole*. My detergent is not *fair game*, okay? I wrote my name and room number on the box right there, see?"

"Oh, freshman," she says with a sigh, and then she turns around and *oh crap*. That face. That is one beautiful face. Long voluminous curls with short, tousled bangs soften and frame her thin, angular face. There's a smattering of freckles across her tan nose and cheeks but it's her bright green eyes that stop me in my tracks. I drop my arms and run a hand through my greasy, unwashed hair, very aware that I had just called this woman an asshole—straight to her beautiful face.

She crosses her arms and lays into me. "Let me tell you right now that if you leave your stuff out, it's public property, even if you write your name on it. No one cares here. If you leave your laptop out in the common room, step away to take a piss and come back to find it gone—no one will feel sorry for you."

I want to keep yelling at her because I'll be damned if I'll let anyone steal detergent from me—it's the good, expensive kind—but her stupid gorgeous face is making it very hard to maintain a consistent level of anger. So I just stand there and think of every possible comeback I could say that would put her in her place as well as make me seem clever and smart.

"Fuck you," I finally say. Okay, so it wasn't my finest comeback but cut me some slack, it's my first day of college and she's completely disarming me. It's that face, and hair, and those cheekbones and that stupid hot mouth. *Ahh fuck* I wanna put my mouth on that mouth.

She turns back to the washer to swipe her Emerson ID card and turns it on. "You're welcome," she says. *Aaaaannnnnnd* now I'm back to being pissed.

"*You're welcome*? Why would I thank you when you just fucking stole from me?"

She crosses her arms and looks down at me—not in the condescending way (well maybe) but the literal way because she has a couple of inches on me.

"I just gave you a valuable college life lesson that most freshmen don't learn until the second semester. So yeah, *you're welcome*."

Oh, this smug asshole is about to get an earful. Just as I open my mouth to insult her, the fucker smiles and it's the kind of panty-dropping smile that gives me full-on tender chicken.[14] I hold firm. I refuse to budge. I know if I try to say something mean, there's a 99 percent chance my mouth will betray me and I'll end up hitting on her, so I just stand there and try to convince her I hate her with my eyes. We stand there in a stare-off in the laundry room until the buzzer on the dryer breaks the tension. She picks up her empty laundry bag from the floor and smiles as she brushes passed me on her way out the door.

When I get back to the room, I tell Lucy everything. "I can't believe she did that!" Lucy exclaims as she neatly fans colorful packets of teas onto an antique floral plate and rests it atop

14 *Tender chicken* is a McHugh-coined term that means a lady wood, a female hard-on, a girl boner. The origin of the term is this: Remy invented the phrase when she was eight years old. Izzy and I went down to the basement one day and saw Remy sitting on top of a pillow while watching a show. She said, "Whenever I see two people kissing on the TV, I get tender chicken and have to stick a pillow between my legs." And in that moment, a legend was born.

her tea cart. I love that thing friends do when they get mad on your behalf at whatever unimportant thing you're complaining about even though they secretly think you're just overreacting. It's cool that Lucy and I are already at this stage in our friendship.

"Yeah, well, now we know to never leave detergent in the laundry room," I admit. My ass buzzes again with a text from Remy.

Remy: Did you get your detergent back?

Elliot: Sure did!

Remy: Coolio! gotta go school supply shopping with Mom. talk this weekend?

Elliot: Wouldn't miss it!

Remy: Miss u, big sis!

Elliot: Miss u too, smol sis.

A pang of homesickness stabs me in the heart as I stare at Remy's last text. Sure, I miss my parents, but they're still parents, which means they sometimes suck—but little sisters? Little sisters are worth missing.

Lucy approaches with caution and sits next to me on the bed.

"You okay?" Her tone is sweet and gentle.

I throw on a big dumb smile for show. "Yep, I'm great, totally great."

"I know we just met, but I'd really like to give you a hug," she says, opening her arms wide, inviting me in. "If that's okay with you," she adds on. I don't usually let strangers hug me, but I've known my roommate for two hours now and we ate friendship-binding Cheez-Its together, which *technically* means we are no longer strangers. I nod and let Lucy wrap her arms around me and I am now enveloped in the warmest hug I've ever been a part of in my entire life. This is what bathing in hot chocolate must feel like. This is what hugging clouds must feel like. I had no idea hugs could be so good.[15]

"Woo!" I say into Lucy's honey-scented hair. "We completely bypassed that whole getting-to-know-you stage of our friendship and went right into the seeing-me-cry stage, didn't we?" Lucy releases me and I'm already missing her warm embrace. I fan my eyes and shake myself out of it. "Where'd you learn to hug like that? That was some next-level hugging."

"I have six aunties and twenty-two first cousins and they *all* like to hug. Not one of them knows how to mind their own business or respect personal boundaries and we meet every Sunday for family dinners."

"I'm assuming I'm invited now that we are eternal soul mates?"

Lucy laughs and shakes her head. "Are you sure you want to be surrounded by twenty nosy Armenians as my aunties force-feed you borscht and my born-again Uncle Stan tries to

---

15 You see, most of my family sucks at hugging, with my dad being the only exception. It's like we're allergic to it. High fives, pats on shoulders or back, meaningful looks with slow subtle nods we excel at, but hugging? Nope, hugging is something we're genetically predisposed to suck at. I don't think Izzy and I have ever hugged. I kind of grew up feeling apathetic toward hugs. So, I am delighted to discover that my new roommate is the world's greatest hugger.

quote you scripture as my grandma pokes your ribs and says you're too skinny, all while my little cousins torment you until you sit and watch them play video games for two hours?"

"Lucy." I take her soft hand in mine. "As painfully loud and uncomfortably intimate as that sounds, I will never turn down *free* food." I take a deep breath—I feel better. Even though I've cried enough today to meet my usual yearly quota, I'm good. I feel good.

"What should we do now?" Lucy asks.

My face lights up the second I get an idea. "Wanna go spy on our neighbors?"

She looks at me and grins. "Hell yeah I do."

Look, I have no data to back up this claim, but I'm pretty positive that I can state, with absolute certainty, that I have the best fucking roommate of all time.

CHAPTER 3

"ARE YOU READY TO DO THIS?" I ASK LUCY AS SHE puts the finishing touches on a small whiteboard we're going to hang outside our door. "What did you write? I really hope you went with *Hello from the other side*—or *Now Streaming: Free Hugs and Tea*."

"I went with *Come on in, the water's fine*." She flips the whiteboard around to show me her handiwork and if her whole marketing/PR double major doesn't work out, she'll have an excellent backup career as a calligraphist/illustrator. She's paired perfectly scripted words with a delightful island beach scene complete with palm trees, a sandy beach, and a sparkling blue ocean. It's *almost* perfect.

"You should draw a shark fin in the water right there and maybe add a little blood around it," I say, handing the board back. She laughs at my suggestion and in thirty seconds she's worked my suggestion in.

"There," she says as she hangs her work of art on our door for all to see. "Now I'm ready." She kicks a floral doorstop under the door—because of course she would think of bringing that with her—and joins me in the hallway, but before we even have a chance to walk the two steps it takes to cross over to our neighbor's door, a loud female voice bellows through a megaphone at the other end of the hall.

"THERE IS A MANDATORY THIRD-FLOOR MEETING HAPPENING IN THE COMMON ROOM RIGHT NOW!"

Neither of us moves and as we look around, nobody else is moving either. For the first time, the hallway is dead silent . . . until the megaphone speaks again.

"Y'ALL KNOW WHAT MANDATORY MEANS . . . RIGHT?"

Lucy and I shrug as we change plans and walk in the megaphone's direction until we reach the common room.[16]

Lucy and I snag seats on one of the leather couches and as more third-floor residents file in, I study the faces of my new neighbors. There's at least four, no, five people I'd like to make out with so far. I'm about to point them out to Lucy when our resident adviser struts in and *oh fuck.*

Fuck.

Fuck.

Shit.

Fuck.

---

16 In case you need a little more world building: The third floor holds a kitchen and two common rooms made to look like living rooms with desks and couches, and the fourth floor also has access to the kitchen lounge via a small staircase. It's pretty awesome.

I shrink into the couch and hide behind Lucy in a subtle attempt to obscure my face. Our resident adviser . . . is the girl who stole my detergent. Our RA, the person who has the power to make my life a living hell, is the same person I just called an asshole—to her face!!!—no fewer than thirty minutes ago.

Cool.

This is cool.

This is totally, absolutely cool.

Given our earlier meet-ugly, I expect her to yell or talk down to us lowly freshmen, but the first thing she does when she gets to the front of the room is throw a bunch of lollipops into the air. Nobody moves at first, but then a guy at the back makes a dive for one, and suddenly there's a stampede as if they were hundred-dollar bills.

The commotion provides great cover for when I whisper to Lucy, "That's her. That's the girl from the laundry room." Lucy glances at our new RA and her eyes go wide as she gives me a *you're totally fucking screwed* face to which I reply with a *think of me after I'm dead* face.

"There, that oughta keep you guys quiet," our RA says as we all settle into our seats again. "My name is Rose Knightley and I'm your third-floor RA. Hang with me for a minute here, I'm supposed to read from this script." She grips a stack of paper and reads from it in a bored, impatient tone. "Welcome new students. Undergraduate Orientation is a week designed to show you the Emerson experience. This week marks the beginning of an important journey you will never forget," she continues. "You will meet professors who will inspire you, build friendships that will stay with you forever, and create memories to treasure for life. The Emerson experience is blah blah blah boring boring boring annnnd scene!" Rose crumples the script and tosses it behind her. She leans back against the wall and shoves her hands into the deep pockets of her white overalls. "Okay, basically *yay*, you're all here, you made it. Woo!"

"Woo!" shouts a dude somewhere in the back and everyone nervously giggles.

Rose adds, "This week is important and it's about getting the lay of the land and meeting your academic advisers and signing up for clubs, submitting your course selections, and all that jazz. I'm not going to read this whole thing because it's all the same stuff that's in your orientation packet, which I'm sure you've all read by now."

I lean over and whisper in Lucy's ear. "There's an orientation packet?" Lucy shushes me, keeping her eyes laser focused on Rose.

"Instead, I'm going to cover the basics and share some stuff I wish I had known when I was a freshman last year," Rose continues. I glance around the room and remarkably, everyone is silent and paying attention to our RA—a far cry from my days in high school where everyone was constantly shouting over the teachers. We either all managed to evolve and grow up over the summer since high school, or (more likely) we're all just too terrified of drawing attention to ourselves.

Rose takes her hands out of her pockets and starts walking around the room like she's giving a TED Talk. "Here's the only *real* important information you need to know: The health center is across the street on the third floor of the building next to the Irish bar. They have free condoms, birth control, and just about every over-the-counter drug you would need, so take advantage of that. If you are on the floor and have a health emergency during closed hours, please come see me or text me. You may also come to me for non-health-related emergencies or if you need help with anything. I am not here to babysit you, but I am here for you for any reason at any time. My room is the single at the end of the hall." She points in the direction of her room and we all turn our heads like meerkats.

Rose continues monologuing. "If I see you with booze or drugs on the floor, I am required by the school to report you, *and I will*, but please don't let the fear of getting caught stop you from seeking my help if you are in a situation that makes you uncomfortable. Okay, now onto some of the smaller stuff." She stops to pick an unclaimed lollipop off the floor, unwraps it, and pops it into her mouth before she keeps going. "Don't forget your shower shoes because, well, you'll see soon enough. Invest in noise-canceling headphones. Don't bother buying textbooks, the library carries everything you need. I'm about to sound like all your moms, but please, *please* remember to eat healthy. Just because we have a cereal bar doesn't mean you should eat from said cereal bar for every meal."

Now *that* gets my attention.

"There's a cereal bar?!?" I whisper to Lucy who shushes me again, a little more aggressively this time.[17] Rose catches me whispering and shoots death rays out of her eyes and I zip it up.

"Okay, one last announcement," Rose continues. "If I even hear *rumors* of someone getting harassed, I *will* get involved and if you are the one who does the harassing, you will damn well regret it. So let's all act like the grown-ass adults I expect you to be and treat each other with respect, okay?" Rose looks around the room, making eye contact with each and every one of us. She's so intense. I am equal parts impressed and intimidated by her ability to control a room like this—I'm actually paying attention for once in my life. "Okay, that's it, you may disperse," Rose says when no one speaks up.

The tension breaks and the room fills with chatter and energy as everyone starts to mingle and sniff one another's butts. Lucy excuses herself politely and dashes out of the common room to take a whiz, and just as I go to strike up a conversation with this hottie with a mohawk, a skinny brown arm hooks in and around my white arm.

"Don't you just love her?" This short, pretty boy asks as if we've known each other for years and are not total strangers.

---

[17] I will soon learn that not only is there a cereal bar, there is also a motherfucking WAFFLE STATION. I love college.

From his taupe wool sweater and fitted corduroy pants to his expertly groomed stubble and combed black hair, everything about him is impeccably stylish.

"Who?" I ask, looking around the room. I'm pretty intrigued by his lack of boundaries so I just go with it and follow his lead.

"The RA, Rose." He says it like I should already know this. "I heard she is majoring in costume design in the stage and screen design department and is already getting scouted by *major* Hollywood producers—and she's only a sophomore!"

"How could you possibly know that? We've only been here a few hours."

He stops midstride and gives me this little mischievous look. "It's my job to know these things." We continue walking down the hall as people pass us by on either side, but we slow down as we approach a room with an open door. "You see that cute girl?" he asks, pointing to the freshmen inside.

"Which one? They're both cute," I remark as I watch the two girls organize and arrange about nine thousand books in their room. I can't help but notice that instead of facing a brick wall and alleyway, their room has a big, beautiful bay window that looks out on the Boston Common.[18]

"The brunette on the left is Aubry, she's a stage management major, but the one I'm referring to is the pale redhead on the right. Her name is Sasha and she's kind of a social media

---

18 Jealousy, thy name is Elliot McHugh.

celebrity with more than half a million followers. You should befriend her immediately." He then spins us around and nods to a really tall white guy sitting at his desk in his room across the hall from Sasha and Aubry. "And across the hall here we have a gangly-looking fellow named Marcel who is in *desperate* need of a makeover. His dad is a big-time Hollywood producer, a fact which Marcel thinks makes him better than everyone here so he will no doubt ask every hot girl on the floor to 'star in one of his student film projects' so consider yourself duly warned." I take a mental note to avoid this room as my mysterious companion spins me around again. "Maggie and Meaghan live in this room. They're both musical theater majors so if you hear singing at two in the morning, it's probably one of them. If you need weed, ask for Foxy in that room, and if you need a login for any streaming platform, go right across the hall to the triple and ask Elissa, Allie, or Rebecca for their login info. And I haven't been able to confirm this, but god willing it's true, it's been rumored that a group of sophomore boys on the soccer team are due to arrive tomorrow." I have no idea who this guy is, but I already love him and the way he seems to feed off gossip.

"You are like the human equivalent of the trivia section on IMDB," I tell him.

He unhooks his arm from mine and offers me his hand. "Micah Dalglish, journalism major."

I give him a firm handshake. "Elliot McHugh, undeclared."

He leans back, shifts his weight to one hip as he looks me up and down. "Really? I totally had you pegged as an acting major."

"Please! I actually *want* to make money for a living," I retort and he laughs.

"Ah yes, with that degree in *undeclared* you'll be making millions in no time."

I pause and give him a once-over. "I like you."

"The feeling is mutual," he says. We link arms again and work our way down the hall until we're outside my room.

"This is me," I say. "Do you know who lives across the hall, in #310?"

"Shockingly, I don't, but let's find out together, shall we?" Micah says and then knocks. My neighbors' door swings open and we come face to face with two walking cans of Axe body spray.

"Wassup?" they say in unison. At well over six feet tall, these two poster boys for country clubs and boat shoes dwarf the doorframe they stand in. Sure, I've encountered their kind in high school—and once my older sister, Izzy, dated one of them—but never in my life did I think I'd cross paths with their kind at a school like this, let alone live right across the hall from them.

You see, Emerson is the kind of educational institution where clusters of trendy, artsy students gather in front of the dorms to chain-smoke Lucky Strikes and compare David

Lynch *films*—not movies, *films*. Emerson attracts the artistic misfit type, not these sculpted creatures—I assumed they only traveled in flocks or herds and lived in pledge dorms, surfacing just for keggers or sport games. But lo and behold: My new neighbors are two living, breathing, football-watching, collar-popping, cargo short–wearing, standard-issue white bros.

Micah and I stare up at them, stunned into silence. Micah nudges me with his elbow and I am the first to speak. "Hello!"

"Wassup?" they say, again, in unison.

Micah reaches out and offers them his hand for a shake but one of them slaps it instead. "I'm Micah," he says. "My pronouns are he or they, whichever you prefer, and this is Elliot. She lives across the hall from you." Micah then says aside to me, "Sorry, I never asked you about your pronouns."

"You're good, you got it right: she/her," I say back.

"Nice to meet you, Ellie," one of the big dudes says, butchering my name. "I'm Brad."

"And I'm also Brad," the other one says. "But my last name is Martin and his is Winthrop."

"Wait, you're *both* named Brad?" They nod, smile, and high-five like having the same name is the coolest thing in the world. I give them two enthusiastic thumbs-up. "Excellent. Good stuff, guys."

Micah stifles a laugh and nudges me as we back away slowly. "Well, it was nice meeting you, gentlemen," Micah says.

"See y'all around," one of them says. I've already forgotten which Brad is which. They close the door and go back to manscaping or eating brogurt or whatever it was they were doing.

"They are *so* going in my report." Micah grins as he pulls out his phone and starts taking notes.

"What report?"

"I'm planning on putting out a weekly recap of all the drama that happens on our floor. You need to keep me in the loop on what happens around here, in case there's something I miss."

"So this third-floor report is like, your version of *TMZ*?"

"Don't you dare compare me to *TMZ*! But also, I like that name, *The Third-Floor Report*, I'm stealing it." He types the name in his phone. "It's something I did in high school, it's what got me into the journalism program, and I'm hoping it's what will give me an edge here over other broadcast journalism majors."

Someone taps me on the shoulder and I jump to the side, thinking I'm blocking the hall, but when I turn around, it's Rose, and she's got that *I'd like to have a word with you* look. I go to beg Micah to rescue me but he's already power-walking down the hall away from me, his arm thrown over the shoulder of some other girl. Reluctantly, I return my attention to my resident adviser.

"You need to take those lights down," Rose says sharply.

"What lights?" I coo.

"The ten-thousand-string lights you have draped all over your room."

"How do you even know about those?" I ask. She looks over my shoulder, into my room. I forgot I've been standing in front of my open door this whole time. *Shit*. Maybe if I ask her sweetly, bat my lashes a little, maybe she'll loosen up? Yeah, sure, let's try it. "Do I *have* to? My roommate Lucy *really* loves them and it's important for her to have a cozy environment."

"Nope, sorry," Rose deadpans. "They're a fire hazard."

"What if we just take down the ones on the ceiling?"

"Take them all down."

"How about we remove the ceiling ones and the strands draped over the window?"

"No." *Damn*. This woman is difficult to negotiate with.

"Okay, fine. What if we keep just one strand, the one hanging behind Lucy's bed? Please? It'll make her so happy." Rose glares at me, opens her mouth, and then closes it again.

"No," she says, her patience meter very clearly starting to run low. "What's your name?" she asks.

"McHugh. Elliot McHugh."

Rose gives me a look. "Did you just *Bond, James Bond* yourself?"

I pause. "Yes?"

"While I have you here, McHugh Elliot McHugh, you are the only student on the floor who hasn't declared a major yet, and I want to talk to you about the classes you've signed up for."

"Do you have to?" I try to persuade her with my tone but she doesn't take the bait.

"Yes," she says right away. "You could talk to the academic adviser assigned to you, but you're assigned to the same guy I had last year and let's just say he is a bit of a talker. This will only take a sec, let me just see what you signed up for."

Excuse me while I go on a tangent.

I knew being undeclared was going to single me out, but I was kind of hoping it wouldn't be that big of a deal. And yet, I am three hours into my first day of college and I've already had three people comment on my undeclared status. You see, most freshmen come to Emerson already knowing what they want to study, which classes they want to take, what careers they want to pursue in The Great Beyond after college. They have dreams and goals and other synonyms for ambitions. Essentially, they know who they want to be when they grow up. I, on the other hand, am not one of those people. I guess you could say I fall into the spectacularly average category of students. I did okay in high school. But just *okay*. I wasn't a standout, I got mostly Bs with a few As here and there and the occasional C. I wasn't a star, but I wasn't a burnout either. I was busy doing other shit like plays, choir, and hooking up with people in the plays and choir.

Perhaps you are wondering, *Why, then, did you go to an expensive private school instead of a big state school if you don't know what you want to do*? And if you are wondering that, then congrats! You and my mom have something in common! So I'll give you the same speech I gave her:

I love pop culture. End of speech.

Lol, just kidding! Okay here it goes: I love pop culture—books, movies, TV, etc. I know I want to do *something* with those things but fuck if I know anything else beyond that. My choices were this: A big school like Ohio State where I would have ended up lost in the void, or a small private school teeming with a bunch of creative weirdos that is so well connected in Hollywood its alumni association is literally called a *mafia*. The day I got my acceptance letter to Emerson was the day I knew I'd be joining the weirdos.

Now, as far as classes go . . . Rest assured, dear reader. While I may not be super great at planning my life four years in advance like Lucy or Micah, I *am* super okay at planning it four months in advance, and here is what I've done about that: To graduate with an undergrad degree from Emerson, you must acquire a certain number of credits that count toward your major and a certain number of credits to fulfill your general education requirements. And since, well, we both know my current chosen major is ¯_(ツ)_/¯, The Elliot McHugh Plan for Academic Excellence in Her First Year at College is to defer taking any classes toward a specific major and instead knock out a variety of gen ed requirements. As easy as that sounds, I still had to pick a set of classes to attend and Emerson's course catalog was so long, it was like picking what you want to eat at the Cheesecake Factory. Are you sure you want that flatbread pizza? Really? I mean, have you even read the descriptions for all nine Glamburgers on page 12? But you know what? I did it. I read through every option very carefully and let me tell you, I chose some *spectacular* courses this semester. So, gentle reader, please indulge me as I take the weirdest courses possible while calling it *getting an education*.

ELLIOT MCHUGH'S MOST EXCELLENT FALL SEMESTER SCHEDULE

PH 205 — Queer Dreams

IN 146 — Making Monsters

SC 114 — Plants and People

HI 115 — The Culture of Burlesque

Amazing lineup, right? I am actually quite proud of myself for being conservative in my choices because I could have (and wanted to) signed up for classes like Literature of Extreme Situations or Deconstructing *The Legend of Korra*. The point is, I deserve copious amounts of praise for showing restraint in not signing up for *the most* ridiculous courses.

Unfortunately, my present company doesn't seem to share my opinion.

I handed Rose my phone and now she's swiping through my courses. "First of all, every freshman has to take Fundamentals of Speech Communication their fall semester so right away one of these has to go," she says while still staring at the screen

"Barf."

She swipes again. "The Culture of Burlesque?"

"It fulfills the history requirement."

"And the plants one?"

"Science, obviously," I tell her. "And I'm not really sure what Making Monsters is but I hope it involves Play-Doh." Rose sighs and shifts her weight to one hip. She hands the phone back and there's this long, silent pause between us, which can only mean one of two things: Either Rose agrees with my plan—or I'm about to be offered some unsolicited advice from someone I don't know very well.

"Elliot—" Rose says.

"Yes, Rose?" I use my sweet, innocent voice just to piss her off.

"You should really rethink this course load." She gives me a condescending look.

"Why? I thought really hard about *this* curriculum. I selected these subjects with great care and thought."

"You basically chose bullshit courses that will be easy As."

"Nuh uh, that is so not true.[19] The course description for Plants and People is deeply academic."[20]

She shakes her head at me. "Elliot—"

---

19 It is. It is absolutely 100 percent true.
20 It is not. No joke, the class description is basically like "we gonna teach you how to not kill houseplants." *God, I love college.*

"Rose—"

"Can I *please* give you some advice?" *Annnnnd there it is.* I never understand why people ask for permission to give advice when they're going to do it regardless. "You need to take this stuff seriously."

I straighten my posture and use the same voice and gestures that usually get me out of trouble with my mom. "What if I told you I selected *slightly easier* classes because I feel as though I am, perhaps, not yet emotionally equipped to handle a tougher course load? That I am feeling overwhelmed by the transition to college life and I want to ensure my grade point average will not suffer while I take a semester to mentally adjust to my new environment and prepare myself for the real work that lies ahead?"

"I'd say you're full of shit," Rose says immediately. I tilt my head back and groan as she continues. "Look, you already have to change one of these to the freshman speech class, so I strongly *suggest* you change out another one while you're at it, Elliot," Rose reiterates.

"Fine. Whatever. I'll think about it."

● ● ●

"So did you take her advice? Did you switch one of your gen ed classes for a core one?" Lucy asks during our first dinner together in the dining center. Emerson is on a swipe system, which means you swipe to get in to eat but once you're in,

YOU'RE IN, and you can eat as much as you can until they kick you out at 9 P.M.[21] The kitchen is buffet style, with different stations that rotate based on the time of day, but the cereal bar and the waffle station stay the same all day, every day. Lucy and I are in a booth in the very back, in the corner that overlooks Tremont and Boylston streets. She's having a grilled tofu Caesar salad with a small side of tomato soup. I'm having a large bowl of Cinnamon Toast Crunch.[22]

"You know," I say while munching on my cereal. "I thought about it, but the way I see it, my current approach will allow me to sample all that this fine institution has to offer. I can take the year to dabble in each department, get to know the faculty, and gain a better sense of the curriculum. It will allow me to test the waters, if you will, to explore my options so that I may be empowered to make an informed decision as to which major I might select."

"So that would be a *no*?"

"Correct. But I did switch The Culture of Burlesque for a class called Love and Eroticism in Western Culture. I hear there's going to be a lot of movie watching involved." Lucy looks up at me from her salad and I give her a big goofy smile, but she's not taking the bait. She has this serious look about her, the kind of look people who have their shit together, like Lucy, get around people who don't have their shit together,

---

21 #Blessed

22 As far as cereals go, the top five are 1) Cinnamon Toast Crunch, 2) Frosted Flakes, 3) Froot Loops, 4) Cocoa Puffs, 5) Honey Nut Cheerios. Don't @ me.

like me. I know I should say something to ease her mind, and quick, because this could become the thing that drives a wedge between us.

"Okay, fine," I say, setting my cereal aside so she knows I'm serious. She folds her hands on the table and listens. "I know I want to do *something* in entertainment but I don't really know what that is yet. The classes I've chosen sound interesting, meaning I might be able to focus long enough to learn something, which is hard for me. I wish I could have career certainty like you, but figuring out what I want to do with my future while also being away from home for the first time seems like an impossible task. Is that okay?"

Her stare is intense but then the corners of her eyes crinkle and her mouth turns into the warmest smile I've seen from her yet. "Of course it's okay! It seems like you've really thought about this—you know what you're doing."

Whoa. I can't believe that worked. I didn't even really think that hard about what I was saying, I was just trying to come up with something that sounded legit. What did I even say? Hold on, let me reread that last paragraph . . .

. . .

. . .

. . .

Okay, yeah. I agree with all of what I just said! Phew!

"What about you? Aren't you worried about balancing school and life?" I ask her.

"I can't afford to worry about it. I'm the first member of my family to go for a bachelor's degree. I took out over $36,000 in student loans to come here."

"Oh, well, that's not *too* bad," I say.

"That's just for the first year."

"Holy fuck!" I slap the table in shock. "I didn't realize it was *that* much."

"I know. Emerson gave me some scholarship money, I got a couple of grants, and my family scraped together what they could, but it was only enough to cover room and board. I've already applied for a part-time job at the Emerson Fund to help."

"Why take on such an enormous amount of debt? You think Emerson will be worth it?"

"Probably not. I'll probably be paying off student loans until I'm dead," Lucy says with a laugh, and thank goodness, because I was starting to feel squirmy like my armpits are getting sweaty. Truth be told, I'm privileged as hell. I didn't have to take out loans to be here—and talk about money triggers my rich-girl guilt—but Lucy isn't throwing herself a pity party, so I won't either. She reaches for her glass of water but it's empty, so I slide mine over to her. "But the loans don't matter," she continues. "It's always been my dream to come here. The marketing program is top-notch and they have a really good teacher to student ratio."

"Plus the abroad program near Amsterdam is in a mother-fucking *castle*," I add.

"Ohmygosh, I know, right?"

"And it's really progressive and queer-friendly."

"Yes! And it has no math classes," she says.

"And the school has no policy on students hooking up with faculty." That last one catches Lucy midsip and she chokes on my water. I reach across the table. "Are you okay? Can I get you something? Do you need a waffle? I think you need a waffle." Exactly three minutes and fifty-seven seconds later, I'm back at our booth with a freshly made waffle and Lucy has stopped coughing water out of her lungs. We start picking at the waffle with our fingers.

Lucy shoots me a curious look. "So, about that . . ."

"What?"

"Emerson really allows students and faculty to have—to be in a relationship?"

"Oh, that? I was kidding, they definitely don't allow it, but it's cool, I'll still find a way to check off *teacher* from my Fuck It List." Lucy nearly chokes again. I reach out and place my hand on top of hers. "I'm sorry. Is this too much for you? Should I withhold all bombshells until you are at a safe distance from foods and beverages?" I slide the water and waffle far away from her—just in case.

"I'm good," Lucy laughs and clears her throat. "I'm afraid to ask, but who is on your list?"

"Oh, the usual suspects—a firefighter, D-List celebrity, author . . . *college roommate*." I wink at Lucy, and she throws the last piece of waffle at me and I catch it in my mouth. "Kidding! It's not so much a list as it is just a piece of paper with one sentence that reads GET SOME. The Fuck It Lifestyle is part of the Horny On Main family of brands and I have been a proud sponsor for the last year."

"Why? What happened last year?" She asks.

"Oh, you know, a classic hard pivot after a bad breakup." I try to stall because this will be the first time I talk about my romantic history with someone who wasn't there to witness it. How far into my backstory should I go? Or can I just hit the lowlights? I opt for the latter. "Here's the TL;DR version: Right before winter break last year I found out my boyfriend had been cheating on me with a girl from another school because I, quote, *wasn't meeting his needs,* and apparently all my friends knew about it but no one told me. I decided to make my list right after that."

"Oh, Elliot . . ." Lucy reaches across the table but I evade her touch and wave her off.

"No, no, it's cool, I learned three important lessons: I needed better friends, serious relationships aren't for me, and you can get it on without getting complicated." I pause as my mind drifts back to four months after the breakup when my ex brought the girl he cheated on me with to prom and I finally met her. I introduced myself when we bumped into each other in the bathroom, we hit it off, and the next morning she woke up in my bed instead of my ex's. Good times. "But you know what? I'm excited to *really* live the Fuck It life, especially now that I'm away from all that drama and the people associated with it. So you see, in addition to the whole figuring out my life thing, here at college, I'm mostly looking forward to getting laid." Lucy laughs as though she thinks I'm kidding—which I most certainly am not. "Lucy, there are no parents, no rules, endless exotic locales for clandestine hookups, and how many people our age living in the Little Building? This place is a bottomless pit of available booty from which I get to call." I hold my arms out wide and wave them around as other nearby freshmen stare. "How can I possibly care about my education when there is all this fresh ass just waiting to be tapped? How could *you*?" I thought she was going to laugh, but instead she looks visibly uncomfortable with the question. She shrinks back into the booth and rubs her lips together anxiously. I reach out and quickly try to put her at ease. "I mean, if that's your thing, of course. If not I can always come up with an appropriately inappropriate list of platonic things to do too if you just give me a moment here . . ."

"I'm not a-spec," Lucy says and then pauses, searching for a way to tell me whatever it is she's about to tell me. "It's . . . Well—I only have one person on my list, I guess. Sorry, I know that's not very exciting."

"Are you kidding? Now I'm totally intrigued. Who? Who? Who?" I badger her.

She reaches for her napkin and starts shredding it into tiny pieces. "Well, actually, I guess, it's just a *boyfriend*."

"Stop, wind it back. You've *never* had a boyfriend? Sorry, let me preface that with a sincere *that's totally fine too, it's your choice, hashtag Feminism hashtag Resist*, but I am just so surprised! A woman as smart, kind, and banging as you should have dudes lined up around the block."

"Oh, they were," she says and it's the cockiest thing I've ever heard her say, but there isn't a single hint of arrogance in her tone. "But it was only ever Armenian boys my family tried to set me up with, and let's just say the pickings were slim and my family does not have the best taste."

"What about at school? There had to have been guys in your class you were into."

Lucy laughs. "I went to an all-girl Catholic high school! And I worked a lot, my Uncle Lev's restaurant after school during the week and my mom's bed and breakfast on the weekends."

"Shit. No wonder you're ready for a boyfriend; you must be horny as hell." I say it as a joke but when Lucy's cheeks flare and she gets this crazy guilty look on her face I know it's for real. "Oh my god, you *are* horny! Well shit, roomie . . . let's get you laid!"

Lucy blushes even harder and hides her face behind both hands. "Nooooo! I'm not ready to get laid! I just said I want a boyfriend!"

"Does this boyfriend need to be Armenian or can we broaden our search terms?" I ask.

"God no," she says. "I mean, sure, my grandma would love it if I married another Armenian but a lot of my cousins have married outside the community and no one has made a fuss about it."

"Let's not get ahead of ourselves," I tell her. "We don't need to find you a Mr. Forever—just a Mr. For the Next Semester." I pull out my phone and scroll through the Emerson events calendar checking for any upcoming social events where I might find an acceptable suitor.

Lucy flops her head back against the booth. "Oh god, what have I done? I have a double course load this semester; this is not what I should be focusing on."

"Don't worry about it! This is going to be the easiest setup ever. We won't even have to do the whole makeover montage or anything," I say just as Micah appears in front of our booth holding a tray full of food.

"What is going to the easiest setup ever?" He asks.

"We're going to find Lucy a boyfriend!" I inform him.

"Oooh, fun!" Micah slides into the booth next to Lucy. I continue to scroll through the Emerson events calendar searching for anything promising.

"Hey, Micah, does Emerson offer any school-sanctioned mating rituals like formal dances? We need a good social gathering with lots of people for Lucy to choose from."

"Why don't you ladies join me at a party in Allston tomorrow night?"

"Where's Allston?" I ask.

"Off campus, of course. All the best parties are in Allston," he says as he starts eating his dinner.

"How the hell did you get an invite to an off-campus party?" I ask him, completely astonished. "We've only been at college for a day!"

Micah flicks his fork at me. "A good journalist never reveals their source." This time it's Lucy who gives him the side-eye. He rolls his eyes and says, "Okay fine, I met a guy who lives at the apartment where the party is in the fitness center this morning and we *might* have made out a little."

"Attaboy," I say and he grins. I love that Micah is one of those people who can make friends with anyone in any situation.[23] "So we're all set then. Well, Lucy? What'll it be? Are you game?"

I look to Lucy and watch as her brain processes the decision before her: Will she continue to let her obligations hold her back or will she take a chance, throw caution to the wind, and go get some vitamin D?

Lucy covers her face in with her hands, which at first I take for her saying no, but then she says, "What the heck, let's do this. Go find me a boyfriend."

Micah throws an arm around Lucy and I raise my glass to them both. "To the hunt!"

"To the boyfriend hunt!" Micah clinks his glass with mine and hugs her tighter.

Lucy squeezes her eyes shut and says, "I think I regret this already."

---

23 And I'm the kind of friend with no qualms about benefiting from her friends' talents. Especially if those talents land her an invite to her first college party.

CHAPTER 4

SO HERE WE ARE: MICAH, LUCY, SASHA, AND I FREEZ-ing our asses off outside an ugly two-story house, while we wait for someone to let us into our very first college party. Micah is rapidly texting, Lucy is looking around nervously, and Sasha, the influencer Micah insisted we befriend, is in the back of our little group, livestreaming on Instagram. She ends her livestream and pushes to the front and pokes Micah. "Are you sure this is the right place? It's pretty quiet."

"We're definitely in the right place. I trust my source com-pletely," Micah assures her. On cue, the door swings open, spilling heavy bass and smoke out into the otherwise still night. A tall, muscular dude wearing the traditional uniform of a native Bostonian[24] opens the door, gives Micah a quick dap, and steps aside to let us all in. Micah winks at me as he slips into the townhouse without making introductions and

---

24 Red Sox hat, Patriots sweatshirt, baggy gray sweatpants.

immediately disappears into the crowd, leaving the rest of us to fend for ourselves. Lucy, Sasha, and I cross the threshold, and in exchange for a five-dollar entry fee, we are handed red plastic cups filled with a mystery liquid that smells like a mixture of Jolly Ranchers and nail polish remover.

I've been inside this house for less than a minute and I can tell you right now that all the parties I went to in high school, all the ones that I thought were so wild and hedonistic, now seem like kids' birthday parties by comparison. I genuinely thought I was prepared to party in college because I had raged a respectable amount my senior year of high school, but nothing could have possibly prepared me for what I've just walked into.

From where I'm standing, I see a shot luge in one room, three people doing keg stands in the kitchen, and, in the living room, a DJ—an actual motherfucking DJ—spinning on a mini-platform while everyone in the room is either dancing or trying to invent new ways to have sex without taking off any clothes. It sounds as if I'm exaggerating, I know, but from where I'm standing, I am in full view of a gratuitous display of grinding and dry humping. I spy one, two, three . . . nay, *five* boners standing at various degrees of attention, and just when I think my eyes have been overstimulated, a half-naked gentleman wearing body glitter and feather wings swoops by our group and offers us edibles.

It's dark and loud and sweaty and dirty.

It's fucking awesome.

I stand there with Sasha and Lucy, the three of us a herd of deer in headlights. We are too overwhelmed to move or think or blink or drink. The guy who answered the door nudges Sasha in the shoulder.

"Yo, you guys look like a fuckin' party pack just standing there like that," he says over the music in a thick Boston accent. He takes a liberal gulp from his Solo cup.

"What's a party pack?" Lucy asks Sasha, but before she can answer, the Boston dude just laughs and shakes his head at us.

"Party packs are groups of freshmen who go to parties but never leave each other," he informs us. "You go around looking like a fuckin' school of fish or some shit because y'all move as a unit. It's the quickest way to get kicked out of a party, or hazed, so if I was you I'd either toss back that bucket juice I just gave you and disperse—or get the fuck out now. Your choice." He crushes his cup and walks away from us until I lose sight of him.

"What's in *bucket juice*?" Lucy asks but I shrug because I don't know either. I've been drunk before, but in high school we drank what was available: occasionally a case of cheap, watery beer courtesy of someone's benevolent older brother or a dusty, half-empty bottle of vodka someone managed to steal from their parents' liquor cabinet that we'd pass around and take nervous sips from.

I put one arm around Sasha and the other around Lucy and ask them, "What do you wanna do? Stay or go?" At this very moment, we look like we're in a soccer team huddle and I think I finally understand what the dude was saying about party packs. I take a step back and try to look cool, casual.

Lucy hands Sasha her Solo cup. "I'll stay, but I'll pass on the bucket juice. I don't really like to drink."

Sasha gives the Solo cup a little shake. "Are you sure you don't want a little liquid confidence?"

Lucy nods. "I'm sure. Thanks, though. I need to get to the bookstore early tomorrow to get all my course materials." For a second I think about making a note to do the same in my phone, but two seconds later I've forgotten what I was supposed to remind myself to do. Sasha shrugs and pours half the contents of Lucy's cup into mine and the rest into her own. I eye it cautiously and sniff it again, just to make sure I really want to do this.

"Ah, hell," I say, raising my cup to my girls in salute. Sasha and I clink cups and swallow the entire contents in one go. It tastes *easy*. The kind of easy that could lead to a morning full of regret. I want more. "All right, ladies. Let's fucking do this," I say to my squad because it's the kind of line I'd want my character to say in the movie version of this moment. And together, we embark on our first college party.

● ● ●

THE
ELLIOT MCHUGH
DRINK SCALE

1 drink = Elliot is feeling warm and cozy

2 drinks = Elliot is charming and hilarious

3 drinks = Elliot is an asshole who will zero in on your greatest insecurities

4 drinks = Elliot wants to DANCE

5 drinks = Elliot is in love with everyone and wants to make out

6 drinks = Elliot is crying in the corner

7 drinks = Elliot is vomiting in what she thought was a trash can but is actually her purse

8 drinks = Unknown territory

Within thirty seconds of entering the party, we lose track of Sasha. Lucy and I walk down a long, crowded hallway full of people standing around drinking, talking, or making out. The air is thick, sticky, and smells like a mixture of cheap beer, cheap cigarettes, and cheap perfume. Someone hands me a shot glass and I don't know if it's meant for me or someone else but I drink it anyway.

"See anyone you like?" I ask.

Lucy's cheeks flare in response. "We just got here! Besides, it's so dark I can barely see anyone's faces."

"Girl, get your eyes checked!" I tell her. "I've already seen four people I'd like to see naked."

Lucy shoots me a look. "You'd like to see *everyone* naked, Elliot."

"True, everyone gives me tender chicken." The hallway leads into the kitchen, crowded with people watching two guys do competing keg stands, so we squeeze through until we make it to the adjoining dining room. "And don't worry, the night is young and there are plenty of boyfriend prospects here. We'll find you someone, I promise."

"Well—" Lucy starts to say but her face goes all red again and I instantly know something is up. I smack her arm to get her to keep talking. "I met someone at orientation yesterday," she says. "At first I wasn't interested, but then we started chatting and, I dunno, he's sweet."

"And cute, I hope?"

"I think so! He lives on our floor, I'm not sure you've met him yet."

"Well that's convenient! Your walks of shame will be significantly shorter."

"His name is Brad Martin. He lives across the hall—" Lucy gets cut off by a loud cheer from the kitchen. The crowd shifts and we watch some guy fall over while trying to do a keg stand. Beer dribbles out of his mouth as he laughs from the floor. Several adjacent dudes laugh and offer him high fives. It's then that I realize that this idiot is one of the Brads, the two dudes who live across the . . . OH NO. I look over at Lucy and say a silent prayer to whichever god happens to be listening. *Please don't let this Brad be* the *Brad my roommate has a crush on*. But by the glint in Lucy's beautiful doe eyes I know right away that this Brad is Brad Martin, the one Lucy is smitten with. *Goddammit*.

"Lucy, no!" I say as sweet as possible. "*That's* the guy you want to remember as your first boyfriend?" We look into the kitchen and watch as Brad tries to shotgun a beer from the floor, struggles to punch a hole into the can, and sprays beer all over his face. Lucy grimaces and sighs. For once, I don't need to explain myself. Brad is making the argument for me. Lucy can't get with a bro like Brad—I mean, look at him, reader! Look at him with your imagination! That man is a total clown, and under no circumstances will I ever let my goddess of a roommate get with someone so loud and so coarse as Brad. I give Lucy a sympathetic pat on her shoulder.

"Come on, my love, I'm sure Brad is a very nice boy, but you can do better. And you will! Let's find Sasha and see if Micah is still here or if he's ditched us." We turn to leave, but it's Sasha who finds us first.

"Ohmygod there you are! Micah sent me. He needs your help." And suddenly, finding a boyfriend for Lucy is the last thing on my mind.

"Is Micah okay? What's going on? What happened?" My questions fly out in rapid succession as I fear the worst. Sasha leads us through a screen door off the side of the kitchen and we step into the backyard where I see Micah bending over in anguish next to a Ping-Pong table. I run to him.

"Micah, are you all right? Where does it hurt? What are your symptoms?" I reach out and lightly rest my hands on his back. He bursts up with a high-pitched wail, spinning away from me. I look to Sasha for context, and she rolls her eyes and sighs.

"He's down one hundred dollars in a Ping-Pong match." She laughs when she sees my reaction. "I *know*, right? I tried to get him to stop when he was way behind, but nooooo. Someone here just had to keep going, didn't they?"

Micah flails and points his paddle at Sasha. "I wouldn't be behind if *you* had played on my behalf like I asked!"

"I already told you," Sasha says. "I play beer-pong, not Ping-Pong—and besides, I don't take bets unless I'm 100 percent certain I'm going to win." Micah huffs and throws his paddle back on the table.

"Are you short on cash?" I start fishing around in my bra for bills. "I think I have enough in here somewhere—"

"Thanks, but you can keep your titty money," he sighs out. "My parents are both architects, so it's not about the money."

"What is this about then?" Lucy asks.

"I don't like losing!" Micah whines. "My older brother is so good at Ping-Pong. He wouldn't be out one hundred dollars right now." I follow him to where he's crouched into a ball. He reeks of bucket juice.

"Well, your brother isn't here. He'll never know," Lucy says to him.

"He *will* when I have to ask our mom to Venmo me one

hundred dollars tomorrow. She doesn't loan me any money without requiring an itemized list of everything it's for."

"Can't you just lie?" I ask him.

"You don't understand," he cries out. "My mother can tell when someone is lying to her. She *always knows*."

I look over to Lucy. "What should we do?"

"Don't you know how to play Ping-Pong?" Lucy asks me. "You told me your dad does."

"Yeah, I mean, I grew up playing with him, but—"

Micah immediately perks up. "Ohmygod you *have* to play for me."

"Dude, no," I say, backing away. "I'm not going to risk losing you *more* money."

"Pleassssseeeeeee." Micah clasps his hands together. "I will so owe you and you know I'm good for it." I take a moment to consider it. Micah is probably going to be the next Anderson Cooper, and it might be good to stockpile a few favors I can cash in a few years from now.

"Fiiiiiine," I groan. Micah throws his hands up and hugs me. His hugs are no hot chocolate bath. They're all bony and sharp angles. "All right, all right. Simmer down now. Who am I playing? Who is this pong hustler that's kicking your ass?"

Out of nowhere, a Ping-Pong ball comes flying across the yard, bounces off the table, and gently flicks my left tit.

"I found it! Are you ready to lose a fourth round?" she says as she emerges from behind a shed in the corner of the crowded yard.

Ahhhhh fuck.

It's Rose.

I spin around and lower my voice. "What the hell is our RA doing here?" I look to my friends for an answer but no one says shit. I thought Rose was all anti-drinking, anti-partying, anti-fun-of-any-kind. She is the last person I want to see right now and yet, here she is—in a floor-length, layered pink tulle dress and gold platform creepers. She's pulled her hair into a topknot, and if I wasn't so annoyed with her, I would be able to admit how cute she looks in that outfit. But I *am* annoyed. So, no. She doesn't look cute. Not even a little.

"Nope, I'm out," I say and hand the paddle back to Micah. I throw the ball to Rose who catches it easily.

"Double or nothing, Micah? Or you can just give up now. I take cash only," she says. And I quickly find that the competitive asshole side of myself is beginning to stir. I don't like it when someone fucks with *my* friends, especially when that someone is doing it in a goddamn tutu.

"All right, fine," I say to Micah, who looks thrilled. "I got this."

"Yassss queen!" he shouts behind me as I take his place at the table across from Rose. She tosses me the ball.

"Double or nothing?" Rose asks me this time.

"Elliot, no! I can't afford to—" Micah starts to say but I ignore him.

"Yes," I say to Rose and then I get a great idea. "But I'd like to make an addendum. If I win, Micah gets his money, Lucy and I get to put the fairy lights back up, *and* you buy me more detergent." Rose looks annoyed. This is not what she wanted. *Good*.

"First of all," she says, "I know you have already put the lights back up so you can't bet those, and second of all, have you changed out one of your courses yet like I told you to?"

"Yes," I say as I toss her back the ball.

"Any classes *other* than the speech one that's required for all freshmen?"

"Nope." I give her an arrogant smile.

"Fine, then," she says, crossing her arms in front of her chest. "I accept the new terms. But if I win, Micah owes me double, the fairy lights come down *for good*, and you *have* to change one of your classes." She tilts her chin up toward me. A challenge.

"Deal," I say.

"Would you like a warm-up point?" Rose asks smugly.

"No thanks, I'm good." I stretch my neck side to side and spin the paddle a few times in my hand, getting a good feel for it.

"Are you sure?" She asks and tosses me back the ball, but this time I spike it over the net with a fast topspin that rockets off the edge of her side of the table. Her jaw drops and all the smugness drains from her face.

"Let's do this." I grin.

● ● ●

". . . sixty, eighty, one hundred. You can claim the other hundred from Micah tomorrow," I say as I reach into my bra to pull out the cash and hand it over to Rose. OH YES, THAT'S RIGHT. I FUCKING LOST. YOU TOTALLY THOUGHT I HAD THIS SHIT IN THE BAG, DIDN'T YOU? WELL, GUESS WHAT? SO DID I. I grew up playing pong with my dad, so naturally I thought I was top bitch with my fancy topspin and my suave undercuts, but here comes that sexy-ass dick of an RA, Rose, who grew up with a Ping-Pong ball *machine* in her house because her grandfather WAS A GODDAMN PROFESSIONAL TABLE TENNIS PLAYER. So, yeah. She smoked my ass out there and now I have to pay up.

"And your class?" Rose stands there with one hip cocked, all self-assured and annoying.

"Seriously? Right now? You want me to change my class while we're at a party?"

"Hey, I'm not the one who bet—AND LOST. So let's see it. Pull up the Emerson app on your phone."[25]

"I strongly resent this," I bemoan as I do as I'm told. I pull open the app and flip it to my schedule and show her the screen, but she grabs the phone out of my hand and starts swiping and tapping. "Hey! What are you doing?" I cry out as I try to get my phone back.

"Annnnd there! Done! I switched one of your classes for you. You're welcome." She tosses the phone back to me and I drop it.

"What did you do? WHAT DID YOU DO?!?" I pick up my phone and frantically scroll through the app to find out what

---

25 My anger right now can only be described in one word: asd;fkjasd;kfjads;kfjdslkfja;aljkshdfl she did to my schedule. "Noooo! You switched out Queer Dreams for what—Screenwriting?!?!?!?!?!?!"

She crosses her arms and looks defiant. "Yes, I think you'd be great at it."

"Based on what evidence?!"

"She'd be great at what?" An ultra-pale girl with waist-length blue hair appears behind Rose and wraps her arms around Rose's waist.

"I think she'd be great at screenwriting," Rose tells her. "Monica, this is Elliot. She's a freshman on my floor. Elliot, this is my girlfriend, Monica." Rose pulls away from Monica to let her shake my hand but Monica doesn't go for it so I don't either.

"Nice to meet you, Monica," I say to her and then to Rose, "May I be excused? Or is there some other way you'd like to make me miserable?"

"Oh, I'm sure I'll think of something later, but for now you can go." I roll my eyes at her and leave in search of my friends who abandoned ship when it was clear I was going to lose.

● ● ●

Back inside the kitchen, I shove my way to the fridge in an attempt to find something, anything with alcohol, but out of the corner of my eye I see a very drunk Brad slumped over in the corner by the trash bags. I try to backpedal out of the kitchen, but he spots me and loses his shit. He points at me from the floor and shouts.

"Elllllliiiiiiotttttttt!"

"Um, hey, Brad," I say, annoyed that he's drawing the attention of the entire room to me.

"Everyone, this is my neighbor Ellioooot," he says to his bros. They help him off the sticky floor and he stumbles and plows into me. He slumps a beefy arm around my shoulders and I get a good whiff of Eau de Drunk Brad. "You're pretty," he slurs into my ear while trying to touch my hair. "Hey, how come you have a boy's name?" I swat him away and remove his heavy limb from my shoulders. I grab an empty chair from the kitchen table and maneuver his hulking, drunk body onto it.

"You're drunk, dude. Maybe you should slow down a bit." I go to fill him a glass of water but he grabs my hand, pulling me back to him. He looks at my hand for a long time and then giggles.

"You have the biggest hands for a girl I've ever seen," he says and then giggles some more. He sounds like a drunk baby when he laughs. He calls out to his boys, "Yooooo! Come look at Elliot's hands! They're huuuuge! Hey Elliot, did you know you have man-hands?" He asks, turning his attention back to me.

"I wasn't aware that hands could be gendered, but yes, I know my hands are big," I say as I wriggle my hand free from his sticky grip so I can get him some freaking water.

"Need some help?" someone says out of frame.

"Could you fill up a glass of water?" I turn around to ask and am pleasantly surprised to find a white guy who isn't a total frat bro. Usually I'm pretty good at sizing people up, but there's something about this guy I can't quite put my finger on. He's very clearly in shape but so obviously not a jock by the way he's dressed in all black and a beanie. He has a tattoo on his forearm that could easily place him with the art scene, but he seems way too outgoing to roll with that kind of crowd. He's the kind of guy you can't easily place at a lunch table in the cafeteria because he could sit at all of them. He's perfect for Lucy. Mystery boy goes to the sink, fills a cup with water, and hands it to the drunk baby, who takes a sip and makes a sour face.

"What this? This issssn't beer," Brad slurs. He stuffs his hands into his armpits like a six-year-old. "I want another beer."

"It's a new kind of *tasteless* beer," I say to Brad and then redirect my attention to this new, yet-to-be-named character. "Thanks," I say to him. Tall, Dark, and Mysterious narrows his eyes and looks at me curiously, like he's trying to see if I'm real or just a mirage.

"You go to Emerson too?" I nod yes. "You a freshman or a transfer?" he asks and I'm surprised he doesn't instantly suspect me of being fresh from the womb.

"Freshman."

"Same," he says. "You live in the LB?"

"Uh, yeah. I'm on the third floor." He grabs two beers from the fridge, tosses me one and opens the other as he pops himself up on the kitchen counter.

"Nice. I live on the eighth floor."

"The eighth floor is nice, but the third floor is far superior," I tell him.

He pauses midsip. "Oh yeah? Why's that?"

"The third floor is the only residential floor that retains some of the original materials and structure of the building. They razed the LB in 2017 because it's old as shit and was falling apart but once they stripped it down, they realized everything up to the third floor could be restored but had to replace all the upper floors. I dunno, I guess I just think that's cool."

He sets the beer down and looks at me blankly. "You're weird, aren't you," he says as a statement rather than a question.

"Probably," I sigh. I eye him, study him, scrutinize him, other adjective for judge him, and right as he opens his mouth to say something else, I get my second brilliant idea of the night.[26] "Hey, are you planning on staying awhile?"

"I just got here like ten minutes ago so I'm not going anywhere," he says. "Why? What's up?"

"Oh, I just have someone I'd really like you to meet. Would you do me a favor and meet me in the living room in five minutes?"

"Sure?" He looks confused but also intrigued. Intrigued is good. Intrigued I can work with. I gulp down the last of my beer and throw the can on the floor among all the other empty cans. Having invented the Elliot McHugh Drink Scale, I am well aware of the state of mind three drinks puts me in, so

---

26 My first great idea was to go double or nothing against Rose and that was obviously a huge oversight, but I'm older and wiser now. I have much more confidence in this next brilliant idea.

I steal someone's half-empty bottle of vodka and pour myself two shots, getting me to level 5.[27]

"Okay, see you in a few!" I call back to him as I scamper out of the kitchen. I find my friends sitting outside on the front stoop. "Wooo!" I shout when I see them. "Who's ready to go dancing?"

Micah smacks me in the arm as I walk past him. "You owe me one hundred dollars!"

"Hey! I never promised you a win. That's on *you*," I tell him. "And by the way, you need to pay Rose back *in cash* tomorrow or she's going to start charging you interest like a bank."

"*And* you lost us our last strand of fairy lights!" Lucy yells next.

"Yeahhhh, okay, that one's on me," I reply, feeling genuinely sorry I ruined my roommate's dream of achieving the perfect dorm-room aesthetic. I need to make things right. "If I rub my butt all up on you on the dance floor, will that make it better or worse?" I ask her.

"Better," Lucy says with a wink, and I am so in love with my roommate and her willingness to forgive so easily. I herd Sasha, Micah, and Lucy back into the house and onto the dance floor and before I know it, everyone has completely forgotten about the Ping-Pong disaster and we're having the time of our lives. The weed fairy floats by again, and this time I take him up on his offer and eat a gummy. While we dance, I keep my eyes glued to the hallway, hoping to spot the mystery guy.

---

27 Also known as the Elliot is in love with everyone and wants to make out stage.

"What are you doing?" Micah dances up beside me.

"Nothing, just dancing," I say innocently.

"You're definitely up to *something*."

I dance Micah out of earshot from Lucy and tell him, "Okay fine, I met a guy I want to set Lucy up with and he's supposed to meet me here any minute."

"Why don't you just set her up with Brad? He's good looking-ish and Lucy told me she likes him."

I stop dancing for a moment. "Are you seriously advocating for Brad the Bro to be Lucy's first boy toy?"

"Sure, why not?"

"Oh, come on," I scoff. "You know how guys like Brad are."

"Well, Brad is straight and I'm gay, so no. I don't know how guys like Brad are. But why are you being so quick to judge? You don't even know Brad."

"You may not know how guys like Brad are, but I do, and I don't want that for Lucy. She deserves someone better than I had for her first time."

Micah concedes to my logic and we start dancing again. "Okay then, where is this guy you're determined to pimp out our Lucy to?"

And just then, he emerges from the smoky depths of the hallway.

"There he is!" I point him out to Micah and his jaw drops.

"I take everything I said back. Well done, McHugh. Well done, indeed." The boy catches my eye and trots over.

"This is my friend Micah," I say, introducing them.

"Hey man, I'm Kenton," the boy whose name I now know to be Kenton says. "Is this who you wanted me to meet?" he asks me.

"Yes," Micah says, looking Kenton up and down.

"Paws off," I say to Micah and shoo him away. "No, he was not who I wanted you to meet," I address Kenton again. I take his hand and lead him into the mass of writhing bodies until I find Lucy and Sasha. Micah, finally getting with the program, does me a solid and runs interference with Sasha so Lucy is dancing alone. I get Lucy's attention and introduce her. "Kenton, this is my exquisite roommate Lucy. Lucy, this is Kenton. He was a true *gentleman* earlier and helped me deal with a slightly annoying situation." Lucy looks Kenton over and her face goes bright red, and I know she has tender chicken.[28]

"It's nice to meet you!" Kenton says and the way this guy is looking at Lucy right now—yeah, he's hook, line, and sinker.[29]

Twenty minutes later, Lucy and Kenton are grinding all up on each other on the dance floor, Micah is making out with the weed fairy on a couch, Sasha got one hundred new subscribers—and me? Well, I'm upstairs in the second-floor bathroom kissing a very cute girl, while I slip my fingers down her pants.

---

28 Symptoms of tender chicken include flushing, intense pressure in the groinal region, biting of the bottom lip, heavy breathing, and, in rare cases, extreme sweating.
29 What? Did you think it was going to take me three chapters to convince this dude to be interested in a hot girl like Lucy? Reader, please. These are drunk, horny college kids here. Matchmaking in college is not that hard.

CHAPTER 5

AN ANNOYING BUZZING SOUND WAKES ME THE next morning, and it takes a second to rub the sleep from my dry eyes and realize the buzzing is coming from my phone. I have twenty-seven texts from Lucy and various other people from my floor wondering where the hell I am. And one text from drunk Brad thanking me for taking care of him last night.

Last night?

Oh, right. The party.

I sit up in bed and it quickly dawns on me that I have no idea whose room I am in. I look over to my right and see the messy hair of a girl fast asleep. I lift the covers to take a peek and yep, I'm naked and so is she. It seems as though Five-Drink Elliot had a lot of fun last night. Self–high five! I reach for a half-empty bottle of water on her nightstand and catch a glimpse of her Emerson ID. Her name is Lottie and she's a sophomore. Well, that's good. At least I slept with a student and not someone random. I mean, someone more random than a random student. I slide out of bed as stealthily as fucking possible, find my rumpled clothes in a pile on the floor. I get dressed, grab my shit, and quietly leave Lottie's room.

It's 8 A.M. by the time I get back to my room, and I'm fumbling for the keys in my bag when the door flies open and I come face to face with a very pissed-off version of my roommate.

"Top o' the morning to you!" I say with a heavy Irish accent.

"Where the hell have you been?" Lucy asks as she yanks me into our room.

"I was with that babe from the party," I say as I start stripping off my clothes again. I expect Lucy to be proud of me but she's not. She looks furious.

"Are you serious?! I was so worried about you! When we left last night we looked for you but you were nowhere to be found. I figured you'd gone home already. We've been texting you all night!"

"Dude, I'm fine! I just got a little carried away with one shot too many and went home with a hot girl. Look, I feel fine! I'm not even hungover!" It's true, somehow I feel totally fine. I have no idea how I got so lucky, because usually my hangovers are fucking brutal.

"I'm glad you're okay and you made it home safely, but seriously, please be more careful next time. At least text me where you're going so I know that you're okay. Will you please do that from now on?"

"Yeah, yeah, okay, I promise I will. Sorry." It's funny. When my parents implemented that same rule in high school it made me feel caged, but coming from someone like Lucy, it just makes me feel loved. Lucy hugs me even though I definitely don't deserve it; I hug her back and thank my lucky stars I have such a forgiving and concerned roommate.

"Good, now here, eat up," she says, tossing me a greasy brown paper bag. "Fresh from Ho Yuen in Chinatown." I peek inside the bag and take a whiff of the doughy treats. They smell sweet and I immediately start stuffing my face with one, and holy shit, either this is the best thing I've ever tasted or hunger is the best sauce.

Lucy pulls her tea cart to the center of our room and makes us coffee as I devour the red bean bun. Maybe it's my adrenaline levels finally cooling off or my body reacting to the first food it's had in over twelve hours, but suddenly it feels like someone cracked open my skull and took a dump inside.

"Okay, I lied," I say as I choke down the last bite. "I do have a hangover. It was just delayed."

"I knew it," Lucy singsongs.

I reach over the side of my bed and grab my hoodie off the floor and put it on, pulling the strings on the hood to make it as tight as possible around my exploding face. I rest my head against the wall and pray for a swift death. Lucy, looking well-rested and showered, hands me a floral-printed mug filled with coffee, and joins me on my bed.

"How are you not hungover right now?" I grumble.

"I got up at six this morning and went for a run to Chinatown, plus I didn't drink last night, remember?"

"Wait a second." I look at her skeptically. "You *run*? Like, on purpose?"

"Every morning since I was in seventh grade." She beams, making me wince. I want to judge her healthy lifestyle so hard right now but I'm too tired to do anything but exist at the moment, and Lucy doesn't seem to mind because she keeps talking at me. "Kenton runs too. We're going to go on a run together tomorrow. I was worried I wouldn't have time to date someone, but we have so much in common that I think this could really work out!"

"Are you going to eat any of this?" I hold out the bag full of Chinese goodies to her.

"No, thanks." She waves me off. "I already had an egg-white omelet this morning." I would roll my eyes at her but they currently feel like they're covered in sand, so instead I just eat more fried dough. While I'm shoving carbs in my mouth, Lucy proceeds to tell me, again, everything there is to know about Kenton. I'm too hangry to write it out in complete sentences so I'll just give you the highlights:

THINGS LUCY
KNOWS ABOUT
KENTON PARKER

- He's from New York.[30]
- He runs (on purpose) too.[31]
- He's a film major.
- He has four tattoos that he designed himself.
- He's an only child.
- His favorite book of all time is *Fear and Loathing in Las Vegas*.[32]
- He has strong opinions about music.[33]
- Some other stuff I don't remember.

"I can't believe you got all that out of him in one night. Your butt must be magic," I tell Lucy when she's finally run out of Jeopardy facts on her new crush.

"After we danced, we went outside for some air and we just started chatting and then we just didn't stop for the rest of the night!"

---

30 Technically Hoboken, New Jersey, but whatever, who am to judge? I'm from a state east coast people refer to as a "flyover state."
31 WHY.
32 Acceptable, but only because it's better than *On the Road* as far as favorite dude books go.
33 I stopped paying attention during this part.

Part of me wants to remind Lucy to take it easy, she only met this guy last night, but then again A) this is what she said she wanted and B) I just woke up in some rando's bed so I am a little unqualified to be doling out relationship advice. So I just keep my trap shut and instead say, "Aww, Luce, I am so happy for you!" Her smile is so big it even starts to counteract my hangover a little.

"What about you? Are you going to see that girl again?"

I tilt my head in confusion. "Who? What? Which girl?"

"That girl you whose dorm room you just came from?"

"Oh, right, Lottie."

"Are you going to see her again?" Lucy wiggles her eyebrows up and down.

"She was a babe, but nah." I take a sip of coffee.

"What? Why not?"

"She's just the girl you hook up with when you're drunk at a party, she's not the kind of girl you bring home to meet your roommate."

Lucy's pout morphs into pity. "Oh, that's too bad. But don't worry, you'll find someone."

I tip my mug and drink the last of that sweet bean water. "That's sweet, but I'm not worried. I just like to have fun. There are plenty of *someones* to find here and I intend to find them all." I brace for impact. It's the kind of sexual philosophy that usually warrants lengthy follow-up arguments from people like Lucy who never quite understand that when I say I *just want to have fun* that it means exactly that and nothing more.

Lucy takes a deep breath, preparing to launch into a monologue, but I am saved when her phone alarm goes off. She hops off my bed and starts putting on a pair of lace-up boots.

"Come on, get dressed!" she commands me.

"What? Why?" I pull my hood down even farther, covering my face.

"We have to get to the bookstore to get our course materials and then we have an orientation presentation at the Majestic Theatre where we're going to take that test on *The Iliad* and then we break out into meetings with our department heads." I get up and start swapping one comfy outfit in exchange for a different comfy outfit when something Lucy said makes me stop.

"Wait . . . what test?"

"The one on *The Iliad*." She keeps looking at me like I should know what she's talking about. "Didn't you get a copy of it in the mail this summer? They sent it to everyone."

"Yeah, but I didn't read it!"

"Seriously? The letter it came with said we'd have a test on it during orientation week."

"WHAT?!?" I start to panic. "A test during our first week of school, before the school part even starts?! Who does that?!?"

"Emerson does that!"

Lucy and I finish changing, then she drags me downstairs to the bookstore next to the Little Building, where in exchange for hundreds of dollars, we're given stacks of textbooks that'll be worth nothing at the end of the semester when we try to sell them back. We drop the books back in our room and then walk a block away to the Majestic Theatre, Emerson's decadent and lightly haunted theater built in 1903.[34] We sit through a one-hour improv show about Emerson's history put on by a bunch of comedy majors, and then those blue test booklets I swear I thought I'd never have to see again are handed out and we take our test on *The Iliad*.

A large screen drops down in the center of the stage and five essay questions are projected onto it along with a clock counting down from forty-five minutes. I look at the screen and read the first question. I read it again. I understand four of the words and none of them are the important ones. I look around and everyone is furiously writing and flipping pages in their little books. Suddenly, I feel hot and sick and sweaty. I clear my throat and wipe my clammy palms on the velvet cushioned seat. I read through the question a few more times before I start writing whatever nonsense I can come up with and by the time I've finished what I hope is a coherent answer, people around me are getting up to turn their books in. I look up at the clock and I have only three minutes left. Three minutes to answer four more essay questions.

So, that's super cool. Less than a week into college life and I've already fucked up. Cool. Awesome. Great. Super. Wonderful.

---

34 The legend goes that one of Boston's mayors died while watching a performance back in the day and now he haunts the place.

CHAPTER 6

IT'S TAKEN ME UNTIL MID-OCTOBER, ABOUT SIX weeks, but I think I finally have a handle on this whole freshman thing. Here's what I've learned so far:

- Don't tell Micah about people you hook up with unless you enjoy having your business broadcasted via his *Third-Floor Report*.
- You'll be asked to help film about 9,000 student films, TikToks, or YouTube videos and 8,999 of those requests will be from Sasha.
- If you're stealthy about it, bring Tupperware with you to the dining center and load it up with snacks for when you get hungry in the middle of the night.

- The classes here may have clickbait-y names, but they are actually way harder than I thought they would be. Even my Love and Eroticism class is hard. It involves zero porn and our entire grade rests on a twenty-page essay that's due at the end of the semester.
- THERE IS SO MUCH WAITING. There is always a line for the shower, the elevators, the stairwell, the laundry room, the dining halls.

In addition to all that, it turns out—and I don't know if this is common knowledge—college kids are super fucking busy! We may live together, but I don't see very much of Lucy now that we have fully acclimated to our new routines. Lucy leads a very structured life—she has to. She's double-majoring, has a new boyfriend, works part-time soliciting donations from rich alumni at the Emerson Fund, *and* she still goes home every Sunday for family dinner. I am only guaranteed an audience with her on Saturday mornings for breakfast, which brings us to the next scene:

"Ahh fuck, I regret this," I say as soon as Lucy and I see the line for the waffle machine on a Saturday morning. I fidget in line, crossing and uncrossing my arms, bouncing on my feet, assessing every person ahead of me in order to estimate how long I'm going to have to wait until my hunger is satiated, when I realize one of those people happens to be Rose. "Fuck it, I'll just get cereal."

"Oh, come on," Lucy says, wrapping her arms around me to keep me still. "There's only five people in front of us now. It won't take that long." The dude at the front of the line has finally finished and now it's down to four, four people between me and my waffles and Rose is up next.

"So I wanted to ask you something," Lucy says.

"Mm-hmm?" I reply but I'm not really paying attention. I shimmy free from Lucy's embrace and stand on my toes to see what's going on. There's a lot of commotion at the front of the line. What the fuck is Rose doing?

"It's about Kenton," Lucy says.

"Sorry, Luce, there's a waffle emergency. I'll make us a waffle, why don't you grab us coffees and I'll meet you in the back." Lucy agrees to the plan and I step out of line and make my way to the front. Rose, dressed in a very poufy polka dot dress and her signature combat boots, is fretting over the iron and wiping batter off the floor. "Do you need help?" I ask her.

"Yeah, thanks," she says. "I don't know what happened." I look at the machine and the batter is sputtering out the sides in mini-explosions and the whole machine is starting to smoke. I pop open the iron and assess the damage. She put so much batter in, there are barely any pockets visible; the whole thing looks more like a bumpy pancake.

"Holy crap, this is way too much batter!" I grab a plate from the stack and the tongs and try to pry it loose from the cast iron but the whole thing is stuck and it's breaking off into little pieces. "Didn't you spray this down before you drowned it in batter?" I ask her as she finishes mopping up the floor with a napkin.

"Oh shit, I forgot to do that!" She says and she looks like she's about to panic. I shake my head and keep trying to get the waffle free with the tongs but it's not working. I reach around and unplug the whole damn machine and roll up my sleeves.

"We're gonna need a scalpel," I tell her. "I have to surgically remove your waffle." She dashes over to the cutlery station, gracefully weaving in and out of people like a dancer. She bounds back and hands me a butter knife. It takes concentration and it isn't pretty, but thanks to the many years of fucking up in the kitchen at home, I am able to excise her waffle out of the iron mostly intact. It flops on the plate and I hand it to her.

"Damn, you are really good at that. I thought it was a goner," she says to me.

"Next time, don't use so much batter, and spray the iron down beforehand." We get out of the way and let the next guy in line have his turn. I turn to go back to my place in line but she stops me and says, "Hey, thanks for helping me. This is my first time making waffles."

"What, are you serious?" I ask her, shocked that someone could live this long without having made waffles before.

"Yeah, I'm more of a pancake girl," she says casually, like there's no difference between pancakes and waffles. Fool.

"Well, that's unfortunate. And here I thought we were going to become good friends."

"Oh? No room in your life for a pro-pancake girl?" She asks.

"Sorry, I'm a registered waffle enthusiast. I cannot be associated with your kind."

"Too bad," she says, and I think this is the first time I have ever seen Rose smile in a way that isn't the least bit cocky. "Enjoy your breakfast," she says and starts eating off her plate as she walks toward the seating area.

Ten minutes later, Lucy and I have a chocolate chip waffle to share as well as roasted salmon on a bed of greens for her and a bowl of Lucky Charms cereal and one banana for me.[35]

"So what did you want to ask me?" I pour milk out of a carton and then start in on my cereal.

"How do you know if you've lost your virginity?" Lucy asks. I choke on my Lucky Charms and cough up some tiny marshmallows onto my shirt.

"I'm sorry, what now?" I wipe my mouth with the back of my hand. She nervously folds and unfolds her hands on the table.

"*Hypothetically* speaking, how do you know if you've *lost* your virginity?"

"What, like you misplaced it or something?"

"No, I mean, like—" Lucy pauses, searching for a way to

---

35 The banana is just for show. You and I both know I'm never gonna eat it.

phrase her next question. "How do you know when you've had *all-the-way* sex?"

"Is there such a thing as *half-the-way* sex?"

"Yes!" She chirps loud enough for the people at the table next to overhear and they give us looks. Lucy lowers her voice. "What I mean is, does it count as sex if it's only the tip that goes in?"

Well, this is officially shaping up to be one of the weirdest conversations I've had at college thus far. But I'm not gonna lie, my interest is piqued. I sit up and lean in.

"So, in this hypothetical scenario, there is peener and cooter penetration, but the hymen isn't broken?"

She thinks about my question for a minute, considers her response. "Yes, exactly."

I set my cereal aside even though I still have a quarter left. That is how intrigued I am by this convo—I am no longer hungry for cereal. I sit up straight and fold my hands together on the table. "How long was the peep inside the hoohah?"

Lucy shoots me a mildly annoyed look. "Can't you just say penis and vagina?"

"I can, but I will not," I say in my most professional voice. "I am a proper lady and those clinical terms are so vulgar. So, tell me, how long was the wiener inside the tiddlywink?"

"I don't know." Lucy shrugs. "Like, a minute, maybe?"

I lean back into the seat and lower my imaginary therapist's glasses to the bridge of my nose. "Now, did either party reach, you know, *completion*?"

"He did," she says quickly and looks down at her hands.

"Interesting." It's funny how losing one's virginity is considered to be a rite of passage, like some form of emotional and physical test one must pass in order to be considered a normal human person. But the question she's asking me is one that has literally never crossed my mind before. How *do* you know when you've lost your virginity? I just have so many questions. I lean away from the table and my eyes travel toward the ceiling as I ponder all scenarios in which a virgin could have sex without losing their virginity. It takes me all of twenty seconds to form an opinion.

"Yes," I finally say. "I do think it still counts as sex, *all-the-way* sex as you call it, even if it was just the tip. I don't think penetration should be the only standard by which sex is defined."

Lucy takes a sip from her mug. "Why not?"

"I think everyone can and *should* define what constitutes as sex and virginity on their own terms. For me, I would define sex as junk on junk. Therefore, even if it is just the tip of the wiener that enters the muffin shop, that's still junk on junk. And as for virginity, I just think that term means you haven't done something before. But that's my own personal definition. Everyone should define what sex means for themselves."

"I like that," she says while nodding, letting my argument sink in. Satisfied with my explanation, I reach for my cereal and resume eating when Lucy says, "I guess by your definition then, I lost my virginity last night."

The soggy cereal gets stuck in my throat and I have to momma-bird it back into the bowl.

"OOOOOOOH MMMMMMMMMY GOOOOOOOOO-OOD." I stretch the reaction out for extra effect because this is the kind of thing that deserves to have words and syllables elongated. When one friend tells another friend that they've just experienced a life-changing moment, it is that friend's duty to turn it into a big fucking deal. "I can't believe you didn't tell me about this sooner! Where did it happen? How did it happen? What did it feel like? Were you scared? Was he respectful? Did you come? Now, using this banana as your constant, please compare and contrast Kenton's length and girth. TELL ME EVERYTHING! But first and most importantly, did you guys use a condom?"

"Did who use a condom?"

In my shock and awe I didn't even notice Micah approach our booth. He sets down his food tray and signals me to scoot over and make room, which I do.

"Lucy used a condom," I tell him, and then turn to Lucy and point at her with my spoon. "At least, she better have."

"Of course we did!" Lucy squeaks and then gives me that *I can't believe you're telling Micah my most personal, intimate details* look and I get it. If Micah hears about Lucy's first v-card swipe, she could be featured in tomorrow's *Third-Floor Report*. Micah senses this, or just becomes aware of our silence since he sat down. He sets his fork aside and looks at us.

"What? I'm off duty right now." I raise my right eyebrow and give him the same look my mother gives me when she catches me in a lie. Micah throws his hands in the air in a show of surrender. "My lips are sealed. Everything said at this booth will be completely confidential."

"You promise?" Lucy asks him nervously.

Micah makes an X with his finger over his heart. "I swear it. Now, spill."

Lucy looks around and lowers her voice, forcing Micah and me to lean in. "Kenton and I had sex for the first time."

Micah salutes her with his fork. "It's about damn time. Good for you!"

Lucy hides her face behind her hands and we wait patiently for her to work up the nerve and tell us the story. "It happened last night in his room—"

"OH MY GOD!" I interrupt and she gives me a look. "Sorry! Continue!"

"I went up to his room to study like we usually do," Lucy continues. I am trying my best to not interrupt her, so I press my lips together and stare at her adoringly. "We took a break after an hour and then we started watching some art house film he had to watch for class, I don't even know what it was. It was all in French with subtitles."

"Hot," Micah chimes in.

Lucy pauses and takes a sip of tea. "Anyways, we start kissing and it's nice, and then we're both undressed and under his covers and I'm on bottom and he's on top—"

"Interesting," Micah interrupts. "I always figured Kenton to be a bottom."

Lucy fiddles with a napkin, tearing it into little bits. "Well, we were kissing and then, I guess, he just put it in? I mean, I definitely felt it go in a little, but it didn't hurt or anything. It was just sort of, *there*, I guess."

"Okay . . . then what?" I coax her. She continues shredding her napkin and I slap my hand over hers, getting her to stop fidgeting and focus.[36]

"I guess he just sort of—came?" She finally looks up at Micah and me, as if either one of us has any explanation for her boyfriend's shortcomings.

Micah sets his plate aside and folds his hands neatly on the table. "So let me get this straight, and I do mean *straight*," he says calmly. "Kenton just gets it halfway in there and then comes immediately?"

Lucy nods.

"What did he say? What did *you* say?" I ask her.

Lucy throws her arms up in frustration. "We didn't say anything! He just pulled out, rolled over, and cleaned up. We didn't talk about it afterward either, we just finished the movie and then I left." She looks at us, distraught.

I squeeze her hand. "How are you feeling about this?"

"I dunno, it's just . . . not what I expected, I guess."

I ask my next question carefully, really hoping it doesn't

---

36 Is this how non-ADHD people feel around me?

offend her. "What did you think your first time would be like?"

She lets out an uncomfortable laugh. "Honestly? I don't know! But I guess I always thought it would be more—*climactic*?"

"That's fair." I nod. "I think we'd all like our first times to be more like how they're shown in movies, but the reality is, the first time for everyone is just straight up awkward as fuck. At least you were with someone who cares about you."

Micah nods as well. "The first time I did it was in the back of a car in the parking lot of a bowling alley. Super romantic."

Lucy learns forward. "Do you think he was nervous or something? He didn't seem nervous."

"I mean, I've never swiped anyone's v-card before so I can't speak to that specific experience, but once I did take this one guy's blow-job virginity." Micah starts laughing as the memory of it comes back to him in vivid, awkward detail. "He was so nervous, he was practically shaking. It was kinda sweet, now that I think about it. But from start to finish it only took ten seconds. I think I set a new world record for fastest BJ ever. I mean, I'm good, but I'm not *that* good."

"We should compare notes sometime," I say to him.

"Have you figured out how to stop the gag reflex? Because I cannot figure that one out."

"Oh yeah! All you need to do is—" Lucy waves her hands in front of my face, bringing us back to the conversation.

Micah—in a surprising show of compassion—puts his hands on top of mine, which are now on top of Lucy's, and gives her a sympathetic smile. "Lucy, darling, there's no need to fret. Men have no self-control when they're horny and nervous."

"You see? This is why I think it's better to have sex with people you don't care about," I say, suddenly very excited to stand on a soapbox. "The second you get to know some-one, there is so much pressure and so many expectations to live up to. Everyone gets all nervous and then the sex ends up sucking!"

Micah scoffs. "That is *so* not true!"

"Hey! You just said so yourself, your first time was super awkward too," I say, feeling pretty good about my argument.

"That's because it was in the back of a car and neither of us knew what we were doing!" Micah laughs. "Everyone's first time is awkward! But eventually we figured it out and the sex got really good. So don't listen to Elliot, Lucy. You and Ken-ton just need to work at it and eventually it'll be great." Micah reaches for his coffee mug and raises it to Lucy. "Here's to Lucy's v-card!"

I start to feel myself gearing up to preach more about the virtues of free love, but then Lucy laughs as the tension finally eases out of her shoulders, and I remember that this moment isn't about me. It's about Lucy. So I swallow my pride and raise my banana and say, "And here's to junk on junk and the shar-ing of bodily fluids!"

"Ew, gross. I'm not cheers-ing to that." Lucy scrunches her face but cheers-es us anyways.

The next day, Sunday, something happens.

[*dramatic pause*]

But first, let me digress. Over the past six weeks, I have learned that college is nothing if not a grand experiment in learning how to tolerate people being all up in your shit. Every dorm room has a lock but no one really uses them here. As a result, I have grown to be comfortable with strangers occupying the space where I roost.

Anyway, I bring all this up because I need you to understand that Lucy and I haven't locked our door since orientation week. We don't really even knock anymore either, we just come and go as we please. If either one of us needs the room for sexy things, we text each other a chicken emoji beforehand.[37] I have never received a text like that from Lucy because she and Kenton are usually in his single on the eighth floor. I am telling you all this because I want it to be clear that what happens next is totally not my fault.

So it's Sunday afternoon and I just got out of one of those free screenings movie studios sometimes set up for Emerson students. As I walk back to my room, I'm reading Micah's latest *Third-Floor Report* post on my phone and I don't bother knocking because it's Sunday and Lucy always goes home on Sundays.[38] So without looking up from my phone, I waltz

---

37 The international symbol for tender chicken.
38 AND BECAUSE I'M USED TO NOT KNOCKING.

right into my room and happen upon Lucy and Kenton getting it on.

"OCCUPIED!!!!!!!!!" Lucy shrieks while Kenton frantically dives under her covers.

"Shit! Fuck! Oh god, sorry!" I slap my hands over my eyes and blindly reach for the door handle behind me but end up knocking over whatever is on top of Lucy's dresser. Objects are falling, Lucy and Kenton are yelling, and I cannot get out of there fast enough.

It takes me seventy years, but I finally find the handle and back out of our room, ass-first. I slam the door shut and yell through it, "I am so sorry!!!"[39]

I wait for a reply but don't get one. I check my phone to see how much juice I have left but it's completely dead. I try Micah's room first, but he isn't there, just his off-page roommate you'll never meet in this story, and neither he nor Micah has a charger that will work with my phone.

I try again, this time down to the other end of the hall toward Sasha's room but she has a *Filming in progress! (PS - Don't forget to subscribe!)* note taped to the door. I think for a second about trying the Brads but they're in the common room livestreaming some extremely loud video game and there's no way I'm interrupting that nonsense. I think about going back to the movie theater and napping in a back row, but

----

39 What's the polite way to apologize to your roommate and her boyfriend whose boobs and boner you just walked in on? Does Hallmark make a *Sorry I caught you and your new boyfriend sexing it up!* card?

then I pass by Rose on my way to the elevators. Since the last time we interacted was when I saved her waffle, I decide to risk it and see if Rose is willing to return the favor.

"Hey, on a scale of good to great, how is your mood right now?" I ask as I fall into step with her. Her outfit today is a pastel rainbow tracksuit that looks tie dyed by hand. Knowing her, it probably is.

"What did you do?"

"Nothing."

She stops walking. "WHAT DID YOU DO?"

"I swear it was nothing!" I throw my hands up. "I wanted to know your mood because I need to ask you a favor and sometimes you can be a lil' scary. By the way, I'm really enjoying this vaporwave look you've got going on today." That does the trick because she softens her tone.

"What's the favor?"

"What kind of phone do you have?" She holds hers up and it's the same as mine. "Can I borrow your charger and also possibly take a nap in your room? Mine is currently . . . *occupied*." We get to Rose's room and she unlocks the door because she's smart and doesn't keep her room unlocked like the fool narrating this story.

"Can't you use the common room?" she asks as we hover just outside her room. "Or go to Micah or whoever else you hang around with?"

"The Brads are using the common room, Micah is out, and Sasha is filming a YouTube video."

She sighs and checks her watch. "You're welcome to borrow my charger, but you can't sleep here. I'm headed to the library."

"Cool, I'll just join you then. That sounds more fun than napping."

"What? No, I wasn't inviting you," she says.

"I know." I give her a charming smile. "I was inviting myself."

Rose glances at her watch again and for a second I think she's going to say no, but she sighs in defeat. "Fine, but I need to work so you have to be quiet."

"Excellent! And don't worry, I will be totally focused and quiet, I promise."

● ● ●

This is my first time visiting the library and I wasn't sure what to expect, so I am surprised to find it packed on a Sunday evening. There are so many students here, nearly every table and study room is full. Rose leads the way as we wind through the stacks until we find a row of small study rooms with glass doors. All of them are occupied, including the one Rose steps into. Monica is here. Ugh, I really don't want to be the third wheel to my RA and her girlfriend, but I really need to charge my phone and well, I've made my bed. Now I must lie in it. I take a seat opposite Rose and Monica and watch as they awkwardly kiss hello. It is the least sexy kiss I have ever watched. It's like watching my parents kiss. I shudder.

Rose opens her bag and pulls out a laptop, a notebook, and

one of those retractable pens with six colors to choose from and gets to work. I clear my throat.

"So, uh, Rose, about that phone charger . . ." Rose reaches into her bag and hands me the long white cord. "Thanks. So, what are you guys working on?"

"An essay," they reply in unison as they continue working without missing a beat.

"Cool, cool. Me too. Well, I mean, I have an essay for my Love and Eroticism in Western Culture class but I haven't started it." Monica sighs in that rude way where she's clearly trying to let me know I'm being a nuisance, but I ignore her. "Actually, I haven't even written the proposal yet; I'm having trouble coming up with a good angle for it. Maybe y'all could help me with that?"

Rose glances at me from over her screen. "Look at you, getting into your classes. I'm so proud."

"There is only *one* class I like and it's not this. The others have failed to inspire me thus far."

Rose leans back very slowly, crosses her arms and cocks an eyebrow while a smug grin spreads across her face. "And which class is the one you like?"

Ohhhhh, no she doesn't.

I shake my head. "Nope, nuh uh."

"It's your screenwriting class, isn't it," she states rather than asks.

"No, it's my Plants and People class," I lie. "I *love* learning about plant structure and growth processes."

Rose smacks the table in excitement and points her pen at me. "Ohmygod! I was right, you do like screenwriting!"

"I do not."

"Admit it!"

"Never!"

"Come on, you can't even give me that one?"

"*Je refuse* . . ."

"Can you two either leave or shut the hell up? I'm trying to write," Monica snaps at us and Rose immediately drops the act, returning her attention back to her laptop. I've only met Monica a few times and she's always been kind of dickish, so either she's a dick all the time or she's just a dick when I'm around. Either way, it really makes me question what Rose sees in her. Watching them together is an uncomfortable experience. I check my phone and sigh. It hasn't charged enough to turn on in the two minutes since I plugged it in. I fold my hands under my chin and try to be quiet for Rose's sake, but you know those annoying people who can't handle uncomfortable silences and must fill every quiet moment with idle chatter? Well guess what? I AM ONE OF THOSE ANNOYING PEOPLE.

"So, anyways, about my essay," I say. "It's the *only* assignment we have for the entire semester and it's worth 90 percent of our grade but the guidelines are pretty loose; we just have to pick a specific topic within the realm of love and eroticism and dissect how it is depicted in media and entertainment. I have to make it good and stand out, but I don't know how to do that."

To my surprise, it's Monica who perks up. "Make it personal."

"What do you mean? Like say *I would argue* instead of *one would argue*?"

"No," Monica says. "Make it about you. Start with your thesis, then move on to examples to support your thesis and then top it off with your own personal experiences and how they compare. I took that class last year, your teacher loves that kind of shit."

"Huh," I say, leaning back in my chair as I consider that option. "That could work."

"So what's your topic?" Rose asks.

"I want to write about what comes after virginity."

"What do you mean?" she asks.

"There are tons of movies and books about people losing their virginity, but no one ever talks about what comes after that. Like, everyone sucks at sex when they're first starting out, but what about people, especially women and queer people, wanting to and learning how to have *good* sex? Where are those stories? So yeah, this could work. I could top the essay off with some personal thoughts about my own experience with good sex."

Rose sets down her pen and leans forward. "So you've had good sex then?"

"Yes, of course I have," I say right away and then pause. "Wait—what do you mean by *good* sex?"

She closes her laptop and looks at me. "Well, what do *you*

mean by good sex? Because for me, I'm not just talking about an orgasm. An orgasm is a nice by-product, but it doesn't necessarily need to be the point or the goal of sex. What I'm talking about is connecting with someone in a moment where the world melts away and there's nothing left but the two of you, your bodies, your heat, your breath, where you open yourself up, let the walls tumble down and reveal yourself to your partner and them to you. And I don't mean the *tension-releasing*, frenetic sex. I'm talking about the slow, hot, *tension-building* kind of intimacy where you take your time and savor every moment. The kind of sex that leaves your knees shaking and your body dripping."

Oh.

Oh, damn.

I don't think I took a breath the entire time she was talking.

I have to clear my throat before I can speak again. My mouth has suddenly gone dry from my jaw being on the floor for the last minute. "Uh, hmm, uh, yeah, no. I don't think I've had that kind of sex before."

"You should experiment then," Monica says and to be honest, I completely forgot she was even in the room with us. "Go have sex with a bunch of people and write about it for your essay."

"Seriously?" Rose furrows her brow at Monica. "*That's* your suggestion?"

"Why, what's so wrong with that?" Monica crosses her arms in front of her chest. I get the distinct feeling that I'm about to be left out of the conversation any moment now, so I sit back in my chair and watch them go at it.

"Your advice for her is to sleep with some strangers and then tell her teacher all about it in an essay? Doesn't that seem weird to you?"

"Not if she gets consent from her partners to write about the experience—and why are you suddenly so against it now? You didn't balk at the suggestion before when I told her to make it personal," Monica argues.

"I wasn't suggesting she have multiple partners, I was suggesting she find *one* person!"

This time Monica looks to me and says, "Oh right, I forgot Rose is a traditionalist."

Rose looks pissed. "I'm not a traditionalist, Mon. I just think a bisexual person—"

I hold my hand up to stop her. "Whoa, who, whoa, hey now. If you *insist* on labeling me, my sexual orientation is horny," I joke and hope they laugh because the fighting is making me feel all prickly and nervous.

Rose offers me an apologetic look. "I'm sorry, it's just that there's this negative stereotype about bi people being . . . promiscuous."

"So I'm not allowed to get messy and explore my sexuality out of fear I might be a stereotype?" I am genuinely interested in what Rose has to say, but Monica cuts her off before she can even start.

"Get over yourself, Rose. No one's type of relationship or sexual activity relates to their orientation. Fuck the stereotype."

Rose blatantly ignores her and says to me, "I just want you to be safe." And now Monica is the one who looks pissed.

"Why do you even care so much?" Monica asks, her voice harsh.

"She's my resident!" Rose yells, her voice rising above Monica's.

"Oh sure, *that's* the reason—"

Rose sucks in a breath between her teeth, like she's ready to strike, and as much as I want to steer the conversation back to stereotypes and sex positivity, it's obvious this conversation is no longer about me now and I should go.

I yank the phone charger out of the wall and hand it back to Rose. "Thanks for letting me borrow this and for the advice and all the other stuff, but clearly you two have . . . *some things* . . . to talk about so I'm going to go ahead and let myself out. Have a good evening, ladies."

I grab my bag off the floor and slowly back out of the room and away from whatever the hell that was. Yikes. I don't know if all that was about me, or them, or sexual experimentation or politics or what but that was some weird-ass energy I do not want to be around.

As I leave the library, I turn my phone back on and it lights up with a text from Lucy letting me know Kenton has left. When I get back to the third floor, I almost walk in the room without knocking again out of habit, but recent events have taught me to do otherwise, so I politely tap my knuckles on the door and wait until I hear Lucy shout, "Come in!" I open the door and shield my eyes, you know, just in case.

"Are you sure it's safe?" I tease. I peek between my fingers, but when I see her sitting on her bed, with her knees tucked up and her head buried between them, I immediately drop the act and go to her. "Ohmygod, what's wrong? Are you okay? Did he hurt you? I will fucking kill him if he hurt you." I wrap my arms around her. Her face is blotchy and wet.

"No, no, nothing like that. He didn't do anything, we didn't do anything. I don't know why I'm crying." She tries to wipe away her mascara but it only spreads even more across her face, making her look like she's auditioning for a goth metal band. I offer her the hem of my shirt.

"I'd be crying too if I was dating a guy with a peep as small as Kenton's." I'm hoping my joke will make her smile but instead she buries her head between her knees again.

"Oh my god you saw it!"

I laugh and rub her back. "Lucy, I swear, I did not see your boyfriend's peep. I was just kidding!" It takes a minute but I eventually coax her out from behind her knees and take her hands in mine. I look her right in the eyes. "What's going on, lady?" She fidgets with the rings on her fingers. I tap the top of my shoulder and she rests her head on it and I lean my head against hers. Her hair smells like she's been stealing my shampoo. I wait as long as she needs to compose herself.

"I took Micah's advice. I invited Kenton over today because I wanted to try again, but we were trying to get him . . . going, you know, and—"

"I walked in," I say.

"Yeah, that didn't help either," she laughs but keeps going. "He wanted to try again after you left but I just wasn't feeling it. So we had a long talk and I told him I felt like we had moved a little too fast and maybe I wasn't as ready as I thought."

"How did he take it?"

"Good, I think. I don't know, he can be hard to read sometimes. I mean, he *said* he was okay with it and then we decided that we'd do . . . *third base* more until I am ready for more."

"Ohmygod, just say *oral,* you nerd," I tease.

"Hey! If you can't say *penis* and *vagina,* I don't have to say *oral.*" She shivers at the word.

"Fair enough," I say and remove my head from hers so I can look at her. "You don't have to do anything with Kenton until you are *both* ready. You know that, right?"

"Yes, I know that."

"Good." I smile and kiss her cheek.

She sits up straight and exhales a steadying breath. "I think it just hit me today, how fast things have changed in such a short period of time. It's a little overwhelming." I nod in agreement as she keeps talking. "I couldn't wait to get here, but now that I am here it's . . . *harder* than I expected, I guess."

"But not as hard as Kenton, amiright?" I raise my hand and

wait patiently until she reluctantly gives in and high-fives me back. Then she laughs and wraps her arms around me.

"I am so glad we got paired together," Lucy says. "I don't know what I'd do without you."

"Probably not get walked in on as much."

"Probably," she agrees.

"And you'd eat less waffles."

"That too."

"And have a cleaner room."

"Okay, okay, okay," she says and finally sits up straight again, wiping away all the tears from her lovely face.

"You gonna be okay?" I ask her again just to be sure.

"I think I just needed a good cry," she says, and even though her eye makeup is a hot mess, she looks better. "So where have you been? I texted you over an hour ago."

"Oh yeah, I've been at the library with Rose."

Lucy scrunches her face. "Hold up, *you* were at the *library* . . . with *Rose*?"

"Yeah it's a short story, but first let me tell you about this essay I'm going to write." I hop off her bed and hold my hands out like I see all the musical theater kids do when they practice in the common room. "I'm calling it *Project Tender Chicken* . . ."

CHAPTER 7

AND SO BEGINS A GRAND UNDERTAKING WHEREIN I, Elliot McHugh, shall embark on a mission of the utmost importance: Project Tender Chicken. And in case you've been skipping over all my *hilarious* footnotes, *tender chicken* is my own personal phrase that essentially translates to lady wood, a girl boner, the female hard-on. It's both a noun and a verb and now it's your new favorite phrase.

Okay, so, here is how this is gonna go. For the next month or two, I am going to get it on. A lot. And the best part is, it's ALL IN THE NAME OF ACHIEVING A HIGHER EDUCATION.[40] My goal? Fully embrace the freedom being emotionally unattached affords me and find the Holy Fucking Grail of Sex. I don't care how much time and energy this will require; all other aspects of my life are now secondary to Project Tender Chicken.

---

40 Lol, let's be honest. The essay is a bonus. I was gonna do this regardless.

It's Rose's question I can't get out of my head. *Have you ever had good sex?* What turns you on? What turns you off? And the truth is, I don't know. How does anyone know? How do YOU know? And it's got me thinking that maybe this is what college is for. Sure, sure, yeah college is also about getting a degree blah blah blah and whatever, but isn't it also about figuring out who you are and who you want to be? And I'm not just talking about a career, I'm talking about who I want to be as a human fucking being. And how else are you supposed to find the answers if you don't go searching for them? So strap in or strap on, my friends! Fuck it, let's do this.

ELLIOT MCHUGH PRESENTS: THE TENDER CHICKEN SPECIAL

☙ ANDERS ❧

I didn't go very far to find my first partner. In fact, all I had to do was walk up one flight of stairs to the fourth floor to find Anders, an acting major who looked like he could play a Swedish viking on TV. I met him outside the Little Building a few weeks ago and I'd been curious to try him on for size ever since. And now, I have.

"How about now?" He asked nicely as he readjusted the

angle of his wiener. He pushed in deeper and it did not feel good.

"Ack!" I cried out from underneath him. "You still keep hitting my cervix. Can we try it from behind instead?"

"Okay!" Anders said. We'd been going at it for nearly an hour and while he was very enthusiastic, we couldn't quite get a good rhythm going. He pulled out, got off the bed, and I flipped over, got up on my hands and knees, and we gave it a go. Unfortunately for me, when Anders came in for a landing, he miscalculated and his peeper nearly slipped into my pooper.

"No, no, no, no! Wrong hole! WRONG HOLE!" I screeched. He jumped back and immediately started apologizing.

"I'm so sorry! Are you okay?" He looked genuinely terrified.

"I'm fine!" I said even though my butt had a slightly different opinion.

"Do you want to keep going?" He asked and I was amazed he still had a boner. I certainly didn't.

"Uh, no, I think this might be a good place to stop." I pulled the sheets up to cover myself while Anders reached for his boxers.

I didn't return his text the next day.

❦ YVONNE & TOBIN ❦

I met Yvonne and Tobin in the darkroom when I got bored waiting for Micah to finish one of his journalism seminars one evening. I started to wander the halls when I saw someone come out of a red-lit room. I had never been in a photography darkroom before and I didn't even realize a class was going on, so I walked right in—but no one seemed to notice I wasn't supposed to be there. I watched as they took these white glossy sheets of paper and gently slid them in plastic trays filled with clear liquid. Look, I get it, current technology is cool and all, but there is something completely captivating about watching a black and white nude photograph of a beautiful woman materialize before your very eyes.

"Did you take this?" I asked as a student used rubber tongs to delicately press the photo paper into the liquid bath.

"Yeah, this one's mine," they said.

"This is really fucking good."

"Thanks," they smiled. It was cool that they weren't totally weirded out by a stranger coming up and getting all critique-y of their work.

"Who is this?" I asked, unable to take my eyes off the photo.

"That's Yvonne, she's my girlfriend," they said with a beam.

"Wow, you are lucky. I could eat her up."

They looked at me, and for a second I worried I had overstepped and been too forward but then they said, "She and I would love that."

And then, for one very successful week for Project Tender Chicken, I was the guest star in an erotic, three-episode arc in Yvonne and Tobin's relationship. Y&T invited me to stay—to be *with* them—but as soon as I was asked for some kind of commitment, all those old, familiar anxieties started creeping up again and I lost all interest. I declined their offer. I haven't seen either since.

❧ EVA ❧

Sasha introduced me to this Puerto Rican girl, Eva Grey. Sasha met her in a creative writing class and from what she told me, Eva writes fantasy stories with super hot sex scenes and has been single for a while and ready for someone new, so I was *really* looking forward to our date.

Lucy went home for dinner like she usually does on Sundays, so Eva and I had the room to ourselves. I set the mood perfectly—I restrung the fairy lights without Rose knowing, and I bought one of those oil diffusers to blanket the room in a vanilla and musk scent. I was just putting on my favorite sexytime playlist when she arrived. I let her in and as soon as I took a seat on my bed, Eva was on me. Literally. She jumped on my lap and straddled me. Her kisses were rough and sloppy and she squeezed my tits so hard it felt like she was going to pop them. Very gently I peeled my face from hers and said, "Hey, hi. So um, mind if we slow this down a bit?"

Her hands flew to her mouth in embarrassment as she got off my lap. "Was that too fast? Ohmygosh, that was too fast. I'm so sorry, I'm nervous. This is my first time with a girl."

"Oh shit, really?" And suddenly, I was nervous because I had never been anyone's first before. There is a lot of pressure and responsibility with being someone's first, especially when it's not *your* first. *If I do this,* I thought, *this isn't going to be some casual experience for her, she's going to remember me for the rest of her life.* With so little experience, there was absolutely zero chance Eva was going to be a mind-blowing sexual partner for me, but this was an opportunity to give Eva something most people never got—a phenomenal first time. I looked at her, standing there all cute and shy and you know what? It would be my honor—nay, my *duty*—to welcome Eva to the queer world with a climactic experience. If I was going to be her first, I might as well also be her best.

"There's no need to be nervous." I smiled at Eva and pulled her back down on my lap. "I'll take good care of you." I wrapped my hands around the small of her back, brought her lips to mine and kissed her.

Eva and I had fun together, but that's all it was: one sweet night. Eva will make a great girlfriend to a lucky lady someday, but I'm not going to be that lady.

🐓 THEO 🐓

I took the Chinatown bus to New York City to spend Thanksgiving with Izzy because it was easier than flying back to Ohio.[41] She hosted her medical school friends in her tiny apartment for Friendsgiving, but she spent the entire night ignoring me, so I started chatting up a hot, Black psychiatry student named Theo. After dinner, Izzy left with her

---

41 You remember Izzy, right? She's my older sister who also moonlights as Satan's mistress.

friends to hit up a bar, knowing full well I was too young to join her, and Theo offered to stay back and help me clean the dishes.

I'm not sure how it happened, but somehow we went from lathering pots and pans to tying each other up in my very first attempt at light bondage.[42] Theo was no Eva. He wasn't a virgin, he wasn't timid or shy. He wasn't an Anders either. He didn't fumble with my bra or stick it in the wrong hole. He was confident, strong, hot. And when I played the dominant role and had him tied to the bed, he was into it, fully committed and submissive. It was fascinating to watch him open up like that and I thoroughly enjoyed controlling the situation, only allowing him to come when I said he could, but when it was my turn and the roles were reversed . . . I just couldn't get there. Something was still holding me back. Don't get me wrong, the whole night was hot as hell and if I lived here I'd definitely put him on my *U up?* text list, but it wasn't the holy grail— it wasn't what Rose had described. I mean, maybe it was for Theo—but not for me.

"To be honest, I don't think I would make a very good sub," I told him after we finished playing our games. We were sprawled on my sister's bed, tangled among the sheets, naked and sweaty and sleepy from all the sex and turkey.

-----

42 Okay, that's a lie, I know how it happened. I was sitting on the kitchen counter drying dishes while Theo scrubbed the pots in the sink and I straight up asked him, "Have you ever had sex while tied up before?" And he said, "No" and I said, "Wanna try it?" and he said, "Oh, fuck yeah" and that was it.

"What are you talking about? You were great!" He reassured me. He reached over and gently kissed the inside of my wrist. It was still red and sore from being tied to the bed.

I flipped on my side to face him. "Theo, I'm a big girl. I can handle the truth."

"You *definitely* don't like being told what to do," he said with a laugh. "For what it's worth, I think you might enjoy it if you found the right partner."

"Why would who I'm with matter? Either you enjoy being controlled or you don't, simple as that."

"When is anything ever that simple?" He rolled onto his side so we were facing each other. "Think about it. In order to let someone control you, you have to trust them, and trust only comes through emotional intimacy."

"Oh god, you're talking about that whole desire versus intimacy thing, aren't you?"

"I am going to be a psychiatrist so . . ."

I roll my eyes. "We studied that in my Love and Eroticism in Western Culture class."

"It sounds like you have an opinion on it," he said.

"Yeah, I do," I said, sitting up in bed. "That whole philosophy is about how desire requires distance and space but in order for intimacy to happen, two must come together, i.e., closing the distance. Therefore aren't you sacrificing desire in order to achieve emotional intimacy?"

His head turned to the side in thought. "I suppose . . ."

"So by that logic then, in order to achieve maximum desire, a.k.a. Boner City, space and distance are required, i.e., zero emotional intimacy." I felt light-headed. I hadn't realized I was getting all worked up in my argument.

Theo debated himself in his head for a moment and then he sat up and leaned back on his palms. "If that's true, then why didn't you come? You just met me, you have no emotional attachment to me, so if your theory were true you should have been able to reach *maximum desire* as you said." The question is so shocking, it hits me like a bucket of cold water. This whole time, I'd been operating under the assumption that I could have amazing sex if I just experimented with different ways to get off with a wide array of people, like throwing a whole bowl of spaghetti at the wall to see what sticks. But it wasn't working . . . at least not in the way I thought it would.

"Wait, hold up. I'm a stranger to you too, right? So how come you *were* able to let go and come so easily then?" I asked, flipping the script on him.

"I don't know," he said. "Maybe I just have an easier time letting my guard down. Or maybe I actually feel emotionally connected to you."

I made a face. "Ew, gross, stop that."

"I'm serious!" He laughed. "I think you're really great. I'd like to see you again."

"Thanks, you're cool too, but I live in Boston and you're here and you're one of Izzy's friends and I think you get my point. But for real, thank you, you've given me a lot to think about." I threw the covers off us and got out of bed. I grabbed one of Izzy's many skater dresses cluttering the bedroom floor and pulled it on, and when I found his pants in the corner, I kicked them up to Theo.

"Are you seriously kicking me out?" he asked.

"Yeah dude, my sister is gonna be back any minute."

"It's Thanksgiving!" He looked at me like he'd never been kicked out of a woman's bed before.

"Sorry, but I've got this essay I need to work on and whatever, you get it. This was fun though, I'm sure I'll see you around sometime, or not. Either way, have a good one." He groaned, but got out of bed and dressed at a glacial pace. He only had one shoe on when I ushered him out the front door.

"You have real intimacy issues," he said as he hopped out into the hall.

"Yeah yeah yeah, I know. Anyways, thanks, doc. See ya." I tossed him his coat and shut the door. I plopped down on Izzy's couch, opened my laptop, and started writing down my thoughts for the essay.

Had I been going about this all wrong? I'd discovered what a whole lot of other people enjoy, but me? What do I want? What do I need? When I started Project Tender Chicken, I was hoping for a strong conclusion, a clear understanding of exactly what good sex is and how to have it, but in the end I was left with more questions than answers.

CHAPTER 8

IT'S THE WEEK AFTER THANKSGIVING BREAK, A month since I started Project Tender Chicken, and here I am, back at the place where all good sexual awakenings begin— the library.

"Can you show me where the sexual fetishes section is, please?" I ask. The student librarian whose cheeks are now two shades redder than they were a minute ago begrudgingly ushers me to the sexual health section at the back of the library.

I'm supposed to be meeting Kenton and Lucy, but I decided to get here early and work some more on my essay. I didn't want to start getting bizarre search engine results by Googling, nor can I buy anything online without the credit card company notifying my parents, so I'm cobbling together information with the material available in the library. Well, lesson learned, because the pickings here are slim. I'm flipping through this old book from 1940 titled *Sex Knowledge Wrecked Lives in the*

Twentieth Century[43] when I spot Anders in the next aisle over. *Shit shit shit shit shit shit.* I throw the book back on the shelf and dart into the next section of the library as quickly and quietly as possible before he sees me. I never responded to his last text.

"I've been looking for you," Kenton says when he catches me hiding out in the classical literature section.

"Oh yeah, sorry," I say, breathless. "I was doing research for a class. Should we grab one of these study rooms?" We walk down the aisle, passing occupied rooms until we find an empty one at the end. I dump my crap on the floor. "Is Lucy here somewhere? I can go find her—"

"She bailed . . . *again*," Kenton says through clenched teeth. "She's doing an extra shift at the Emerson Fund and then she's going home to help her grandma remodel her kitchen or some shit."

"Wait, I thought she went home last weekend to help her grandma?"

"She did *and* she's going again today," Kenton grunts. "Do you mind if we don't talk about Lucy?"

"Excuse me?" I glare at him.

He attempts a recovery and offers me a humble smile. "Sorry, things are just . . . frustrating right now. I feel like I never see her."

I reach across the table and put my hand on his arm.

---

43 This is a real book, by the way.

"Dude, you got to spend Thanksgiving with her, but I do know what you mean. The closer we get to finals, the less I see her. I think she's got too much on her plate. I mean, it's been great for my project to have the room to myself so much, but I miss Luce."

"Oh right, your *project*." Kenton leans back in his chair and looks at me curiously. "Lucy told me about that but didn't go into detail."

"It was just supposed to be an essay, but now the professor wants us to *present* our essays to the class as part of our final grade. I had this whole final bit about my own experiences, but I wasn't able to come to any sort of firm conclusion. I'm hoping if I spice up the presentation, the lack of definitive substance in the essay will be less noticeable. All I know is I cannot wait to see the look on my professor's face when I start talking about the female orgasm." I wait for the same shock, awe, and applause I usually get from everyone else when I explain Project Tender Chicken but Kenton doesn't look shocked—he looks bored, which weirdly bothers me, so I try another angle.

"I've decided to dedicate a whole section to S&M . . ." This time he perks up.

"Interesting." Kenton leans forward and rolls up his sleeves. "Will you be focusing on one particular discipline or on the relationship between doms and subs?"

"Oh, uh, neither, actually." I side-eye him. How come Lucy never told me he was into S&M? "The S&M stuff is a small part

127

of it; it mostly just covers its portrayal in movies and my own brief dabble with it."

"What does that mean then? You tried out S&M and wrote about it?" he asks.

"Yep! I tried a lot of things with a lot of different people over the past six weeks, but I'm only going to talk about a few of the more memorable experiences in my essay." I lean back in my chair and look him up and down. "But the bigger mystery now is, how come *you* know so much about this stuff?"

"Have you been to The Dungeon in Downtown Crossing? They have a pretty wide selection of toys if you want to include props in your presentation." His smile is weird as he adjusts the beanie covering his floppy black hair. There's a look in his eyes right now, something ignited, frantic even. As long as I've known him, Kenton has had the emotional range of a block of ice. I've never seen him get excited about, well, anything. But then again, that could be my own fault. I have made a point of limiting our interactions to the occasional dinner and whenever I walk in on him and Lucy. Maybe I just haven't gotten to know him all that well.

"How about tomorrow night?" he asks.

"What about tomorrow night?" I've been so lost in my own thoughts I didn't realize he was still talking.

"Do you want to go to The Dungeon tomorrow night? I can reschedule dinner with Lucy if you want." He pulls out his phone and starts texting Lucy.

I reach across the table and swat the phone out of his hand. "Don't you dare cancel on Lucy! Besides, I have plans tomorrow night with Micah. I'll check it out some other time though, thanks for the recommendation." He puts his phone away and we fall into an awkward silence for the rest of the hour. I don't get much done. It's hard to focus when you discover your best friend's boyfriend has a secret sexual fetish. I wonder if Lucy even knows. If she doesn't, there's no way I'm going to be the one to tell her.

But I do tell Micah the next day when we pay a visit to The Dungeon.

● ●|●

"Wait, I thought you were still pursuing that guy from MIT—what was his name?" I ask Micah the next day during our visit to the sex shop. We move from the cabinet of ball gags to the wall of whips. I pick up a short, black riding crop and play with it.

"His name is Eric," Micah reminds me. "And haven't you been keeping up with my *Report*? I quit that game a few weeks ago. He's straight."

"I told you that whole 'gay by May' thing wasn't going to work." I rest the tip of the riding crop on his chest. "Now, bend over and accept your punishment for not listening to me." He sighs, bends over, and I smack his ass a few times. I set the whip back in its place on the wall and walk over to a clothing rack filled with an array of apparel.

Micah picks up a pair of leather assless chaps and hands them to me. "You should wear these during your presentation. Your ass will get an A."

"Oh, I didn't realize that's what the A stood for. B must be for boobs, not butt, then."

"And C is for clit and D is dick."

"And an F means you're fucked." We laugh a little too loud and an embarrassed-looking customer checking out the nipple clamps shushes us, which only makes us laugh even more. We put the chaps back and skitter off to a different section of the store. The Dungeon is bigger than I imagined, not that I have been to that many fetish shops in my day, but it is surprisingly tasteful. It's well-lit and each department has been carefully merchandised—despite its name, The Dungeon is anything but.

"What about you?" Micah asks as we approach a table neatly arranged with dildos and vibrators in a wide variety of shapes, sizes, and colors. He picks up a giant pink monstrosity—it's unclear which hole it is meant for—and waves it in my face. "Are you in the market for one of these or will you be paying a visit to one of your playthings again? Maybe you should give Anders another shot . . ."

"I don't take victory laps. I do have some standards."

Micah pushes the button and the vibrator violently spasms out of his hands, falls onto the floor, and starts scooting away from us. Micah picks it up, blows the dust off, and offers it to me. "Here, you'll need this then. I bet you can get it half off since it's been on the floor."

"Hard pass."

Micah heads to the back while I continue exploring the front of the store. I walk the aisles, run my fingertips over leather floggers, silk blindfolds, and feather ticklers for another ten minutes until I get bored. Something about this place is bumming me out. I work my way to the back of the store and find Micah trying on a shiny black latex catsuit over his clothes.

"We should go. I already have some of this stuff, I don't need any more," I say as I take a seat on a purple velvet couch and watch as he admires himself in the mirrors.

"You're not gonna get anything? Why are we even here then?"

"Kenton recommended this place and I was curious. As you know, I've spent the last month on a journey of self-discovery."

"Yesssss," Micah says as he twirls in front of the mirror. I'm not sure if he's being supportive of me or himself in this scenario.

"I've learned quite a lot, actually, about what other people like. This one girl on the fifth floor only likes having her nerps tweaked. That's it! Nothing else! And over Thanksgiving break, I went down to New York to spend time with Izzy and I got with one of her med school friends and we tried out some light S&M. And there's this one dude on the digital culture floor who likes to hook up with *American Psycho* playing in the background. At first I thought it was just a coincidence, like he already had it streaming and just forgot to turn it off, but the second time he stopped us mid–make out in order to put it on."

Micah spins to face me. "Ohmygod, are you talking about Brendan Fromme?"

"Yes! How'd you know?!"

"We totally hooked up the second week of school! He put on *American Psycho* with me too! He is so weird—hot, but weird."

"I know!" I nod. "I've been trying to stay open-minded about everyone's predilections but that was one I just could *not* get on board with. But I dunno, I think I might be done with Project Tender Chicken. Or at least I think I need to put it on the back burner for a while."

"No sign of the holy grail of sex then?"

I sigh. "No, no holy grail. I mean, I got what I needed out of it to write up what I think is a decent essay and I've had fun, but it's not quite right. I had some pretty good sex, but none of it was *great*. There was just something . . . missing for me, and I don't know what it is. It's weird but I just spent the last six weeks being with all kinds of people but I feel . . . lonely. Know what I mean?" I look up to see if Micah is listening but he tuned me out some time ago. I watch as he spins around and around, trying to grab the zipper in the back, but he can't reach it. "Do you need some help?" I get up and try to unzip the back but it keeps getting stuck over his clothes. "How did you even get in this by yourself?"

"It's a skill."

"Who else besides *American Psycho* boy have you hooked up with here?" I ask him as I tug on the zipper. "I need to keep a list so I don't get any more of your sloppy seconds."

"Oh, I'm done with Emerson boys. I'm widening my network. If I'm lucky, I'll bag a trust fund gay at Harvard, and maybe then my parents would forgive me."

"Forgive you? For being gay?"

"They don't care that I'm gay, they only care that I chose journalism over architecture. But they might be able to forgive me if I *marry* an architect since I won't become one."

"Didn't they see your front-page article in *The Daily Beacon* on the college tuition debt crisis in America? I thought it was crazy bold of you to call out Emerson for increasing tuition costs by 54 percent in the last ten years alone."

"I emailed my parents the article, but I doubt they've read it," he says, and his eyes drop to the floor.

"You should print the article out and mail it to them. That's the only way I've been able to get my dad to read my favorite comics. Text me your parents' address; I'll mail them a copy on your behalf. Now, hold still or you're gonna be stuck in this suit forever."

Micah spins to face me again. "Wait. Did you say that *Kenton* told you about this place? As in the same Kenton that has totally vanilla sex with Lucy?"

"I was just as shocked as you. Can you even imagine a guy like Kenton in a place like this?" I hold my arms out wide.

"I can't figure that boy out." Micah puts his hands on his hips, his fingers squeaking against the latex.

"I know, right? You *cannot* put that in your *Third-Floor Report*, though. Lucy would kill us. Now turn around and let's get you out of this thing before they make you buy it."

●●●

A week later, it's finals week and three things happen:

1) Micah puts out a new *Third-Floor Report* divulging the highlights of Project Tender Chicken.[44]

2) I present Project Tender Chicken to my Love and Eroticism in Western Culture class. I incorporate fun movie clips into the performance and my classmates *love* it but . . . it's quite possible I make my male professor *suuuuuuuuuuper* uncomfortable when I pull out the bondage props.

3) Boston. Boston happens. A December snowstorm threatens to shut the city down and Rose holds an emergency third-floor meeting in the common room on Monday night.

"Listen up, everyone," Rose has to yell to be heard above all our chatter. "Due to the impending snowstorm—"

---

44 At first I was pissed that he aired my dirty laundry for the floor to see but honestly, most everyone on the floor knows about it already because some of them have participated.

"Snowpocalypse!" One of the Brads shouts from the back and high-fives his twin.

"Yes, thank you, Brad," Rose deadpans. "Due to the impending 'snowpocalypse,' all finals next week are being rescheduled." The room immediately erupts into cheers. I myself am personally ecstatic and relieved because I spent so much time working on my Project Tender Chicken essay, I completely forgot about all my other classes and haven't studied for a single test yet. This is a *huge* relief.[45]

Rose remains silent at the front of the room, waiting for us to simmer down and when we do, she continues. "I'm not done, people. Because of this, your finals will now be held *this week*."[46] This new piece of information hits the room like a bucket of ice water and everyone starts to panic.

But me? I'm totally fine.

This is fine!

This is all just totally, 100 percent, absolutely, perfectly fine.

Twenty minutes later, Rose finds me hyperventilating in a toilet stall in the girl's bathroom. She knocks on the door. "Occupied!" I croak out. Just as I realize that I forgot to lock the door, it starts to open. "Hey, hey, don't come in here, it's occupied!"

---

45 Thank you, Boston! I no longer hate you!
46 I take the last footnote back. Fuck you, Boston. I'm now officially rooting for the Yankees and THAT'S ON YOU.

"You're not even doing your business, Elliot." She slips in next to me and shuts the door behind her.

"I'm going to have to kindly ask you to leave," I tell her. "This stall is reserved for people who are freaking out."

"Elliot—"

"WHAT?!" I screech.

"You need to calm down." Rose rests her hands on my shoulders. "We've lost like what, seven extra days to study for our finals? If you don't know the material by now what makes you think you'll know it after only one week of studying?" She looks at me expectantly but there's nothing I can say. I am so ashamed.

I take a deep breath and tell her. "I don't know the material."

"What do you mean?" She looks genuinely confused, like it's inconceivable for someone to be a total slacker. I am about to deeply disappoint her.

"My method in high school was to cram all of my studying into the weekend before finals and then just memorize everything so I could regurgitate it back. And, well, this semester I got distracted and spent way too much time working on that essay you and Monica gave me the idea for, and I haven't paid much attention in my other classes and was really banking on this extra week to cram." I wait for her to respond but she just stares at me. "Do you think I'm screwed?"

She thinks about it for a second. "No, I don't think you're screwed." I breathe a sigh of relief. But then she adds, "I think you're fucked."

FOUR DAYS LATER

Rose was right.

I got fucked.

Look, I don't really want to talk about it.

Let's just say, it was a motherfucking bloodbath, all right?

ELLIOT MCHUGH'S
FIRST SEMESTER
FINAL GRADES

WR 101 Fundamentals of Speech Communication: D+

SC 114 Plants & People: D

SW 101 Beginning Writing for the Screen: B

IN 106 Love and Eroticism in Western Culture: C-[47]

---

47 Do you remember that essay I spent nearly two months working on? Well, I got a C-. A FUCKING C-. Here's what the professor said: *While I admire your commitment to exploring your own sexuality and bravery in sharing it with us, this essay failed to incorporate the texts we studied over the course of the semester in a meaningful way. This essay aims to only explore the eroticism side of the class, but neglected the love aspect. Most in your class met with me for office hours at least once this semester to discuss their essay. I wish you would have too.*

CHAPTER 9

THE ELLIOT MCHUGH DRINK SCALE (A REMINDER, JUST IN CASE YOU FORGOT.)

1 drink = Elliot is feeling warm and cozy

2 drinks = Elliot is charming and hilarious

3 drinks = Elliot is an asshole who will zero in on your greatest insecurities

4 drinks = Elliot wants to DANCE

5 drinks = Elliot is in love with everyone and wants to make out

6 drinks = Elliot is crying in the corner

7 drinks = Elliot is vomiting in what she thought was a trash can but is actually her purse

8 drinks = Unknown territory

Hello, I am drunk.

You know what's a great way to forget that you just bombed your first semester of college? Tequila. Tequila is great. I used to think vodka was a great idea but then Kenton introduced me to *good* tequila tonight and now I'd like to publicly declare my burgeoning relationship with tequila. I think I love tequila the most because I get to eat a bunch of salt with it and there is nothing better than salt. Except for dancing. Tequila and dancing. It's been an hour and a half and I'm somewhere between four and five shots of tequila and having the time of my damn life.[48] We're at some sophomore's apartment only a few blocks from the Little Building. Lucy went home after finals but thanks to Micah, tons of people from the third floor who don't normally go to off-campus parties are here. One of the Brads and Sasha are in a bedroom getting it on because apparently that's a thing that's been happening for a few weeks now, Micah is mixing drinks in the kitchen with Kenton, and even Rose is here with her scary girlfriend, Monica. And me? Yes, well, I am dancing my motherfucking ass off.

Someone turns off the overhead lights in the living room and turns on one of those tired-ass party strobe lights. Normally, I'd make fun of the cheesiness of a strobe light at a house party, but I'm in that agreeable fifth-drink stage of drunkenness where everything is amazing and I want to make

---

48 Have I told you, dear reader, how much I love you lately? I do. It's super cool that you've made it this far into the story and I just love you, a lot. Five stars on Goodreads, please.

out with everyone. More people join in on the dancing and things start heating up. I shed my top layer, a long-sleeved crop top sweatshirt, and reveal this shiny, gold, backless leotard I borrowed from Sasha. Others seem inspired by my costume change because suddenly clothes are flying everywhere and the party is now 25 percent more naked. *Hell, yes.* Some girl I have never met appears out of nowhere with a bottle of gin. She and I must be at the same level on the drunk scale because when she sees me she shouts, "Friend!" and I yell, "Friend!" right back at her and now we are friends. She takes a drink straight from the bottle, hands it me and I do the same. And just like that, she disappears and I go back to dancing. This party is quickly turning into one of those nights that could go down in my memory bank as one of the best parties I have ever been to.

The song changes from Robyn's "Dancing on My Own" to Ginuwine's "Pony," a motherfucking classsssic, and everyone collectively loses their damn mind. People go from, well, dancing on their own to partnering for some dance-floor dry humping—a natural and expected by-product of "Pony." I close my eyes and lose myself in the music and in my own body. All the bullshit from finals melts away. I'm not worried about telling my parents about my grades. I'm not worried or stressed about anything. Instead, I feel sexy, uninhibited, confident.

Whatever vibes I am putting out there must be working because suddenly, I feel the heat of another body behind me. I keep my eyes closed, I don't really care who it is, I am feeling this moment so hard and whoever this guy is, he knows how to fucking *move*. Strong hands grip my hips, pulling me in closer and I lean back into him. The heat, the song, the flashing lights, the energy of the room, his hands, my body. This particular moment is thrilling because the next time I play never have I ever and someone asks, "Have you ever given a guy a boner while dancing?" I will finally be able to take a drink. Our bodies move as one to the beat of the song. His hands slide up my hips and over my torso until his fingers graze my breasts. Feeling devilish, I press my back into his front a little harder, making *him* a little harder, knowing full well in the back of my mind that the second the song ends I plan on abandoning ship. I'm only in the mood to tease tonight, not to play for real. The song ends and I peel my body off his. I *was* planning on playing it cool and walking away without looking back, but now I am *waaayyyyyy* too curious to see whose boner I had the pleasure of sponsoring. I turn around and the world stops.

It's Kenton.

The guy I've been grinding all up on is my best friend's boyfriend.

What the fuck.

What the fuck.

What the fuck.

What the fuck.

What the fuck.

What the fuck.

What the fuck.

What the fuck.

What the fuck.

What the fuck.

What the fuck.

What the fuck.

What the fuck.

What the fuck.

What the fuck.

What the fuck.

What the fuck.

I get out of the living room and away from Kenton as fast as I can. I push my way passed blurred faces until I find an empty bedroom where all the coats have been tossed on the bed. I close the door behind me and try to steady my heart rate as I pace back and forth over the creaky hardwood floors of this shitty apartment. I can't believe I just gave my roommate's boyfriend a boner. That was not friend-dancing. That was vertical fucking. *Shit.* I wish I was sober right now. And I *so, so, so, so* wish I had not had that last shot. I can't steady my breathing, and the lack of oxygen is making me light-headed. The room tilts on its axis and I stumble. I collapse on the bed and stare at the ceiling, hoping that if I focus my eyes on one spot the world will right itself.

I don't know how long I've been here—maybe an hour, maybe a minute—but suddenly, the door opens. Piercing light and noise flash for a moment before the door is closed again, swallowing me back into darkness.

But I'm not alone.

Someone is in here with me.

"Elliot," he says. *Shit*. It's Kenton. He's in here with me.

"Go away," I try to say, but my mouth is too dry and the words shrivel on my sandy tongue. After last year, I swore I would never put myself in a position to be cheated on again, but right now I am giving Kenton the false impression I am someone who is comfortable with cheating. I need to sober up RIGHT NOW. I force myself to get off the bed and go to the window. I stumble again but I manage to push up the dirty window and stick my head out.

The sudden shock of cold air is like a force-quit to my system. I feel clearer, more aware. I reach for my back pocket and feel the comforting shape of my phone. Thank god I have this with me.

"Elliot," he says again. "Can I talk to you for a second?"

"I really wish you wouldn't." I try to sound polite but it comes out sharp, too sharp.

This is really bad. Here are the facts: Kenton and I were seen dancing and then we went into a bedroom together and shut the door. The longer we're in this room together the worse it's going to look. I suck in a few final sobering breaths of icy cool air before I turn around and face him.

"What happened back there was—" Kenton takes a step toward me but I cut him off.

"Nothing happened, Kenton. Okay? Nothing. I would really like to be alone now, if you don't mind."

"Elliot—" He takes a step toward me. He's too close now. I look around for an exit but the only way out of this room is through the door behind him. I hold my hand up to stop him but he still takes another step closer.

"Fffine then. *I'll* leavvve," I slur. I make a move to walk around him but he cuts me off, backs up, and blocks the door.

"I'm trying to talk to you," he spits out at me.

"And I'm trying to leave," I fire back.

"I felt something back there," he says pathetically. I roll my eyes at his bullshit.

"Look, I didn't know it was you, okay? It was a simple mis-understanding. Nothing happened."

"Don't lie to me, Elliot. I know you wanted it, the way you moved your body against me." He takes another step forward and lowers his voice. "You liked it when I touched you."

"Are you fucking *serious* right now?"

"No one has ever gotten me hard like that. Lucy and I only had sex once and that was months ago."

"So fucking what? You think you're *owed* because Lucy wants to take things slow?"

"Lucy has never even come close to turning me on as much as you did, and I've seen the way you look at me when I'm with her. Don't deny it, Elliot. You want me. I know you want me." I'm too slow to dodge him. He grabs my hand and brings it to his crotch. His breath is hot and moist on my neck. "God, do you feel how *hard* I am for you right now?"

I freeze, my entire body stiffens. I become hyperaware of this moment. The smell of the thick, heavy coats on the full-size bed behind me. The orange glow from the floodlight in the alley streaming in through the dirty glass window. The heavy bass vibrating the slightly sticky hardwood floors below me. The superhero movie poster on the wall to my right. The muffled sounds of the crowd chanting just outside the door for someone to drink. The smell of Kenton's overly scented, spicy cologne. His chapped lips and clammy tongue on my neck. His one hand skimming over my shoulder as he pulls down one of the straps of my gold leotard. His other hand on top of my own as he moves it up and down the outside of his terry-cloth sweatpants. His erect penis. I take stock of it, of all of it. Every detail carves out a place for itself to live in my brain forever. But even though I am still way too drunk, I consider the situation, my options. I weigh my choices and their possible outcomes. This is not the time to play games because there really only is one clear choice right now.

So I choose. I decide.

As his mouth travels from my jugular to my ear, he lets out a heavy moan and I know that this might be the only opportunity I'll get. I cannot waste this.

"Kenton," I say in his ear.

"Elliot," he groans again, thrusting his penis harder against my hand.

He's badly misjudged this situation.

"Kenton," I say again, this time a little louder. "I am only going to say this once so please listen." I take a deep breath and enunciate each word slowly, clearly. "Get your fucking hands off me."

He immediately stops licking my ear, but doesn't release my hand from his crotch. He leans back and though it's dark in here, I can see his expression clearly. This is the moment I worried might happen. His face confirms it. The raw, unfiltered lust has soured and curdled into white-hot rage. Spit flies from his mouth and lands on my face as he snarls, "I don't fucking get you. You open your legs for everyone else—"

I don't let him finish.

Instead, I give him what he wants.

I wrap my hand around the full length of his dick and feel how hard he is.

And then I twist it as hard as I can.

He screams and doubles over in agony but I don't let him go. I take a steadying breath, then calmly and slowly address him. "Here is what's going to happen, Kenton. I am going to release you and then I am going to leave this room and after I go, I suggest you take a moment and think things through because you'll have a choice to make. Your first option is to break up with Lucy. Tonight. I don't care what excuse you have to come up with, you *will* break up with her tonight and never see her again. I mean it—you will not call her, you will not text her, you will unfollow and block her on all social media. If you see her in the halls, you will turn and walk the other way. If she tries to reach out to you, you will ignore her. You will disappear from her life for good. And your second option is, well, you don't have a second option because if you don't break up with Lucy, not only will I tell her *everything,* I will also report you for sexual assault, you pathetic piece of shit." I give him one last excruciating squeeze before finally letting go. Kenton falls to the floor, his knees curling into his chest as he whimpers and cries.

I almost feel sorry for him.

Almost.

I step over him to get to the bed where I dig through the pile of coats until I find mine. I hear the door open and assume Kenton has fled, but when I turn around, Rose is standing in the doorway. It's dark, but the lamplight from the alley illuminates her face enough for me to witness the moment her eyes flick back and forth between Kenton and me and she puts it together. Rose presses her lips together in a tight line.

"What happened?" she asks slowly.

"She *assaulted* me!" Kenton shouts from the floor.

"I'm not talking to *you,*" Rose spits down at him. "What happened?" She directs her question to me with an intensity in her eyes I have not seen before.

"Can we talk about it later? I just want to go home," I beg her. I can't do this right now. I'm too drunk and too shaky to deal with my RA interrogating me.

"Fine. I'll find you when I get back, but I need to speak with Kenton for a moment." Her jaw clenches as she stares down at him. Every fiber of my being is screaming to stay and inflict more pain on Kenton, but right now I'm more afraid of Rose. She is practically vibrating with rage. Without another word I grab my coat from the bed and leave.

When I step outside the bedroom, I am hit with the reality that the party continued, as if I hadn't been getting groped by my roommate's boyfriend five feet away. I push my way through the hot, muggy hellhole of an apartment. Someone bumps into me and spills beer all over my pants and it takes every ounce of energy I have left not to scream. I want to crawl out of my own skin. It's too fucking hot, the music is too loud, people keep shouting at one another, there are too many fucking bodies in here. I need to get out. Sasha calls to me from the kitchen, but I don't hear what she says. I run into Monica who asks where Rose is but I don't answer her. I'm just about to get to the door when Micah blocks my way.

"Ohmygod, how drunk are you? And are my eyes deceiving me or did I just witness you come out of the same bedroom that Kenton went into a while ago?"

"Not now, Micah. I need to get out of here." I try to sidestep him but he blocks me again. I can feel a cube of anxiety get stuck directly in the middle of my throat. "Can you *please* let me go?" I choke out. I am *dangerously* close to losing it.

Micah crosses his arms in front of his chest. "Not until you spill the tea and tell me what's going on." He thinks there's gossip to share here. He thinks this is fun, something he can use in his *Third-Floor Report*. I start to panic and hyperventilate and the desperate wail that's been building inside me makes my head burst at the seams. I squeeze my eyes shut, open my mouth, and spew hot lava all over Micah.

"GET OUT OF MY FUCKING WAY, MICAH!" I scream. My voice booms over the music, over the voices, and people all around stop what they're doing and watch us. Micah looks hurt and that only makes me feel worse, but I don't apologize.

He doesn't say a word. No one does. He steps to the side and lets me leave. Someone shuts the door behind me and the party resumes. I know I left my sweatshirt somewhere in the living room along with my purse containing my wallet and student ID but I don't go back. I need to get as far away from here as possible. I push my way out of the building and stumble on the snow-covered lawn. I run to the end of the block and immediately throw up on the sidewalk.

• • •

Think of the biggest fuckup you've ever made in your life. Remember that hot, tingly feeling of shame and guilt in the pit of your stomach? Now imagine that—plus vomiting. That's how I feel right now. I am not one of those people who vomits gracefully. You know those people, the Puke and Rally types—the ones who can quietly upend the entire contents of their stomach and then go on as if nothing happened. No, I am the opposite. My upchucks are violent affairs—I am loud and I cry, my entire body sweats, and I have no control over the projection of my bodily fluids.

 149

So here I am, snuggling a toilet in a shared college bathroom, purging all of this semester's mistakes in a sweaty, tearful, pathetic display of human indecency. And that's not even the worst part. The worst part of it is hearing the people I've lived with for the last four months come and go, do their business and pretend like they don't hear me dying in the last stall.

When my body finally stops dry heaving, it's three in the morning. No one has come in the bathroom in a while, so I peel myself off the toilet and crawl across the moldy tiled floor until I reach one of the shower stalls. I try to stand but my legs are shaking and I slip and fall so I just reach up and turn the nozzle on. Water jets out in hard, icy cold bursts that stab my body. I don't bother taking my clothes off—there's puke and beer on them, and I never ever want to wear these clothes again. I tuck my knees in and squeeze my eyes shut as the memory of Kenton's disgusting penis flashes before me. I start to cry again and it quickly turns into uncontrollable sobbing. I can't believe how much I've fucked up this semester. Everything that had worked for me before isn't working now. After the way things ended in high school, this was my chance to build new friendships, ones that would last a lifetime, and now I don't know where I stand with Micah and I led Lucy straight into the arms of a complete piece of shit. And I spent so much time sleeping around with people I don't even care about and for what? I never found what I was looking for, and it did absolutely nothing to help my essay. My parents are going to kill me when they find out my grades—they might pull me out of school. They *should* pull me out of school. I don't fucking deserve to be here. I haven't earned any of this. I cry and cry and cry until the water turns hot, until my clothes are heavy and cling to my skin. I lean my head against the shower wall and close my eyes. I've almost fallen asleep when I hear a voice.

"Elliot? Are you in here?"

I have to spit water out of my mouth. "I'm here," I say. My throat is sore from crying, my jaw is tight from clenching my teeth. "I'm here," I say again, a little louder.

I hear footsteps approach and the shower curtain slides open. Rose stands over me, a glimmer of that same fury still in her eyes. *Fuck.* She's going to yell at me. I know it. I immediately start crying again. "Rose, I'm so sorry," I choke out. "I'm so sorry."

But she doesn't yell or get mad or lecture me. Instead, she steps into the water, squats down and wraps her strong arms around me. "Shh, it's okay, you don't need to apologize," she says. "Kenton told me everything."

I squeeze her forearms tight, rest my weary head on her shoulder and cry harder than I ever have before.

And we stay like that, in each other's arms until I let it all out and the hot water runs cold again.

INTERMISSION

WELL, SHIT.

That was intense, wasn't it?

Why don't we all just take a quick pee break, put on an aloe sheet mask, hug a puppy, and drink a pamplemousse LaCroix.

CHAPTER 10

LESS THAN THIRTY-SIX HOURS AFTER THE PARTY, Kenton drops out of Emerson and I land in Cincinnati. I opted to let the school handle the situation instead of reporting the incident to the police, but now that he's dropped out, there's nothing left to do but move on.[49] As soon I land, I take my phone off airplane mode and it lights up with a slew of texts from Rose.

> **Rose:** Hope you have a safe flight. Wanted you to know that your Title IX complaint has been updated to reflect that the student (aka Kenton) withdrew— and it includes the notation "pending disciplinary."

---

49 I know this decision isn't going to sit well with many of you, and I can accept that. Filing criminal charges would have meant a long, drawn-out process where I'd have to relive the experience day in and day out while also having my own character called into question. It would define me. It would consume me. I absolutely, 1,000,000 percent believe in a person's right to justice—but I also believe in a person's right to move forward. And Kenton will have to explain to his family why he suddenly decided to leave Emerson. I hope that will be enough of a punishment. I hope this was the one mistake that changes his behavior. I hope.

Rose: I don't know what pending disciplinary means but I'll try to find out. Either way, there will be no investigation, your privacy will be protected.

Rose: None of this needs to change how you feel about him or the situation, just thought you should know.

Rose: If you need to talk over winter break, I'm here. If not, I hope you get some rest and family time. Be kind to yourself, Elliot. See you in the new year.

So, I guess that settles that.

I get off the plane, pick up my suitcase at baggage claim, and when my Lyft pulls up at the arrivals curb, I send the Lyft link to my dad so he'll know my ETA. Somewhere along the drive on the barren highway between northern Kentucky and downtown Cincinnati, my mind starts to wander, and it dawns on me that I have been forgetting one massive, huge, enormous piece of this whole unfortunate mess. Lucy. I forgot to tell Lucy. She doesn't know.

I look out the window at the gray sky and start to panic at the thought of telling my best friend that not only did her boyfriend try to cheat on her, he tried to do it with me—without my consent—and now he's dropping out and she'll probably never see him again. My heart leaks acid into my stomach. I have to tell her. Right now, before I get home. This isn't the kind of conversation I want to have in front of a random Lyft driver but both my sisters are home and my mom will be in full holiday-panic mode, so I can't do it there either, my house is too chaotic. I take my phone out of my pocket, change the destination in the app and the driver is pinged. He taps the blinker and veers onto the next exit ramp as he takes me toward Alms Park.

●●●

I don't know why a park was the first place I thought of to talk to Lucy. It's cold as shit and the sky looks dark and angry, as if it's about to take a massive snowy dump on my face, but it doesn't matter. I'm here. It's now or never.

I find a place to sit, on a bench that overlooks the muddy Ohio River and call Lucy. It rings four times before she picks up. "Hi, Elliot," she says. Weird. Normally she greets me with a *Hello, my love.* Something's not right.

"Uh, hey." I clear my throat and try again. "Hey, Luce! Did you make the drive home okay?"

"It's only a ten-minute drive." Silence. Something is *definitely* off. "What do you want, Elliot?" Snow starts to fall and the temperature drops. I pace to keep warm—and to calm my nerves. Shit, I shouldn't have called her until I knew exactly what I wanted to say. I take a deep breath and clear my throat. Here goes nothing.

"So, um, I need to tell you something about Kenton. I don't know how to—"

"Save your breath," she says, cutting me off. "I already know." Her voice is cold and brittle.

"Already know what?"

"I know about you and Kenton, Elliot."

Fuck fuck fuck fuck fuck fuck fuck fuck fuck fuck fuck.

"What? How?" I start to panic. "How did you find out?"

"Micah's blog," she hisses into the phone. "Micah posted all about how you and Kenton were all over each other at the party and then you went into a bedroom together."

"That—that's not what happened," I say quietly. I can't catch my breath.

"And I got a text from Kenton this morning telling me he's dumping me AND moving back to New York."

"That's not what happened," I say again but she's not hearing me.

"God, you don't give a shit about anyone but yourself, don't you?" Her words are corrosive. I have never heard her talk like this before; I have never even heard her swear. "I've done nothing but go above and beyond for you and this is how you show your gratitude? I bring you food and coffee and help you study and give you my full attention as I am forced to listen to every single one of your hook-up stories. Meanwhile you have never, not even once, gone above and beyond for me."

I know I shouldn't get defensive right now; she's only reacting to what she believes is the truth, but I can't stop my mouth. "How could I? If you weren't with Kenton, you were at class or working at the Emerson Fund or running or going home to one of those family dinners you never invited me to. I barely had a roommate all semester!"

"Of course you would make my needing to take care of my

family and study and work about you. You never spent any time or effort doing any of those things! And you know what kills me? You don't even care that you're at Emerson! College is just an afterthought to you."

"That is not true—"

"Some student didn't get a spot in this school because *you* took it."

"I earned my spot at Emerson, just like you did, Lucy."

"That may be true, but you take it for granted. Some of us don't have rich parents who can afford the tuition, Elliot. Some of us have to take out loans and then work for decades to pay them off. Some of us don't have the luxury of doing nothing all semester but partying and sleeping around. College isn't the world's most expensive sleepover camp, for me it's the greatest opportunity I will ever have, and you act like it's a chore. Some of us want to *learn*, Elliot. But apparently, you don't. So why are you even there?"

My face grows hot and my throat swells. It's hard to swallow. My heart hurts so much. It's so cold, my tears are starting to frost on my lashes. There's a long pause before Lucy speaks again.

"I have to go, Elliot," she says, and I can feel her drifting further and further away from me.

"Wait!" I say. "Please don't hang up. You are right—about everything, but—"

"I don't want to hear anything else from you, Elliot," she says as she seethes.

I start to panic. I am about to lose my best friend. I can't believe this is fucking happening—again.

"There is something I need to tell you!" I cry out.

"I'm hanging up now—"

"Please," I get out in between sobs. I take a chance. "You don't need to talk to me, but please talk to Rose. She knows the truth." Lucy doesn't say anything and for a moment I think she's going to stay on the line and give me a chance to explain, but she doesn't.

She hangs up.

I don't call her back.

●●●

Instead of calling my dad or another Lyft to pick me up, I decide to stash my suitcase under the bench and take a walk to clear my head. The snow is falling in heavy clumps and the ground has already turned white. Frankly, I don't give a shit if I freeze to death out here. I know I should go inside and not get caught outside in a snowstorm, but I feel out of control and reckless and agitated and sick and desperate to do something, to feel anything other than this hot, blistering shame.

I don't know what hurts more: the fact that my best friend hates me because of a rumor my other best friend spread, the fact that I bombed my classes, or the fact that I couldn't see for myself who Kenton really was. Logically, I know that what happened wasn't my fault, but logic and reason provide no

comfort when I feel completely stupid. And angry and humiliated and frustrated.

And sad.

And alone.

And hurt.

I cut into the woods, taking a snowy path I like to hike with
Remy and my dad, until I come to this old, abandoned stone
lookout I used to love playing on when I was a kid. But now it
seems no one has tended this part of the park for years, and
the view is obstructed by overgrown shrubs and trees. I brush
snow and fallen branches off one of the stones and take a seat,
pulling my jacket around me tighter. A cold gust of wind slaps
me in the face. Hot tears sting as they trickle down my frozen
cheeks. And just as I get settled in for a good long cry, I hear
the unmistakable sound of crunching footsteps behind me. I
spin around and there's my dad, waiting for me in the snow
with a red thermos in one hand and a round, purple sled in
the other.

"Dad?!?"

"Daughter?"

"What are you doing here?"

"We're going sledding!" He grins and tosses me the sled.

● ● ●

"Nope. Nuh uh. There is no way I am sledding down this, it's
way too steep."

Dad and I are standing at the top of a hill on the other side of the park, surveying the precipitous slope below us. He hands me the thermos and I take a sip. Hot apple cider slides down my throat and warms my insides. I hand the thermos back to him and he takes a sip.

"Come on, it'll be great!" he says.

"How are *you* gonna sled? This saucer only fits one person."

"Oh, I'm not going down *that*," he says casually, as if I should have predicted this. "Do you see how sharp that drop is there at the bottom?"

"What the hell?!" I retort. "Why do I have to do it then?"

He drops a hand on my shoulder and looks me in the eyes. "Because sometimes in life you have to do things that are scary. Or because I said so. Take your pick."

"What if I get hurt?" I can't help but notice that the hill ends at a very rocky creek.

"Psh, you'll be fine. I'll see you at the bottom." He doesn't wait for me to argue; he takes off at a trot and hops down the hill at an angle. When he gets to the bottom he waves both of his arms over his head and *god-fucking-dammit*, I can't believe I'm about to sled down *this* hill in a saucer.[50] I set it down on the ground, climb on, and look down to the spot sure to be

---

50 Have you ever sledded in one of these things? YOU HAVE NO CONTROL. It's essentially a close-your-eyes-and-pray-you-don't-die situation. Once, when we were younger, our dad sent Izzy down a hill in one and she came so close to hitting a tree at full speed, my dad pissed himself in fear. Now that I've recalled this memory, I really have to wonder why the hell we still own a saucer.

known in the future as the location where Elliot McHugh perished. *Ahh, fuck it.* I close my eyes and push off.

● ● ●

"I can't believe you bailed at the end. You are such a wuss." Dad shakes his head at me as we warm up in his car in the parking lot.

"Are you serious?!? I would have flown straight into the creek if I hadn't!"

"Psh! You would have been *fine*." He waves me off. "You do, however, get ten extra points for the dismount. You were quite graceful when you launched off that mound and did a flip in the air."

"It was less graceful when I landed right on my tailbone and cried."

"Yes, well, we can work on sticking the landing tomorrow," he says.

I roll my eyes at him. "No way, I'm never going down the hill of tears again."

I reach across the dashboard and flick the butt warmers on and pray the heat will keep my ass from bruising. I lean back in my seat, reveling in the renewed feeling in my outer extremities.

"Okay, let's do the thing," he finally says, and I sigh.

"Do we have to?"

"Where would you like to start?" Dad leans his car seat back to match mine and puts his feet up on either side of the steering wheel. He's offering me a great courtesy by not forcing me to make eye contact. He tucks his arms behind his head and keeps his gaze up and out the moonroof.

"Well, I guess, my first question is how the hell did you know I was here at the park?"

"Lyft," he says. "My phone notified me you changed your destination and I figured something was up. I saw your bag by the hike entrance and knew where you'd be." I don't say anything, I just nod. "So, what's up?" He asks.

I fiddle with the zipper on my coat. "I don't even know anymore."

"Well, why don't you try telling me why you went out in freezing weather without proper winter gear and without telling anyone?"

"I needed to make a tough phone call and I didn't want to do it at home. I dunno why I came here, it was just the first place that came to mind, I guess." I pause and look out the window long enough for my mind to start wandering back to the events of the past few days. I start to feel queasy and anxious again. I sit up, pull out my phone and check the clock. "Shouldn't we get going? It's almost dinnertime, don't we need to get home to help Mom?"

"Enough, Elliot." He swipes the phone out of my hand and puts it in his pocket. "Start talking, *now*." But when I still don't, he reaches over the center console and holds my hand. And that does it. That gesture, so small and so loving, cracks me open and releases everything that's been building up inside these past four months.

I cry.

And then, I tell him everything.

I tell him about the fight with Lucy.

I tell him about how Micah spread rumors about me.

I tell him about my grades.

I tell him about Kenton.

I tell him about my shame.

I tell him about how lost I am.

And he listens. He doesn't interrupt or scold me or share his own freshman year stories. He just listens. I talk and cry until the thermos is completely empty—and then I talk and cry some more. I talk until the snow accumulates enough to completely cover the windshield. And when I've said all I can say and my tears run dry, Dad finally speaks.

"You ready for some dinner?" He pops his seat upright and turns the keys the rest of the way to ignite the engine. The windshield wipers fail miserably at clearing away the snow.

"What? That's it? You're not going to give me advice or tell me what to do or do whatever it is parents do when their middlest child royally screws up?"

"Nope," he says as he pulls on his seat belt and puts the car in reverse.

"I don't understand," I tell him. "I need help; I thought that's why you came out here."

"It sounds to me like you're figuring things out just fine."

"Am I though? Because 99.9987 percent of the time I feel like I am flailing through life."

"Good," he says.

"Good?"

"Yes, *good*. If you weren't flailing then I'd say you weren't doing your freshman year right."

"I—I don't understand," I say.

He puts the car back into park. "Would you like me to go all Father Figure on you and rant and rave? Because I can totally do that," he says jokingly, but part of me wishes he would. "What would you like to hear? That you're not in high school anymore? That your friend Micah behaved no differently than he normally does? That the only reason Lucy is mad at you is because you didn't immediately do the right thing and tell her the truth? That the choices you make as an eighteen-year-old have real consequences? Honey, I don't think you need to hear that kind of speech because you already know all of this."

"Izzy didn't screw up her freshman year—"

"Stop that, this isn't about your sister!" he snaps, and I instantly regret interrupting him. Sometimes I forget that he can be stern. "Everyone makes mistakes, all right? Stop deflecting and own up to yours, Elliot. Yes, you've made some bad choices and chances are you have a few more ahead of you, but you have to at least start recognizing when you've made a bad choice and learn from it so you don't do it again. And when it comes to your grades, I will give you one more shot to pull those grades up or you will have to find an alternative source of funding for your sophomore year. I'm not spending thousands of dollars to send you to a fancy, east coast private school just so you can slack off. You hear me?"

"Yes . . ." I slump even farther into my seat and start picking at my nails. Neither of us says anything for a full five minutes. My dad is not the type of man who regularly raises his voice, so when he does it visibly unsettles him and he always needs a moment to collect himself.[51]

When he's ready, he says, "You're not alone, Elliot, but you do have to start taking care of yourself. I can't have my middlest going out in a snowstorm and freezing to death." My dad reaches out and gives my hand another squeeze before returning it to the wheel. "And as for that fuckface Kenton, well, he can just go eat shit and die."

It's so unexpected and aggressive and something my dad would normally never ever, ever, *ever* say. I burst out laughing and he smiles as he puts the car in reverse and we take off for home.

"I really missed you a lot this semester, Dad," I say when we pull into the garage ten minutes later. He turns off the engine, reaches over, and we hug awkwardly.[52]

"You are tough, Elliot. You are *my* kid and I didn't raise you take shit from anyone," he says as we continue to hug. "Well,

---

51 In the McHugh house, my mom is the one who usually doles out the verbal reprimands and after all the times I snuck out of the house in the middle of the night during high school, she's gotten really good at it too.
52 Like I told you back in chapter 2, the McHugh family are terrible huggers.

anyone except for your mother. She's going to want to talk to you about those grades, by the way."

"Any chance you could talk her out of yelling at me?" I ask as I pull away. He smiles at me and it gives me more comfort than he could ever know.

"Like I said, sometimes in life you have to do things that are scary."

CHAPTER 11

BEFORE WE RESUME THE SECOND ACT OF THIS STORY, which begins at the start of my second semester, let's do a little montage and recap the past two weeks of my life.

ELLIOT MCHUGH PRESENTS: THE WINTER BREAK SPECIAL

December 18

The second I walked in from the garage, I was thrust right back into the chaos of the McHugh household. Extreme new-age Christmas music played on the surround sound; our dog, Bugsy, a big shepherd mutt, was going apeshit at the sight of me; Remy was in the living room, curled up in our dad's red leather chair playing on her phone while our morbidly obese cat, Fred, was swatting at her hair from his perch on top of the chair; all while my mom was stress-baking two hundred Christmas-themed sugar cookies *and* preparing a turkey for dinner.

"Elliot, welcome home!" My mom greeted me in her Kentucky drawl from across the big kitchen. "Where've you been? I thought y'all were going to be home by four?"

"Hey, mom." I waved to her as I set my suitcase down.

"GIRLS, YOUR SISTER IS HOME!" she yelled while dumping a cup of flour into the stand mixer. She turned it on high, then started going to town on some carrots. Without even looking up she said to me, "Can you reach up and grab another cutting board? And don't leave your suitcase there, take it down to the basement."

"The basement?" I asked as I grabbed the cutting board out of the cabinet and handed it to her.

"You and Izzy are sharing the pullout couch in the basement—Remy! Get over here and welcome home your sister!" she shouted across the room to my little sister.

Without losing eye contact with her phone once, Remy got up from the chair, walked over to me, said hello, punched me in the butt, and then went back to her chair. Bugsy finally got over my return and trotted after Remy into the living room and laid down by her feet, while Fred, having abandoned his perch atop the chair, started scooting his butt across the hardwood floor. I turned back to my mom, who was shoving vegetables into the business end of an uncooked turkey.

"Why do I have to sleep in the basement with Izzy? What happened to her room?"

"We were going to convert it into a guest bedroom for you two, but since neither of you came home for Thanksgiving this year, I turned it into my painting studio."

"Can't I sleep with Remy?"

"No," she grunted as she lifted the heavy roasting pan into the oven. She set the timer and zipped over to the dinner table and started decorating cookies. "Nana is coming in tomorrow and she'll be sharing Remy's room. Now go and get your stuff out of here before someone trips and breaks their neck." I picked up my suitcase and made my way to the basement steps, careful to avoid stepping on Fred. Before I got very far, my mom called out to me again from the kitchen.

"And Elliot?"

"Yeah?" I grumbled.

"I'm so happy you're home," she said sweetly, then set down the cookie she was icing and gave me a look that sent shivers down my spine. "But after dinner tonight I think you and I have some things we need to discuss."

Fuck.

I left the kitchen and descended into the basement where Izzy was sprawled on the pullout couch mindlessly scrolling through Netflix. Her clothes and shit were everywhere. She glanced over at me for a second before returning her attention to the TV.

"Are you gonna make room or what?" I asked as I dropped my suitcase at the foot of the bed.

"No thanks, I was here first," she said casually.

"Are you serious?"

"You can share with me if you want, but I like to sleep naked."

I shuddered at the thought. "Ew, gross. Never mind, I'll take the floor." I grabbed a pillow and a blanket Mom had left for us and started setting up a makeshift bed on the floor.

"How did finals go?" Izzy asked while she continued to scroll through movie options.

"Let's just say . . . there was room for improvement."

"So, you bombed?"

"Pretty much." I looked over and Izzy was trying to stifle a laugh. "Mind your own business, Izzy."

Izzy tossed the remote aside and flopped onto her stomach. "You know, your GPA is fucked now. Starting off low is really hard to come back from—"

"Iz, for real, can we not talk about this, please?"

She grinned, so satisfied with her ability to stir shit up. "All right then, let's talk about Theo. You remember him, don't you? My friend you slept with in *my bed* over Thanksgiving?"

My face burned. "Oh, so, uh, you know about that."

"Yeah, he wouldn't shut up about it. I mean, damn, Elliot. Theo is one of the biggest players at Columbia Med, but he spends one night with you and now he's a total wreck."

"Oh please, he's fine. He knew exactly what that night was about."

"I dunno," she teased. "Ever since Thanksgiving, whenever I see him in labs, he always asks why you haven't called him back."

"Why would I take his calls? It was just one hook-up, and besides, the dude lives in New York. What, does he think I'm gonna take the bus down there every weekend and be his *girlfriend*? Please." I finished making my floor bed and shoved all of Izzy's crap into a corner in order to make room for all of my crap.

"Just call or text him that you aren't interested and put him out of his misery already."

"I already did! It's not my fault he can't take a fucking hint and get over it."

"Whatever," she muttered. "You still didn't have to do him in my bed."

"Consider it pre-payment for you not sharing the pullout with me." I kicked my shoes off and laid down on my new floor-bed while Izzy flipped over onto her back again. She resumed looking for something to watch until she scrolled past *Mad Max: Fury Road.*

"Wanna watch *Fury Road*?" she asks me.

"Always," I said, and then for the next two hours, we watched *Fury Road* in silence until Mom called us upstairs for dinner.

December 19

My nana arrived from Louisville, Kentucky, with a back seat full of presents and a trunk full of bourbon. Over dinner that night, she asked me if I had a boyfriend up there at that school and I told her no. My nana, master of the backhanded compliment, replied, "Oh honey, don't worry! You'll catch one soon enough with that sparkling personality, but I'd mind the waffles, my dear. It looks like you put on a few extra pounds."

December 20

Why is it you always run into people you don't want to see when you look your absolute worst? I was at Target, putting random shit into my cart that I had no intention of purchasing, when in the tampon aisle I ran into three of my friends from high school. The same friends I hadn't spoken to since I found out they knew the entire time my ex was cheating on me but didn't say anything. I tried to back out of the aisle before being spotted, but my red cart knocked over a row of Tampax and caused a scene.

We exchanged pleasantries, they asked how I was doing at Emerson, I lied and told them I was *killing it,* and they updated me on their new lives as well. The one I had been closest to, Jane, said, "We should get coffee and really catch up some time," and I said *sure* even though I don't think either of us had any intention of sticking to that plan. And that was that.

For the past year, I had been so angry and hurt by what they did. But what's interesting was even though seeing them reopened old wounds, the pain from their betrayal didn't feel quite as acute anymore. The second I found out they didn't have my back, I dropped them. I didn't think twice about it. It felt right. I thought I was better than them, that I couldn't possibly keep a secret like that from my best friend. And yet, when I had the opportunity, I didn't tell Lucy the truth right away either. And so, I began to regret being so rigid in my belief that cutting them out of my life was justified. Maybe it was, maybe they had been assholes for knowingly keeping me in the dark. Or maybe I was the asshole for never giving them the chance to explain. Both of these things can be true.

I don't know how long I stayed in that Target, wandering the aisles, lost in my thoughts, but by the time I left I had decided I would find a way to tell Lucy the truth and I wouldn't cut Micah out. I've seen what happens to a friendship if neither side fights for it and I can't let that happen again. Lucy and Micah are friends are worth fighting for.

December 21

I attended the winter solstice party at my Uncle Bo's house with my entire extended family—all forty of us. As per annual tradition, we gathered in the backyard to light the ceremonial firework that contained just a sprinkle of my dead grandfather's ashes.[53]

---

53 It all started in 1975 when my grandfather bought this radio station—ahhhh fuck it. That story is way too long. Yes, yes, my family's weird. We do shit like cremate our loved ones and turn them into fireworks. The end.

December 22

Izzy caught the flu playing her and Dad's annual See Who Can Roll Around in the Snow Longest While Wearing Nothing but a T-Shirt and Shorts Game while my mom and I finally had that chat about my grades. I will spare you the details of that scene. Let's just say if I don't bring my grades up soon, this book will end very prematurely.

December 23

Remy and I had a heart-to-heart while doing our laundry together. And Remy, oh, Remy. My little sister isn't so little anymore. In the span of four months, she managed to grow two inches and sprout some chicken cutlets for boobs. We used to be so close, she was my little shadow for all of her life but even though we video-chatted every week, I had missed out on so much of her life.

"No, Lucy and I didn't exchange gifts this year," I told my little sister as we did our laundry on Christmas Eve *Eve* morning. "We, uh, we decided to save money this year."

"Izzy told me you had a fight with Lucy," Remy said as she turned the dial on the washer.[54] "Don't be mad at Izzy, she didn't give me details, she just said you're having a rough time and I should be nice to you."[55]

"Izzy really said that?"

"Yep. Do you want me to send you back to college with

---

54 Fucking Izzy.
55 Dammit, how does Remy always know my thoughts?

some dryer balls? I just got these new ones and they are much better than dryer sheets."

"I'm good on the balls, Remy, but thanks." I started sorting the next load. Remy squatted next to me in her trademark pose she likes to call *Frog-oonie* and helped me sort.

"Are you gonna be okay, big sis?" Remy asked sweetly, and it knocked the wind out of me. If someone as innocent and optimistic as my little sister was worried about me, then that really means shit has gotta change.

I poked her with my elbow and smiled. "Hey. We're the McHughs. And what does that mean?"

"That we're competitive and quick-tempered?" Remy suggests.

"No, that's not—"

"That we suck at cooking and can't digest dairy?"

"Yes, but—"

"That we need to wear sunscreen with a higher SPF because we're so pale and have a higher risk of getting skin cancer?"

"Dammit, Remy!"

"Don't say *dammit*."

"Being a McHugh means we're resilient. It means when things fall apart, we put them back together. When the going gets tough, we get tougher. When the shit hits the fan, we pop open an umbrella."

"You need to work on your metaphors," Remy said.

"So I've been told."

"And you shouldn't say *shit*."

December 24

Dad and I spent the majority of the day locked in a Ping-Pong battle in the basement. After my epic loss to Rose at the beginning of the semester, I spent a significant amount of time practicing in the student rec center and as a result, I only lost to my dad 50 percent of the time.[56]

December 25

We exchanged gifts in the morning and I tried to show appreciation for the weird thing Remy got me this year.[57] In the afternoon, everyone in the family went for a five-mile jog—except for me and Nana. We stayed back to bake some key lime pies and while I did all the work, Nana sipped on Manhattans and told stories about the time the nuns caught her making out with an altar boy in the confessional booth.

December 26–December 30

Family dinners, a James Bond movie marathon, more family dinners, sledding, bickering with Izzy, more Ping-Pong, sleep.

December 31

My family went to some fancy New Year's Eve party my dad's hospital was hosting downtown but I stayed home instead. Alone for the first time in a week, I finally had time to torture myself by replaying every single event of my first semester over and over in my head. I tried calling Lucy again to wish

---

56 But then he switched the paddle to his dominant hand and I swiftly went back to losing 100 percent of the time.

57 It was a used squirt gun in the shape of a hand and a plastic bag full of tiny green army men. And dryer sheets, of course.

her a happy new year but she didn't pick up. This was the first night I cried myself to sleep.

January 1-4

I caught Izzy's flu and stayed in bed for days. On the plus side, I managed to crank my way through a shitload of new TV shows I had missed last semester.

January 5

Finally feeling less like death and more like myself, I decided it was time. Time to put my shitty little life back together.

So I did two things. First, I made a plan. On a piece of paper, I made two columns. On one side, I listed every single mistake I made last semester—at least the ones I was currently aware of. And on the other side, I listed every single thing I needed to do to make things right. And second, I changed my flight so I could get back to Boston a day early and get a head start on said plan. And you know what? I think there's a chance that maybe, possibly, potentially . . .

I can do this.

ELLIOT MCHUGH'S
7 STEP PLAN TO
GETTING HER SHIT TOGETHER

1 PICK A FUCKING MAJOR.
2 Study my motherfucking ass off.
3 Call Remy more often.

4   Eat 40 percent less waffles and 60 percent more vegetables.

5   Take my ADHD medication instead of selling it.

6   Find a way to forgive Micah.

7   Accept that Lucy may never forgive me even though it's not my fault.[58]

But before you go and queue up the Confidence Boost playlist on Spotify, let me warn you. I don't expect this to be one of those redemption arcs where I come out of this better off than where I started, I'm just trying to get back to neutral. When you start your freshman year, your slate is clean. Whoever you were in high school, whatever drama you were caught up in—none of that matters. You can reset, if you want to. New school, new friends, new attitudes, new life. You get the chance to *choose* who you want to be and then you have the opportunity to *become* that person. It's a moment with weight. It's a moment that demands reflection. But I got so caught up in the *newness* of it all that I completely forgot to take the time to figure out who the hell I want to be. Looking back on that first month here . . . *shit* . . . I experienced so many firsts. My first time away from home. My first time living with someone. My first time living in close proximity to booty calls. My first

---

58 That last one is . . . I feel that last one deeply. I think I have to prepare myself for a future reality in which Lucy and I are no longer friends. That future may already be here. I don't know.

time having to make my own decisions regarding my health and well-being. My first time being responsible for setting my own schedule and studying on my own.

And the truly shameful part of all those firsts is that I was so goddamn lucky to get them. Everything Lucy said the last time we spoke was 1,000,000 percent correct. I am *lucky* to have a family to go home to. I am *lucky* to even be able to attend the school of my choice. And what have I done with all that privilege? Lucy was exactly right. I took it all for granted. I took an opportunity so few get and I pissed all over it. I haven't taken any of it seriously. My friendships, my education, my relationships. I went through life as though none of my actions had any consequences.

I wasted my fresh start, so now I don't get a do-over. Instead, I have to dig myself out.

And I think I am finally ready.

CHAPTER 12

IT'S WEIRD BEING IN THE DORMS WITH NO ONE ELSE around. I've already unpacked all my clothes and roamed the empty halls of every single floor in the Little Building. I even discovered and made friends with the new family of mice that have taken up residence in our common room because someone left a pizza box under a couch. I've had plenty of time to emotionally prepare for everyone's return tomorrow, but I don't know if I am ready to face Lucy. Every time I think about it, I start to panic. So I'm gonna go do the one thing that truly relaxes me—the one thing I *know* I can do when I'm the only one on campus.

Masturbate.

Kidding! It's laundry, I'm gonna do my laundry.

"Have you forgotten this already? We talked about it last week. You should really handwash your unmentionables, but if you're going to put them in the washer, use the delicate spin cycle," I tell Remy over the phone as I transfer my wet bed-sheets into the dryer.

"Can bras go in the dryer?" she asks and I nearly drop the sheets on the floor. *My little sister is asking about bras?!?!?!?!??!* I steady my voice and try to play it cool.

"You should just hang dry bras. Unless they are sports bras, those can go in the dryer." I fiddle with the box of pine-scented dryer sheets Remy got me for Christmas, stalling for time as I come up with a thoughtful, sensitive way to ask my next question. "Remy, I think it's so amazing you are old enough now to experience the joys of womanhood, but locking your melons in a boob prison all day isn't exactly the most comfortable experience. Until those little honeydonts develop into some honeydews, why not save yourself some money and pain and just go braless?"

"Because!" Remy blurts so loud I have to hold the phone away from my ear, and I almost miss her saying, "Some girls at gym class saw that I didn't wear one when we were changing in the locker rooms and then they told these boys who then made fun of me."

I ball my hands into fists and slam the dryer lid shut. "Give me the names of every single boy and girl who made fun of you and find out if they've seen *Taken* because if not, I have the perfect monologue to use when I find them."

"No, Elliot! I don't need you to fight my battles," she scolds me from nine hundred miles away. "I just need to tell them they hurt my feelings and they should be more mindful of how they treat others." *Whoa.* For a little kid who is six years younger than I am, she's a lot more mature. I set the dryer to permanent press, load the quarters, and hit start. Seems like no one has bothered getting the dryers fixed because they are still loud as hell.

"Hey, Elliot, I gotta go. Mom is calling me down to dinner," Remy says.

"Okay, talk to you tomorrow—but wait! For reals though, don't wash your bras in a machine. I know it's a chore, but wash those titty shields by hand, okay?"

"Okay!" She says and hangs up. I stuff my phone in my pocket and go to my other basket and start filling the washing machine with another load.

"So what's a *titty shield*?" a voice asks from behind me and I jump out of my skin.

"JESUS H. FUCK!" I screech as I age about ten years. I turn around to see Rose standing in the doorway. "Christ on a cracker, Rose. You scared me." I rest my hand on my chest, trying to steady my defibrillated heart.

"Sorry about that," she says as she drags in one of those blue IKEA bags absolutely stuffed to the brim with clothes. On laundry day, most normal shlubs wear sweatpants and a ratty-ass T-shirt, but not Rose. Her laundry-day outfit consists of a floor-length red silk robe and a black and white old-timey hair wrap. The whole getup makes her look like she's on the set of a 1930s movie. All she's missing is a long cigarette holder and a Judy Garland accent.

"What are you doing here?"

"RAs have to be back from winter and spring breaks at least one day before everyone else. That and I have an interview tomorrow morning for a summer internship in New York with the costume department for *Law & Order*." She pauses to cross her arms. "But the bigger mystery is why are *you* back so early? The dorms don't open until tomorrow; I'm surprised the security guards let you in."

"Bob and Earl? Yeah, I bribed them with whoopie pies from Mike's Pastry."

"Smart, those are the best ones in town, but that still doesn't explain the *why* part, though."

"I guess I wanted to give myself some time to readjust. It's jarring going home for two weeks, falling back into old routines, and then coming right back here. Plus, it's a great time to do some laundry before everyone gets back."

She kicks at her IKEA bag and I notice there's no detergent on top of that mountain of clothes. "I see you've got a few loads going already," she says and I catch her eyeing my brand-new box of detergent.

I rest my hand on my detergent, pull it close, and very reluctantly ask her, "Do you need to borrow some detergent or something?" *Please say no please say no please say no please say no.*

She reaches deep into the bowels of her blue bag and pulls out a little bottle of the cheapest detergent ever. "I swear, I'm not here to steal your bougie detergent again. I'm just here to wash some clothes." She bends over and starts overstuffing the washing machine, then dumps in way too much detergent. She slams the lid and turns the dial to the boil-all-of-my-belongings setting.

I take a seat in my favorite spot on the windowsill. "For a person who wants to work with clothes for a living, you really don't know how to care for them."

"Oh, I know how to care for them," she says as she reaches up and pulls on her hair wrap. Frizzy curls cascade over her shoulders. "I just choose not to."

I narrow my eyes at her. "That is—deeply frustrating."

"Yeah, you and Monica have that in common. She is always on my ass about laundry." She jumps up to sit on top of the washer in one slick movement that makes me think she's one of the more athletically gifted students here at Emerson.

"So, how was your holiday?" she asks me.

"It was . . ." I shrug. "I dunno, it was weird. Good; it was nice to be away, but it was weird. Sorry, I know that's not a real answer."

"Did you get a chance to talk to Lucy?"

I look away from her and focus my gaze out the window. "I tried."

"I'm sorry, Elliot." She pauses. "Do you want to talk about what happened?" I don't know if she means the fight with

Lucy or what happened with Kenton, but I'm not really in the state of mind that's prepared to talk about either. So I shake my head.

"Did you get to spend time with your family over the break?" she asks, and I am so grateful she's changing the subject.

"Yeah, it was good, cathartic even." I perk up. "I learned a new spin move in Ping-Pong I want to try out on you sometime, got yelled at by my mom, set off some of my grandfather's ashes, ate a lot of spiraled ham . . . You know, the usual holiday traditions."

"Wait, wait, wait." She waves her hands in front of her confused face. "Did you just say you *set off* your grandfather's *ashes*?"

"And if you think that's weird, you should come out to the family's Halloween celebration where we get the biggest pumpkin Ohio has to offer . . . and then blow it the hell up. I've heard talk from my cousin Sadie that next year Uncle Bo wants to drop it out of a helicopter and blast it midair."[59] I pull out my phone and start typing a note to myself. "This reminds me, I need to learn how to fly a drone by next fall so I can record the whole thing on a GoPro." When I finish saving my note, I set my phone aside and look up at Rose. She's giving me a look I can't interpret. It's either a *smiley*-smirk, like she's entertained by me, or the *smirky*-smile, like she's judging me. Sometimes there's a fine line between patronization and appreciation.

....

59 Oh, and to those who are wondering—yes, my Uncle Bo is on the ATF's People We Should Probably Keep an Eye On list.

"What?" I ask.

"Nothing," she says.

"What?!?" I ask again. Her smirk slips away and now it's just a full-blown smile, but she doesn't say anything, and I need to change the subject because people who are comfortable with awkward silences make me so damn nervous, so I go with the first thought that pops into my head.

"So have you met Neo, Trinity, Morpheus, and Agent Smith yet?" I ask and immediately cringe.[60]

"Who?"

"The family of mice living in the common room."

She stares at me. Her expression is blank. "There's a family of *mice* . . . in the common room . . ."

". . . Yes . . ."

". . . And you gave them names . . . ?"

". . . Yes . . . ?"

Rose tilts her head back and groans. "Ughhhhhhhhhhhhhhhhhhh, gross! Why does no one here clean up after themselves? Dammit, now I'm going to have to get pest control in here before everyone gets back and freaks out—"

"Awww, can't you just release them in the alleyway by the Majestic Theatre or something? They don't need to die." I pout.

"Fine, but I'm not going anywhere near them. I'll see if Bob and Earl can help us get them out." She shakes her whole body and her hair twirls all around her. "Ick, ick, ick! I hate mice!"

....

60 WHY DID I CHANGE THE SUBJECT TO MICE? WHY.

"Aww, they're not so bad, they're pretty cute. I think Trinity must have given birth in the last few days or so because Neo, Morpheus, and Agent Smith still look quite fresh."

"What's up with those weird names?"

"I know, you're thinking I should have gone with names from something classic like *The Great Mouse Detective* or *Ratatouille*, and I hear you, but I had to honor my fave, so I went with *The Matrix*."

She squints her eyes at me. "Isn't that, like, twenty years old?"

"Yeah, so?"

"I haven't seen it," she says.

"Whoa, what?" I hop off the window ledge and power walk over to her because this conversation just took a very serious turn, and I can't tell if she's just fucking with me. Whenever my mom catches me in a lie, it's when she's looking at me directly in the eyes, so I get up close to Rose and look at her straight on. "Are you joking right now? Tell me the truth."

"Nope, sorry. Never seen it," she says calmly, like this isn't a big deal. I take a step back while my brain explodes. I am trying my very best to keep my face calm, so I take a deep breath and ask my next question very slowly.

"Are you *seriously* telling me that you—a human person— have not seen *The Matrix* before?"

"I'm *seriously* telling you I have not," she says and I immediately lose my cool.

"NEVER?!?!?!?!" I screech.

"Uh, no," she says, looking a bit startled. "Should I have?" She leans away from me a little, like I might get screechy again.

"YES!" I yell as I smack her arm. I start pacing the little laundry room, hands in the air, completely appalled that some- one my age with readily available Internet access hasn't seen the greatest cinematic achievement of all time. "How is this even possible? You want to be a costume designer for movies and you haven't seen the greatest cinematic achievement of all time? I am shocked, Rose—SHOCKED! I mean for good- ness sake, Rose, Lilly Wachowski, one of the directors, WENT TO EMERSON. It stars my boy Keanu Reeves as Neo, Carrie- Anne Moss as Trinity, Laurence Fishburne as Morpheus, and a bunch of other actors whose names I can't remember because they're Canadian and never really had careers after the fran- chise, except for that one guy who plays Agent Smith, he went on to be in *Lord of the Rings*, but none of this matters because I cannot believe you haven't seen *The Matrix*! This is unaccept- able." I shake my head at her as I keep pacing.

"What's it about?" she asks and suddenly, I get an idea. I can't let her keep living without having seen this movie. It is my duty to be the one to usher her into the world of *The Matrix*.

"Unfortunately, no one can be told what *The Matrix* is. You have to see it for yourself," I say, so proud of the way I seamlessly worked a quote from the movie into our conversa- tion, but the moment is completely wasted on her because the damn woman has never seen it. Without a word, I turn on my heel and march out of the laundry room.

"Hey! Where are you going?" Rose calls after me.

I backpedal into the doorway. "Stay right there for a minute, I'll be right back." I sprint down the hall and bust into my empty room. I grab my laptop, two pairs of headphones, and a headphone splitter and power walk back to the laundry room. When I get back, Rose has moved from her perch atop the washer and is inspecting my box of detergent. "Is this stuff really all that good? It just seems like good branding—" she starts to comment but I cut her off.

"Yes, yes, yes, it's great, now put that down and get over here. I hope you have nowhere to be for the next two hours because I'm making you watch *The Matrix*." I pop myself up on the washer and pull up the movie on my laptop.

"What—right now?"

"Yes," I insist. "Why, you got somewhere else you need to be right now?"

"Nope," she says with a smile. "Let's do this."

I scooch to the side to make room for her on the washer and she hops up, adjusting her red silk robe as she settles in next to me. I offer her my fancy noise-canceling headphones while I take my shitty, in-ear backup pair. She slides the headphones on and her hair is so thick you can barely see them. She's giving me that smiley-smirk again and for the first time, I notice when she smiles like that her dimples show. I smiley-smirk back at her and press play.

●●●

"Annnnnd?" I ask as we take off our headphones and I put my laptop away. "What did you think?"

She starts counting on her fingers. "Two things. One, why didn't you name one of the mice *Mouse* after the character? It seems like a missed opportunity."

"Oh fuck, I can't believe I didn't think of that."

"And two, I'm not sure I understood it."

I let her off the hook. "Oh, no one ever gets it after the first viewing. To be honest, I don't think I understood what it was really about until my fourth or fifth viewing."

"Fourth or *fifth*?" She jerks her head back and looks me over. "How many times have you seen this movie?"

"Counting right now?"

"Sure."

"Thirty-two times," I confess.

"*Holy shit*," she says while laughing. "That is either very impressive or very obsessive."

"I prefer to think of it as impressive." I nudge her with my elbow and suddenly, I am keenly aware that the sides of our bodies have been touching for the last two hours. How did I not notice that before? "So, um, what was your favorite scene?" I ask her, desperate for a distraction.

"Hmm," she hums. She crosses her right leg over her left and the slit in her red robe slips over her knee, exposing her leg. Either she doesn't notice or doesn't care because she doesn't go to cover herself up. My eyes travel from her knee, up and up and up her thigh. Her skin looks like it would be soft to my touch. I almost forgot I asked her a question and jolt when she starts talking again. "Well, first I have to say that I absolutely love the costume design. It's a unique intersection of goth and fetish wear—I don't think I've seen another film with a look such as this. But if I had to pick a favorite part, I really liked the scene at the end when the woman, what's her name—"

"Trinity," I choke out as I clear my throat.

"Yes, Trinity. I loved how, in order to save Keanu, she unapologetically confesses and expresses her feelings for him. It was a nice juxtaposition against the whole computerized, soulless world. And besides, that kiss was hot."

"Of all the incredible scenes in *The Matrix*, including the opening sequence, and the lobby fight, and the slow-mo bullet limbo, your favorite was . . . *the kiss*?" I need to swallow because it seems my throat has gone dry.

"Yeah, it was a simple kiss, but sexy."

And now I am thinking about the kiss.

And her.

And the kiss.

And her lips.

And what it would be like to kiss her on the lips.

Oh.

Oh my.[61]

Let me just pause this scene for one second and clarify something.

------

61 Tender Chicken Mode has been activated.

Up until this very moment, I have absolutely, definitely, 100 percent never once thought about kissing my resident adviser, Rose. She's my RA! She's kind of a dick! And most importantly, she has a girlfriend! And while I may be open-minded, I am no homewrecker. I mean sure, I have objectified the hell out of her, but I do that to everyone! But now that the thought of kissing her has entered my head, I can*not* stop thinking about it and *shit fuck*, I just looked at her tits and she saw me do it too and—*ahhhh, goddammit*. It is suddenly way too hot in this laundry room. My armpits are starting to sweat. I lightly pat my cheeks with the back of my hands in a fruitless attempt to cool myself down. I haven't gotten my jollies off since Thanksgiving and suddenly it's like I've forgotten what being horny feels like. Jesus Christ on a cracker, McHugh—PULL. YOUR. SHIT. TOGETHER.[62]

The buzzer on the dryer goes off and I jump at the chance to put some physical space between us. I can't be thinking about kissing Rose. I pop off the dryer, start pulling out the hot clothes, and stuff them into my hamper. "Right, so, anyways, yeah, thanks for watching that with me. It was a nice distraction, otherwise I would have spent the afternoon fretting over my *please be my friend again* speech for Lucy's return tomorrow."

"Listen, it might take some time until she comes back, but your friendship will work itself out."

....
62 It has just occurred to me, just now, right this very moment, that I am incredibly thankful that I don't get boners.

I stop what I'm doing and look at her. "What do you mean *until* she comes back?"

Rose grimaces. "Shit, I thought you knew. Lucy called me this morning. She's going to commute in for classes for a while."

Whoa. What?

"What does *a while* mean?!?"

"It means she'll come back when she's ready," Rose says, but she senses my unease with this new information. "Give her time, okay? And for what it's worth, you and Lucy are lucky. Most first-year roommates struggle to simply coexist and you two became instant best friends. I'm very jealous, actually. My first freshman-year roommate barely spoke to me and woke up at six every morning to practice her Irish dancing in our room. If I could get through that, you can get through this."

"And what if it doesn't work out?" I ask her but then change my mind. "Never mind, don't answer that. I don't want to know the answer."

Rose slides off the top of the washing machine and gently rests her hand on my arm. "You got this, Elliot."

"I hope you're right."

"I usually am," she jokes. "Now for real though, we need to get rid of those mice."

CHAPTER 13

I SLEPT WELL LAST NIGHT. I REALLY DIDN'T THINK I would. The news that Lucy is staying home until further notice was like getting slapped in the face with a slab of frozen bacon, and I'm constantly fighting every urge to text her ninety times a day, but Lucy's return isn't something I can control. And maybe it is Rose's belief in me that *I got this* or maybe it's leftover endorphins from running all over the floor chasing mice late last night, but I woke up today feeling energized— motivated, even. I've already submitted my course selections for the semester and it's not even 8 A.M. yet. As I start syncing my new class schedule with my phone, it dawns on me that this will be my last chance until May to shower without waiting in line. This opportunity shan't be wasted. I quickly strip off my nightie, wrap myself in a towel, and run out my door straight into Brad. Or more specifically, I run into Brad's back and bounce right off it because Brad is shredded. In surprise, I take a step back and my ankle lands weird and I fall over, dropping the towel in the process.

"Oh, hey, Elliot. Did you have a nice—" He starts to turn.

"NO! DON'T TURN AROUND!" But he does and for a second he sees me sprawled on the floor. Naked.

"Shit! Oh, uh, I'm sorry!" Brad blushes and quickly turns around but he does something unexpected. He moves in front of me to block any potential onlookers from seeing my goodies. "Are you okay?" he asks without turning his head. "Do you need help getting up?"

"I'm fine!" I squeak as I frantically rewrap myself and get up. I try to stand on my ankle but it's too sore to bear any weight. "Ahhhh, shit balls. Brad? Do you think you could help me get to the ladies' bathroom? My ankle seems to be uncooperative at the moment."

Brad turns his head slightly sideways. "Uh, yeah, sure. Are you decent?"

"Yeahhhh, I'm *decent*," I grumble. I lift my arm so he can put his shoulder under it to act like a crutch but instead he swoops one arm under my legs and another against my back, lifting me up, bride-over-the-threshold style. "While I appreciate the drama, you don't need to carry me like this is *The Princess Bride* or some shit," I tell him as he ferries me down the hall.

"I love that movie!" he says.

"Nuh uh, not buying it, no way."

"Yes way! We watched it in one of my film classes last semester. I really love it."

"Yeah, so do I," I say in a daze. *Huh.* I did not expect a bro like Brad to love an old-timey romantic movie like *The Princess Bride*. "You're a film major, right?"

"Yep! I thought I wanted to be a director when I got here, but I think I like screenwriting more."

"I took Beginning Writing for the Screen last semester and was surprised by how much I enjoyed it. It's the only class I didn't completely bomb." He sets me down gently in front of the bathroom door.

"Yeah, I know. I was in your class," he says and . . . *huh.*

"You were?"

"Yep."

Double *huh.* I think—no, scratch that—I *know* I've misjudged him. Sure, Brad exhibits all the symptoms of being a total tool, but I have never, not once, seen Brad be rude or callous toward anyone. Even when he told me I had man-hands, it wasn't malicious—and he wasn't wrong! I do have huge motherfucking hands! So maybe I need to add this to the list of things I need to do to make amends.

"Thanks for the ride," I say.

"No problem at all." He pivots and walks back down the hall. I think about it for a sec and call after him.

"Hey, Brad! We should hang out sometime—you, me, and the other Brad too."

His face falls. "The other Brad dropped out after the semester, actually."

"For real?"

"Yeah, he decided to transfer to a school closer to home."

"Well, shit, that sucks," I say and he looks sad, so I try to rescue the moment. "Well, I guess it'll just be you and me then." It works, his face lights up in a cute smile.

"I would love that."

● ● ●

Honestly, I did not think my second semester of college would kick off with me lying face down on a metal slab with my butt exposed to the world while I wait for a nurse to come and give me a shot in my ass . . . and yet, here we are.[63]

Here's a thing no one tells you when you go to college: Shaving your legs is a huge pain in the ass. I know. It seems as though this simple problem should have an equally simple solution, but the reality is vastly different than the theory. I am used to having a bathtub or a shower with very safe, very clean spaces to rest a foot in order to shave my legs. But in college, you don't get that luxury. There is no safe space to rest your foot because everywhere is covered in mold. Thus, all year long I've been doing what Lucy, Sasha, and just about every

---

63 Aren't you so glad you've joined me on this journey?

other girl on my floor does—shave my legs in the sink. But then my collision with Brad happened, and while I could easily shave my left leg in the sink, I couldn't put any weight on my left ankle and I needed a solution for my right leg. So instead, while showering in one of those tiny-ass shower stalls, I used my caddy to prop up my foot and bent over to shave my legs.

And then my bare ass touched the wall. And now I have a motherfucking bacterial infection on my motherfucking ass. And that pretty much brings us up to speed on the whole lying-bare-assed-on-a-metal-slab situation.

"Okay, Elliot, I'm going to need you to stay as still as possible." A very old, very cranky, very unsympathetic nurse enters the room with a tray that contains the largest needle I have ever seen. "I have to inject the entire syringe slowly, so please refrain from clenching."

I honestly wish doctors and nurses wouldn't tell me what's about to happen, you know what I'm saying? I mean, think about it. If you know you're about to be stab—AHHHH MOTHERFUCKING FUCK SHIT GOD SHIT FUCK. I glance over my shoulder and watch as the nurse pushes all the antibiotics out of the syringe and into my ass.

When she's done, she slaps a bandage over the injection site and pulls a paper sheet over my butt. "Please remain as you are for the next few minutes, then you'll be free to go. And try not to bend over in the shower anymore, okay?"

"Yes, ma'am," I call out to her as she leaves the room. She kicks the door closed behind her, but it doesn't fully close and

I can clearly see out into the hall, which means people can clearly see inside this room. But I'm not allowed to move, so I just have to lie here and pray that no one walks by and sees my semi-bare ass—which, of course, happens IMMEDIATELY. I see someone blip by my room and at first I think I'm safe but then they double back.

"Elliot? Is that you?" *Oh, Lord. Why hast thou forsaken me?* It's Micah. Of course it's Micah. I haven't seen him in the Little Building yet, and we haven't spoken since the night of the party.

"Yeahhhh, it's me."

"Can I come in?"

"Umm, honestly, please don't. I'm kind of, uh, *indecent* at the moment," I say, borrowing Brad's delightful word for nudity.

"What happened? Are you okay?" He asks from beyond the door. I think about lying to him, making something up that's 99 percent less embarrassing, but who am I kidding. I didn't choose the slug life, the slug life chose me.

"Oh, it's nothing, I just have a minor infection on my butt because I tried and failed to shave my legs in the shower. I'm fine. This is fine. It's alllllll *fine*." I hear Micah very diplomatically clear his throat to stop himself from laughing. "So what brings you to the infirmary?" *Please, God, let him be here for an equally pathetic reason.*

"Free condoms, of course. Are you sure you're all right?" He nudges the door open a little and starts to come in. "Look, I know we haven't spoken since—"

199

"NO! DON'T COME IN HERE!"

"—that night at the party and OH MY GOD. THAT'S YOUR BUTT."

I bury my face in the crook of my elbow. "I warned you! I'm sorry, but you'll never be able to unsee this now."

Micah keeps trying to look away, but unlike Brad, he's no gentleman. He flicks my one non-diseased butt cheek. "Damn, Elliot. I never really noticed how much you were packing back there."

"Toss me my pants, please? They're on the floor over there."

"I meant that as a compliment." Micah gathers my sweatpants and tosses them to me.

"I know, I took it as one." I slide off the table and pull my pants up. "Can you do me a favor and *please* don't put this in your *Third-Floor Report*."

Micah takes a seat on the nurse's stool. "Actually, I'm glad I ran into you. I've been meaning to talk to you about that. Do you have a sec?"

"Sure," I tell him as I gather my ID and phone. "But can we walk and talk? I need to get back to get my shit for class in half an hour." The pain from the injection eventually subsides and I do my best to avoid clenching my butt as I limp back to the lobby. I think I prefer walking when having a serious conversation, it gives you an automatic reason to not look someone in the eye because you have to focus on what's ahead of you instead.

"Look, I want to get my facts straight about that party,"

Micah says. His tone is more solemn and serious than usual. "I ran into Rose yesterday and she told me what I posted that night was wrong, but she wouldn't say what really happened."

"I don't know if I'm ready to replay that night again," I tell him as we get to the elevators and swipe our IDs. "I just want to put it behind me." I know I promised to find a way to forgive him, but I'm still not sure I can trust him, and those are two very different things.

"So something *did* happen then?"

"Yes something happened, but not what you broadcasted to the entire school. Lucy read your post, you know, and now she refuses to talk to me. She hasn't even come back to the dorms yet because she thinks what you put out there was the truth." As we step out of the elevator, I turn right to go toward my room, but he stops me.

"I know—I'm trying to fix that and apologize," he says.

I turn on my heel and confront him. "By pressuring me into telling you a story that you haven't earned the right to hear?!" A couple of our floormates walk by and give us the side-eye, whispering as they pass by. I don't need to get into a screaming match with Micah outside everyone's rooms so I lower my voice. "I can't do this right now, I have to go to class."

"I really want things to be okay between us, Elliot." Micah looks desperate. "May I come by your room after dinner tonight?"

I look down at my watch and realize if I don't get going, I'm going to be late. "Fine, I'll see you then."

I spend the next four hours fighting distraction and use every last ounce of mental energy to focus in my classes.[64] Sitting in a lecture hall trying to listen and comprehend during back-to-back two-hour monologues on History of Media Arts and Principles of Sociology instead of letting my mind wander to my impending discussion with Micah requires so much effort on my part that by the time I get back to my room, I completely pass out and miss dinner entirely. I wake up only after I hear someone kick the bottom of my door. I slide out of bed and find Micah standing out in the hall, wearing one of those shortie silk robes, holding two mugs of coffee. He shoves one in my hands and lets himself in.

"Nice robe," I tell him as he takes up residence on Lucy's vacant bed while I sit down on my own.

"Thanks, it's from the Jane Fonda Collection," he says, and then we settle into one of those nice, awkward silences I hate. He crosses and uncrosses his legs. At least I'm not the only one who's nervous.

"So, how do you want to do this?" He asks, breaking the silence.

------

64 I know I've only mentioned it in passing but I have ADHD, and not in the casual, problematic way people like to self-diagnose. I am clinically diagnosed and have struggled with it all my life, and yes, prescription medication helps, but it's not a miracle cure. I don't like being on meds; they make me feel flat and robotic, which is why during most of high school and all last semester I sold my meds instead of taking them. But I need them and now I'm choosing to be better about taking them.

"What do you mean?"

"We could start with a casual, neutral conversation until a few hours go by and we eventually work our way to the real reason why I'm here, or we can skip the foreplay and just jump in, feetfirst."

"More like headfirst, but sure, let's shorthand it," I reply. "What's the real reason you're here?"

"To be your friend again."

I lean against the wall and cross my legs in front of me. I look down at the coffee-oil swirls in my mug. "I don't know, Micah. How do I know I can trust you?"

"Because I owe you," he says and then pauses, collecting himself. "And because I'm shutting down the *Third-Floor Report*." Whoa. I was not expecting that. I look up at him. He continues, "The day after I went home for break, my dad pulled me into his study. At first I thought he was going to give me his typical *Why aren't you like your brother* speech, but then he went to his desk and pulled out a printed copy of my article from *The Daily Beacon*—the one on the American tuition debt crisis—the one *you* printed and mailed him before winter break. Elliot, he wanted to tell me how proud he was of my article." Micah tilts his head back and starts fanning his eyes.

"It's so weird seeing you have feelings," I joke because it's true. This is a side of Micah he has never shared with me before.

"Shut up and let me finish," he says sweetly. He reaches for a tissue on Lucy's desk and dabs his eyes before continuing.

"Elliot, my dad has never, not once, told me he was proud of me, and he's been especially angry with me ever since I chose to go to Emerson instead of USC like he and my mom did, like my brother did. So when my father told me he was proud of my article, I felt seen and supported for the first time in a long, long time."

"That's great, Micah, honestly," I tell him. "But I don't really get how this is about what you did to me and shutting down the *Report*."

"Because I owe you. After the thing with my dad, I spent the rest of the break thinking about how much I enjoyed writing that article and how the *Third-Floor Report* is no longer serving its purpose. I mean, yeah, I love writing about all our trashy lives, a part of me will always love trash, but it isn't fulfilling me like it used to and it isn't helping me stand out in the program like the tuition piece did."

I drink the last of my coffee and set the mug aside. "Here's what I don't get: If you're shutting down the *Report*, why are you still pumping me for details about that night? How do I know you won't change your mind next week and post about it then?"

Micah's face collapses. "Because when Rose told me that what I wrote about you and Kenton was way off base, it made me sick to my stomach. I don't want to be that kind of journalist and I don't want to be that kind of friend. So, this is me, taking the extremely long-winded way of saying I'm sorry. I am sorry I said those things and I am sorry for any damage

I may have done to your friendship with Lucy." He finishes talking and takes a huge breath. He wraps one hand across his waist and rests his head in the other. I've never seen him so vulnerable before. I came back this semester vowing to find a way to forgive Micah and if I don't do it now, I never will.

I get off my bed, walk the three steps across the room, climb onto Lucy's bed, and settle in next to my friend.

"Do you want to know what happened that night?" I ask him quietly.

"Only if you want to tell me," he says.

"I do."

So I tell my friend.

And my friend listens.

● ● ●

It's been three weeks since the second semester started and Lucy and I *still* haven't talked. It was rough there those first few days; coming home to utter silence has left me feeling . . . lonely. But I'm doing my best to branch out and make new friends. Brad and I are both in the Storytelling and Writing Short Scripts class and we've partnered up for a project. We met a couple of times at the library and together we wrote a script for an animated short based on a hilarious theory Remy concocted about dogs and why they sniff one another's butts. During the first brainstorm session with Brad, Remy called and I was going to send it to voice mail but Brad insisted on talking to her, so I put Remy on speakerphone and listened while Brad and my little sister came up with this insane story that we then turned into a script. And now, I guess we're friends—or at least friendship-adjacent.

And as for my other classes? Well, I'm taking another media arts core class, Introduction to Visual Arts, and the other two courses fulfill more of my gen ed requirements—Literary Foundations and Introduction to Ethics. I'm not gonna lie to you, reader, they are bone dry and not as fun as screenwriting, but I am doing everything I can to pay attention and learn.

And I've been trying to eat healthier too. Vegetables are still disgusting and kale can go fuck off, but I haven't touched the cereal bar once—NOT ONCE—in these past three weeks. At first, I wanted to die from sugar withdrawal, but it turns out, if you eat healthier food, you kinda start to feel less like a slug. On Thursdays, both my classes are over by two in the afternoon, so I've made a habit of setting up shop in the dining hall after class for lunch and staying through dinner to study.

And that's where I am now—huddled in the corner of the booth, facing the window, with my hoodie up and my head-phones on, as I work on a paper for my Literary Foundations course. But out of the corner of my eye I see a tray slide onto the table. The tray has a bowl of potato and kale soup with a small side salad. I know who eats like that. I pull my head-phones off and swivel around to see Lucy standing by the booth holding a second tray of food.

"Can I sit here?" she asks politely.

"Of course," I reply. Lucy takes a seat opposite me and slides the second tray over to me. On it is a chocolate chip waffle and a bowl of Froot Loops. I almost start crying right then and there but stop myself because I know those tears are reserved for whatever conversation we're about to have. Lucy reaches for her soup and starts eating while I dig into the waffle.

"I don't think I've ever seen you eat real food for dinner," Lucy says in between sips.

"Why would anyone eat *real food* when there's breakfast available 24/7? But also, I had some steamed broccoli, like, four hours ago," I say tentatively, unsure of the steps to this particular dance. Are we friends? Are we not friends? Are we roommates? Does she still hate me? Every heartbeat feels like a punch in my chest. We eat in silence for a few minutes and when we've finished, she looks up at me.

"I spoke with Rose," she says, pausing to take a breath. She looks uncomfortable, like she too would prefer to pretend the past had never happened. "She told me what really happened with Kenton."

"Oh" is all I say. I can feel heat creeping up my cheeks, and a rock is working its way to the middle of my throat as another wave of shame washes over me. I can't look her in the eyes, so I reach for a napkin and start shredding it into tiny pieces. "You know, then?"

"I know. I am so sorry he did that to you," she says.

"I should have told you right after it happened."

"Yes, you should have. I spent the entire break blaming you for why Kenton and I broke up. I was so mad at you, Elliot. I hated you."

My heart drops to the pit of my stomach. The truth fucking stings. "That's why you haven't been sleeping in the dorms?"

"No," she says, her voice getting soft again. I look up at her. "I called Rose the day before the semester started to tell her I'd be finishing up the year off campus, and that's when she told me the truth."

"Wait, if you knew this whole time, why have you been staying away?"

"Because I am heartbroken!" she cries out. She doesn't even care that people are looking. "I gave Kenton everything, Elliot. *Everything*. The Kenton I knew could never do something like this."

"It's not just you, Luce—no one saw this coming."

"Maybe I didn't *know* him at all," she sighs. "Because I can't stop asking myself the same questions over and over. How could he do this? *Why* did he do this?"

I start shredding the napkin again. "I've been thinking about that a lot too. I know it's not my fault for what happened after I told him no, but I can't help think maybe it was me."

"What do you mean?" she asks.

"There was something he said that night that I can't get out of my head. He assumed I'd be open to hooking up with him because of Project Tender Chicken. I dunno, I guess I never thought people might misinterpret my intentions with it—especially at a place like Emerson."

Lucy shakes her head. "Even if that were true, that wouldn't give Kenton a pass to do what he did. You can't let what happened with Kenton stop you from doing what you want."

"I'm not, I haven't," I tell her. I lean back in the booth and look out the window down at the snowy street below us. "I stopped Project Tender Chicken before the Kenton thing, actually. It was fun, but something about it didn't feel right in the end. I started feeling lonely, like it wasn't enough. I don't know, I'm still trying to figure it out."

"So what happened that night hasn't put you off sex?" she asks.

"Hell, no!" I say boldly and we both laugh. "I haven't been with anyone since Thanksgiving, Luce. THANKSGIVING. I'm afraid if I go any longer my lady cave is going to start collecting cobwebs." Lucy smiles but there's a hint of sadness behind it. I reach out across the table and hold her hand. "And you? I hope Kenton hasn't ruined the whole concept of dating and relationships for you."

She takes a moment to think about it and then says, "No, I don't think so, but I think next time I have to get to know someone first before I decide to give them my heart. But . . . can I be honest with you?"

"Always."

"I *hate* that I miss him. Because I do, I miss him so much," she says and she starts to cry.

"Maybe you don't miss Kenton. Maybe what you miss is the relationship, the feeling of belonging to someone and them belonging to you in return."

"Maybe," she says through her tears. "But it's more than that. I'm angry too. Angry that my first time wasn't meaningful, important, or special. Angry that I won't be able to look back on my first time without feeling anything but regret that I gave it to someone who tried to rape my best friend." She finally looks up at me and tears are streaming down her cheeks.

I want to say something, anything that will comfort her, but I am having a hard time processing her experience in all this. I spent so much time assessing my *own* feelings I forgot that Kenton was Lucy's first boyfriend. Kenton may have tried to hurt me, but he *betrayed* her. It's so easy for me to hate him but it's so much more complicated for Lucy.

I squeeze her hand. "There's nothing I can say right now that will make this part of your life fast forward but I wish there was. I would take all this pain away for you, if I could."

"Thank you," she says, pulling her hand away from mine and then tucking her hair behind her ears. I slide out of my side of the booth and scooch in next to her. She folds her hands into mine and I rest my head on her shoulders.

"I'm really glad you're back," I tell her. "As nice as it is having the room all to myself, it hasn't been the same without you."

"Same," she says and she rests her head against mine and

we stay like that for a moment until she lets out a deep, cleansing breath. "I'm relieved to be back, actually."

"Oh yeah?"

"I can't stay at home anymore, my mom is driving me *insane*," she laughs.

"No way, Carol is a total babe. No one that hot in their forties is allowed to be annoying."

"And yet, she is!" Lucy jokes. "But I'm serious, I told her and the rest of the family that I am not coming home on the weekends anymore." I sit up straight and give her a skeptical look.

"Whoa, for real? But your family is so important to you."

"They still are, but if I am willing to take on this much debt to pay for student housing, I might as well live here and get my money's worth. I may be the first one in my family to *go* to college, but in a way I haven't even left my home yet."

"I can be your *new* home," I say and she smiles.

"You already are."

She wipes her eyes and her fingers come back smudged black. Lucy reaches across the table and grabs a clean napkin. "Don't ever buy into the marketing hype. Waterproof mascara is total crap," she says as she dabs her eyes. I wrap my arms around her waist and squeeze her. "Ugh, Elliot, I thought we practiced this," she grunts as she wriggles free from my grip. "You're hugging way too tight. Here, let me show you." She embraces me and it's 100 percent pure hot chocolate. I melt into her arms.

"I missed you so fucking much," I coo lovingly into her hair.

"You know, we've only been on a friendship break for, like, a month," she says.

"I don't care. Anything longer than a day feels like a lifetime apart from you." I close my eyes and squeeze Lucy even tighter.

And just like that, I have my best friend back.

CHAPTER 14

MOST MORNINGS, LUCY AND I ARE GENTLY LURED from our dreams by the smooth, nutty aroma of freshly brewed coffee trickling from Lucy's programmable coffee maker. But this morning, at 2:30 A.M., a mere one week after my life finally returned to normal, we get blasted out of REM sleep by the ear-shattering screech of the fire alarms.

"WHATTHEFUCK?!?" I yell, disoriented by the flashing, red strobe light on our ceiling. I squint over at Lucy but somehow she is still asleep. "Lucy," I croak to her and when she doesn't stir, I grab one of the pillows beneath my head and throw it at her from across the room.

"Heyyyy," she grumbles when it hits her face. "What the hell?" It takes her a second but her brain finally catches up and registers the alarm. She grimaces in pain as she covers her ears.

"Is that the fire alarm?" she shouts.

"Maybe it's a false alarm? I don't smell anything," I yell back. Lucy shrugs sleepily and falls back down on her bed, pulling the comforter over her ears. But a moment later, Rose kicks open our door and smacks the light switch.

"What the fuck are you two still doing in bed?!" Rose shouts at us. Lucy pokes her head out from under the covers while I take a peek to see if Rose is wearing some kind of sexy nightgown or at least something totally bizarre and Rose-ish, but I'm disappointed to discover she's already dressed in head-to-toe winter gear. Unhappy with our lack of progress, Rose stomps over to Lucy in a huff and rips her blanket off. "GET YOUR ASSES OUT OF BED!"

I glance out the window and gesture to it. "But it's snowing," I whine.

Rose closes her eyes and balls her hands into the tiny little murder fists I am so familiar with. "I swear to god, Elliot . . . as soon as I'm done making sure you are safe . . . I am going to kill you."[65] She turns on her heel and stomps from our room to Brad's room and we hear her start the whole routine again. Lucy is the first to move. She gets out of bed, goes to her dresser, changes into the running outfit she laid out for herself just a few hours ago, then pulls on the snow boots she always leaves by our door.

"Rose can be a real dick sometimes," I complain to Lucy as I blindly reach under my bed for something to wear from the

---

65 See what I mean? Murder fists.

fine selection of dirty clothes that have accumulated there. I throw on some boxers and whatever shirt I grab first. I quickly scan the room for my snow boots but my side of the room is a mess and I'm running out of time, so I suck it up and shove my feet into Lucy's back-up pair even though they are two sizes too small and bedazzled in silver sequins.

We abandon our room and head down the hall toward the line of bleary-eyed freshmen waiting to get into the stairwell. Once in line, Lucy and I glance around and realize we forgot to put on our coats. At least Lucy is in a sweatshirt and tights, I look down and sigh at what I'm wearing: two disco balls on my feet and a long, hot-pink sleep shirt that reads ORGASM DONOR in big block letters across my boobs. *Why must I be this way?* I often ask myself. *Why?*

"Do you think I have time to go back and change?"

"Or at least get our coats?" Lucy also suggests but the line behind us pushes us forward and down the stairwell we go. The second I step outside, my teeth start to chatter and my nerps squinch into icicle tips and it looks like I'm smuggling two frozen Hershey's Kisses under my shirt. I pull my arms inside to help keep warm but cold bursts of wind slip inside.

Lucy and I are separated almost immediately as we're shoved out of the way by hundreds of pissed-off, under-slept students filing out of the Little Building. I push my way across snowy Boylston Street as I try to find Luce, but I end up running into Micah.

"You look like you just got a massage at a day spa," I say in regards to the thick, white terry-cloth robe he is wrapped in.

"I did," he says with a grin and pulls the fluffy robe tighter around his body. "And it came with a happy ending too," he adds and tilts his head in the direction of a hot guy talking on his phone.

"Nice pull," I say to him. "Emerson?"

"Thanks! And no, he goes to Tufts."

"Tufts?! You got a Tufts boy to come all the way downtown on a Tuesday? Impressive." I give him a golf clap and he curtsies in his robe. The wind picks up and curls all around my exposed limbs, and I lean into Micah, expecting him to be a friend and share his robe with me, but he doesn't budge.

"Come on," I whine. "Share the wealth!"

"Nuh uh," he says and shakes his head.

"Please?????" I beg but that bitch is stubborn.

"Go snuggle up to that guy, he's wearing even less than you," Micah says, nodding toward a guy in the crowd who's wearing nothing but a towel and flip-flops. His back is turned toward us so I can't see his face, but his towel is pulled tight around his waist and I can perfectly see the shape of his butt and hot damn, that is an ASS. But I don't make a move. Standing ankle deep in snow at three in the morning waiting to see if your dorm is about to erupt into flames is not exactly the ideal time to be making moves. Micah, however, has other opinions on the matter. He bends down, picks up a fistful of snow, compacts it into a ball and throws it at the guy's perfect butt. Mr. Good Butt yelps and turns around, looking to see who hit him but Micah hides behind me.

"Seriously?" I whisper over my shoulder to Micah.

"You'll thank me later," my annoying friend replies as he backs away from me to join his lover, who has been taking shelter under the awning to the train entrance. While that's happening, Mr. Good Butt leaves his group of friends and approaches me and *holy tenderest of chickens*, his front is even hotter than his back.

"Did you just throw a snowball at me?" Mr. Good Butt, Face, and Body asks. He's close enough for me to count his abs. There's six, no seven, of them. Is it even possible to have seven abs? I don't know, sorry, I'm rambling. He's so fucking pretty it's making me nervous.

"Sorry, that was my friend over there. He's a real big asshole," I say, shivering in Micah's direction. This absurdly handsome specimen in front of me looks me up and down and I'm suddenly very aware of the fact that I am wearing, quite possibly, the most boner-killing of all outfits. I try to look anywhere except his beautiful, hot face but my eyes land on his groin and THAT BULGE! *Goddammit*, there is no safe space to rest my eyes on him, so I turn my whole body sideways and stare at a streetlamp instead.

"Cute shirt," he says.

"Thanks." I blush. "I like yours too." He looks down at his bare chest and laughs at my dumb joke. *Huh.* Maybe I was wrong, maybe standing half naked in the snow in the middle of the night *is* the perfect time to flirt. I rotate away from the lamppost, pull my arms out from within my shirt, and face him. "So do you sleep naked or did you dress specifically for the occasion?"

He laughs again. "Yes, but I was actually in the shower when the alarm went off." And that's when I notice his wavy, black hair is dripping water.

"What the hell are you doing showering in the middle of the night?"

"Couldn't sleep," he says.

"I thought I was cold as shit, but you must be freezing your ass off."

"Yeah, I am." He looks down at me and gives me a panty-dropping smile. "But I know how we can warm up." Well, I know where *this* is going. I take a step closer to him and bite my bottom lip.

"Oh yeah? And how's that?"

"This." He steps toward me and I can't believe I'm about to be kissed out here when instead he drops down, picks up a clump of snow and smushes it on top of my head.

"Oh . . . you . . . mother . . . fucker!" I squat and arm myself with two handfuls of snow and launch them at him but he easily dodges and they hit some kid in the crowd. Everyone in the vicinity freezes—

And then I find myself in the middle of a giant snowball fight in the middle of the street outside the Little Building at three in the morning.

Everyone is running around picking up snow, throwing it, and trying not to get hit. It's chaos. Snowballs are flying left and right but the half-naked man and I stay together and form a team. I take a hit for him, he takes one for me, and I can't help but be impressed by the fact that he's been able to run around like this while still holding his towel in place. I mean, it sucks for me because I'd really like a preview, but good for him. The RAs and the resident director, with a megaphone in hand, finally come out of the building but no one listens when he pleads for us to stop throwing snowballs at them. We don't slow down until two fire trucks roll up and we make room for them to get inside our dorm, but the second they're inside, the fight resumes.

"I'm Elliot," I finally tell him as we hide behind a tree to catch our breath.

"Nico," he says. "It's a pleasure to meet you, Elliot."

"So what do you think, burnt popcorn?" I ask him. He looks confused. "The fire alarm! Ten bucks says someone burnt popcorn in a microwave."

"No way, at three in the morning? I bet someone lit a candle and forgot about it."

"I hope you're good for the money because there is *zero* chance that happened. We're not allowed to put up fairy lights in our rooms, let alone burn candles."

"You really think everyone here abides by the rules at all times?" he asks as a snowball whizzes by his head.

"No," I say and then add, "but we're kinda forced to on the third floor."

"You're on three?"

I nod. "Yeah, I'm in number three hundred eleven."

"Lucky! That means you only have two flights of stairs to go down every time the fire alarm goes off."

"*Every time*? You think this is going to happen again?"

"I'm surprised this is the first time it's happened this year! This must be a record or something because last year it went off six times."

"You're a sophomore?" I ask.

"Yeah, I live on the tenth floor in a suite with some other international kids."

"You're an *international* student?" I look at his face again and study it more closely this time, trying to place his origin. He doesn't look white but beyond that I have no clue. All I do know is he's gorgeous, with a thick head of black, wavy hair and eyelashes so dark that maybe it's Maybelline or maybe it's just killer genetics. "Where are you from?" I ask, but we're interrupted when the firefighters come out of the LB and the resident director gets on the megaphone again.

"ALL RIGHT, FOLKS. FALSE ALARM. EVERYONE GET BACK INSIDE," he says and the snowball fight ends in cheers. As Nico and I enter the mix and shuffle our way into the building, I run into Lucy looking warm and cozy in a huge, oversize men's coat.

"Where the hell did you get that coat?" I ask her.

"From Brad!" Lucy says and for the first time I spot Brad catching up behind her. "He saw us leave without our coats on so he went back to his room to grab us ones to borrow." Lucy burrows inside the hulking parka while Brad hands me his other coat, just as we finally get inside the LB.

"Wow, that was really sweet of you, Brad," I tell him. "But your timing sucks."

"We looked for you but then the snowball fight broke out," Brad says. I look over at Nico and we both grin. The line moves slowly, but we eventually get upstairs to the elevator bank on the second floor, where I spot Rose herding students into one line.

"So what was it?" I call out to her as we get closer to the elevators. "What set off the alarm?"

"Someone lit a candle on the sixth floor." Rose shakes her head in dismay.

Nico smacks me in the arm. "I knew it! I totally knew it! You owe me ten dollars."

I roll my eyes at him. "Will you take a check? I'm fresh out of cash and I don't do Venmo."

"How about you buy me a coffee instead, after we have dinner this weekend." He says it so casually I nearly miss the invite.

"You two are going out?" Rose asks us.

"Oh, um, no. I mean, we just met outside—" I start to say to Rose but then Nico cuts in.

"That's a no then?" Nico asks, looking sad.

"No—I mean yes, I mean—I dunno. Ask me again when I'm not wearing a soaking nightgown covered in melted snow."

"Yes, ma'am." Nico grins and for a moment I think about kissing him right here, right now, but I stop myself when Rose taps me on the shoulder.

"Elliot, quit holding up the line," Rose says. "Third and fourth floor residents can just take the stairs, let your friend here wait in line for the elevator."

Lucy, Brad, and other kids from my floor step out of the line and head for the stairs while I turn to Nico.

"Well, that was . . . I don't know if fun is the right word because I think I may have frostbite now, but that was fun-adjacent," I tell him.

"Sweet dreams, Elliot," he calls to me as I walk to the stair-well entrance and I blush again.

●●●

Four hours later, I wake up for class and find a note under my door from Nico, asking me out. And two days later, we go on our first date.

CHAPTER 15

WHEN WORD SPREAD I WAS GOING ON A DATE— a *real, grown-up, intimate as hell* date—everyone was suddenly very keen to be involved, either because they were genuinely supportive of my first attempt at romance or because they wanted a front row seat to the inevitable *Elliot Fails at Love* show.

Lucy coordinated with the entire female student body of the third floor to help me try on everything I own—and everything *they* own, because apparently my own wardrobe was deemed either too slutty or too baggy for a date of this magnitude. My Big Date Night Squad eventually settled on a white button-up shirt, a crisp black blazer, a green miniskirt and thigh-high boots. Classy and sophisticated, with just a hint of *do me*.

And now it's Friday night, the night of Le Big Date and my makeover is almost complete. While Lucy transforms my hair from a mess of tangled headphone cords into a neat bird's nest at the nape of my neck, Sasha finishes applying a second coat of rose-colored lip stain to my lips. It is such a treat to be made up like this because my usual makeup routine involves dyeing my eyebrows with a box of Just For Men mustache and beard dye once a month and occasionally dragging a clumpy mascara wand from a year-old tube of CoverGirl LashBlast over my sparse lashes.

"Now rub your lips together for me?" Sasha says, her face only inches away from mine. The girls step back and inspect their hard work. I do as I'm told but Sasha must see something because she grabs one of her many hot pink–bristle makeup brushes and starts sweeping it over my forehead again. "Do you think she needs falsies?" she asks Lucy, who has been supervising this entire metamorphosis. "I can glue some on."

Lucy checks her watch. "There's no time for eyelashes, she's supposed to meet Nico downstairs in the lobby in ten minutes. I think we're done here." I get up from my desk chair and take a look at myself in our full-length mirror.

What can I say? I look like a hot-ass bitch.

But there's just one problem . . .

I can't stop sweating.

It's like my armpits are crying.

"I'm nervous, oh god, why am I so nervous?" I don't know why, but the sudden realization that I'm about to go on a grown-up date is making my heart race. I pace back and forth in our room, unable to get my sweat glands to stop betraying me.

Lucy puts her hand on my shoulder and in a very stern voice says, "Elliot, you need to calm down *right now*. And stop fanning your pits." I lift up my arms and show her the situation. The sweat has started bleeding all the way through the blazer. "Good god, woman!" Her eyes widen and she reaches for a box of tissues. "Keep fanning! Keep fanning!" she shouts.

I try to take deep breaths but that only seems to make things worse. "Just give me one minute," Lucy says. She jumps off her bed and swings open her wardrobe. She swiftly scans through her clothes and yanks one of her own white shirts off a hanger. Lucy approaches me with an intense look I've never seen before and it's kinda hot, kinda scary. She puts her hands on my chest and at first I think this is the moment she's going to finally give in to her unrequited feelings for me, but then she apologizes. "I'm sorry, but we're running out of time. You have no choice." She proceeds to rip open, yes, rip my shirt open like a stripper. We stand there, staring at each other after the dramatic moment. I think she expected buttons to go flying.

"You didn't realize the buttons were snaps, did you."

"No, I did not," she says politely. "But you still need to throw this shirt away because it's ruined now."

"Fine," I say as I peel the pit-soaked blouse from my torso. Lucy hands me a fresh one but within one minute, it's soaked again. "Fffffffuuuucccckkkkk! What should I do? Should I cancel? Should I put on a hoodie?"

"No!" Sasha and Lucy yell in unison.

Sasha perks up and gasps. "I know! Go see if Rose can help! She fixed one of my favorite shirts so I wouldn't show any more boob sweat when filming in my room because it gets so hot in there and—"

"Sash," Lucy interrupts. "I absolutely want to hear the end of your story so please hold on to it, but right now we are out of time. Elliot, give me your phone. I'll text Nico that you need a few more minutes. Go right now down to Rose's room and—"

I throw my phone at Lucy and dart out the room before she even has the chance to finish her sentence. I sprint down the hall and knock on Rose's door.

"It's open!" she says and I go in. This is the first time I've ever even seen Rose's room. I'm not sure what I was expecting but "tantric spa" seems to be the general decor theme. It's filled with warm, vibrant colors and patterns. Damask gold curtains frame the window, and a deep red comforter and about a thousand throw pillows have turned her bed into a soft, plush shrine. A tufted Persian rug covers the ugly navy carpet, and piles upon piles of fabrics and clothes are scattered throughout her single. And in the middle of all that is Rose, sitting on her bed next to Monica. They both look up when I walk in. Both their brows are furrowed and there's a weird, caustic vibe in the room. Monica looks pissed—I mean, Monica always looks kinda pissy, but right now she looks legit pissed.

"Oh, hey, Monica," I say to her, feeling suddenly sheepish for walking in on what was most definitely a fight.

"What can I do for you, Elliot?" Rose asks flatly.

I shuffle my feet in her doorway. "I'm sorry to bother you. I, uh, I have a date tonight and I kinda have an emergency pit-stain situation going on here and I could really use your help, if you aren't busy."

"I'm not busy," she says, and anger flashes across Monica's face. Monica gets off the bed and stomps past me out the door.

"Come on, Monica," Rose calls after her girlfriend. "Don't be like that."

"Like *what*, Rose?" Monica growls.

Rose's eye catches me staring and she quickly softens her tone. "Can we *please* talk about this later?"

Monica throws her hands up in the air and says, "Fine. Whatever." She slams the door on her way out.

I feel ssssuuuuuuuuper awkward being here right now, so I start to back out of her room while saying, "I'm sorry, you are very clearly busy right now."

"It's fine, Elliot. What's wrong with your pits?" She sounds snippy and I consider leaving. I don't want to bother Rose, especially when she's in a bad mood but . . .

"Yeah, I'm having a bit of a problem." I lift my arms and show her the damage. "Can you resuscitate or should I just pronounce myself dead?" She squints from across the room, reaches into her pocket, and pulls out thick-framed glasses I didn't know she wore. Then she hops off her bed and walks right up to inspect the damage.

She looks at me over the top of her frames. "Damn, Elliot."

"I know, I know. I just have this thing where I sweat when I'm nervous, and I don't really know why I'm nervous, I mean, I haven't been on an actual *date* date in a long time and I'm a bit rusty but it's just one date! Why should I be so nervous over one date? Ugh, I dunno, the point is my sweat glands are rebellious little fuckers who express themselves at the most inopportune times and as you clearly see, I sweat when I'm nervous. And also I apparently talk when I'm nervous and now my outfit is ruined but was this even a good outfit to start with? I mean, you're wearing head to toe denim and somehow that looks awesome and now I'm thinking I should go change into all the denim I own and I'm sorry, I'll just shut the fuck up right now." I start frantically fanning my pits because they started pissing all through my shirt again during my breathless monologue.

"Who are you going on a date with?"

"Nico, the half-naked gentleman from the night of the fire alarm."

"Really? You're going out with that guy?"

"Uh, yeah," I say, taken aback by the sudden change in her tone. "Why, do you know him?"

"This is a small school, everyone kind of knows everyone here." I stop moving long enough to look at Rose. I want to give her the benefit of the doubt. She was just fighting with Monica when I barged in but I'm starting to feel like I'm under attack because right now because she has this sour, hostile look about her.

"What? What is it?" I ask.

"Nothing, it's nothing. I shouldn't have said anything," she says, trying to backpedal, but I don't let her.

"But you didn't *say* anything. Instead, you gave me the most condescending look."

She arches a brow, silently asking me if I really want to challenge her, and you know what? I do. When I don't back off, she shrugs and says, "I just think you're being a little bit ridiculous."

"*Excuse me*?"

"This isn't you!" Rose cries out. "Since when do you give a shit about what you wear or how you look? You are getting all worked up, and for what, a date with some guy?"

"It's not just a *date*. I want to be in a relationship with him."

"A *relationship*?" She lets out a small laugh and my insides start sharpening into blades. "I thought you weren't about that? I thought you preferred to keep things casual?"

"What I was doing before wasn't working for me anymore. I'm allowed to change my goddamn opinion, Rose," I say, getting in her face. "And I don't think there's anything wrong with trying to find a little happiness."

Rose takes a careful step back and crosses her arms. "And you think this guy, *Nico*, is the one who can make you happy?"

I throw my hands up. "I have no clue if Nico can make me happy, but I'm going to try. Is that okay with *you*?"

Rose looks away, removes her glasses, and starts to clean them with the sleeve of her button-down denim shirt. "Yeah, sure, do whatever you want. But for the record, I don't think he can make you happy."

"You don't even know Nico." My voice gets louder with every word that comes out my mouth, but I can't stop myself now.

"I *do* know him—and trust me, he's not right for you."

I cross my arms. "Oh really? And why's that?"

"Oh, come on! You need to be with someone you can be yourself with, someone who won't let you walk all over them and a guy like Nico will never push you, he will never challenge you. He's a doormat, Elliot."

I lean forward and get in her face. "What the hell is your problem? One minute you're nice to me and the next you're basically calling me a bitch." I turn to leave. I need to get out of here right now. I am bad at this, bad at arguing. I get way too angry way too fast and I tend to lash out.

"Where are you going?" She calls out to me like she's mad that I'm leaving.

"I'm not really in the mood for another one of your lectures."

"You see? This is what I'm talking about!" Rose says. "Elliot, you are a good person who means well but doesn't always do well and whenever someone tries to call you out on your shit, you immediately write them off as an asshole instead of someone who loves you enough to tell you when you're wrong."

"Have a good night, Rose," I tell her in a flat, sober tone. I never thought Rose would be capable of offending me like this and if I stay any longer, I'm going to cry and ruin all of Sasha's hard work. I turn on my heel and open the door but she stops me.

"Elliot, wait—*please*." She reaches out a hand and I pause, my hand visibly shaking on the knob. "I'm sorry for upsetting you. Who you date is none of my business and I shouldn't have said anything."

I think about leaving, I *want* to leave but . . . this is Rose.

She has *seen me* at my worst.

She has *helped me* through my worst.

I can't leave it this way, not like this.

She's only trying to help. She's only trying to help.

If I leave, if I run away from this, I'm only proving what she already knows to be true about me. I don't want to be someone who lets Rose down. It takes every ounce of strength I have to swallow my pride. I turn around and face her. "I'm sorry too. I shouldn't have jumped down your throat like that."

She looks down at the ground and clears her throat. "So, are we, uh, are we good?"

I'm unsure, my insides are still on fire, but the flames are starting to fizzle out. "Yeah," I say. "We're good." I finally look Rose in the eye and see warmth return to her face and it feels like a step in the right direction. I shake out my whole body, trying to release us from this spider web of tension when I catch a whiff of my armpits and oh, sweet Jesus, I completely forgot about the whole reason I came here in the first place. I lift my arms again to show her. "So, then . . . can you help? I'm desperate."

"Oh, right! Yeah, I have just the thing. Stay there." She climbs on her bed and starts tossing pillows behind her head until she finds what she's looking for: the tiniest leather backpack I have ever seen. I mean, what is the point of a backpack that small? It's not even big enough to hold a McDonald's Egg McMuffin. Rose pulls the strings on the little satchel opening and slips her thumb and index fingers inside like lobster pincers and pulls out two wrapped panty liners. "Here you go," she says, holding them out to me on the palm on her hand.

"Panty liners?" I look down at my crotch. "What, am I leaking *down there* too?"

"No," Rose says, failing to stifle a laugh. "They're for your shirt. Stick them on the inside of your sleeves so the soft part touches your skin."

"*This* is your solution?!"

"Take it or leave it, but it's a trick that has never failed me."

I bounce anxiously in place. Am I really about to put pads on my pits? I grab Rose's wrist and check the time on her watch. Oh shit. I'm so fucking late. "Screw it," I sigh as I strip off my blazer and start unbuttoning my top. I get the last button undone and peel off the moist shirt, revealing my black, lace, date-night bra.

"What are you doing?!" Rose's lower lip drops open a little as her eyes start darting around the room, looking anywhere but at me.

"Sorry, do you mind? I'm out of time and I need to make sure I put these on correctly." I hold the shirt out to her and she hesitates, but helps put the pads on. I slip the shirt back on and Rose quickly fastens the buttons while I adjust the blazer over my shirt. When I think everything is where it should be, I ask, "How do I look?" She takes a step back, puts her glasses on, and eyes the length of me.

"You look . . ." She trails off. She clears her throat and

starts to try again when there's a knock at the door and Lucy lets herself in.

"Elliot, ohmygod, what the heck are you doing?" She shrieks. "You were supposed to be downstairs ten minutes ago!"

"Thanks, Rose!" I barely get out before Lucy drags me by the arm into the hall. She places my phone, student ID, and wallet into the pockets of my winter coat and shoves it into my hands, then pushes me into an open elevator and hits the lobby button.

"Have a good time!" she chirps as the doors close.

And off on my date I go.

● ● ●

Twenty minutes later, Nico and I are seated at table by the front window in this cozy, romantic-as-fuck Italian restaurant in Boston's most tender-chickeny neighborhood, the North End. The whole place is warm and dark, lit only by tealights twinkling on every table. He looks handsome and relaxed, like he didn't just spend all afternoon getting ready.

"I'm minoring in art history," he reveals to me over our shared appetizer. "It's my passion, but it won't pay the bills, or so my parents seem to think, so I'm majoring in sports communication instead."

While I watch him try to skewer a tomato, I find myself zoning out, unable to get Rose's comment out of my head. *Is Nico wrong for me?* I don't know the answer to that yet, but she is right about one thing. Beyond his preference for midnight showers and snowball fights, I don't really *know* anything about Nico.

"What else should I know about you?" I ask him with a coy smile.

"What else would you like to know?"

"Hmmm." I rest my chin on my hand and think about all the things I could ask him. *So what's it like to make out with you? How much heat are you packing? Are you a doormat? Can we get the check and go back to your room already?* But of course, I don't ask him any of those things. Instead, I ask, "You said you were an international student, right? Where are you from?"

He grins. "Canada."

"Canada?!" I cry out a little too loud. I lower my voice to a more delicate decibel. "Does Canada even count as *international*? Wait—" I stop myself from being insensitive. Maybe he's from a really remote and Canadian-y part of Canada like Nova Scotia or Saskatoon or some shit. "Where in Canada are you from?"

"Montreal," he says, and I snort really loudly.

"MONTREAL? That's *barely* in Canada! It's what, a four- or five-hour drive from here? I mean, for fuck's sake, Ohio is farther away than *that*!"

He lets out a deep, hearty laugh. It's so hot. "If it makes you feel any better, I wasn't born there. I was born in California, just outside San Diego. When I was five, my parents split up and I had the choice to stay in California with my dad or move to Canada with my mom."

"Damn, I can't believe you had to make a choice like that at such a young age."

"It wasn't much of a choice, really." He sounds distant and stiff. Looking away from me, his eyes fixate on the tealight in the middle of our small table. "My dad made it pretty clear he had no interest in being a father."

"Shit, Nico, I'm sorry," I tell him and it's not eloquent, I know, but I don't know what else to say. *Why did I have to dredge up Nico's past?* Dammit, I suck at this. Maybe Rose got it the other way around—maybe I'm not right for Nico. Any trace of tender chicken I had before is long since gone now.

He forces out a smile. "It's fine, really. I've had years of therapy to deal with the whole absentee-father issue and I'm okay with it now. I go my way, he goes his, and I'm okay with that." He reaches across the table for my hand and I flinch at first but ultimately let him take it. I rack my brain for new topics of conversation, anything to get past the heavy reality of his childhood (and the intense uncomfortable feeling I am experiencing) but luckily I don't have to. He does it for me.

"What else should I know about *you*? What's your major?" he asks. I take a nervous sip from my glass of water to stall for time. I knew this question was going to come up and yet it still makes me squirm.

"Uh, yeah, I'm still undeclared actually, but I'm leaning toward something to do with film and television. Maybe screenwriting? So far it's the only class I'm kinda sorta good at? I dunno, we'll see how I do this semester."

"You must be taking a lot of random gen ed courses then? Last year I took this one called Queer Dreams." He offers me a generous smile and I relax a little.

"Yes! Thank you! I was totally signed up for that last semester too but my RA made me change it to screenwriting."

"Your RA *made* you change it?"

"Well, kinda. It's a long story but the short version is she advised me to change the class and I declined to take her up on that advice and then I lost a bet, so I had to change it. She's incredibly bossy."

"It sounds like she was trying to help you," he says sweetly and I'm immediately fake-repulsed.

"Noooooooooo! You agree with her? Damn, dude, I thought you were cool."

"Yes, I agree with her," he teases. "She had a good point! I was undeclared as an incoming freshman too, and I did exactly what you did and it completely set me back a semester. I wish I'd had an RA like yours to guide me last year." I sink back into my chair and think about that for a second. I mean . . . I *guess* if it wasn't for Rose I never would have even thought of taking a screenwriting class. I should probably suck it up and thank her for that.[66]

"Who is your RA? Is it Taylor J.?" Nico asks as our waitress appears, setting steaming plates of pasta down before us.

---

66 Meh, or not. She doesn't need to know she was right.

"No, it's Rose. Rose Knightley. She was the one who confirmed the source of the smoke Tuesday night."

"That was Rose? Huh . . ." He looks surprised and a bit confused as he digs into his pasta.

"What?"

"She's dating Monica Gallagher, right?"

"Yes . . . and?" I urge him on.

"Interesting."

"Dude, spit it out. What is it?"

"It's not a big deal," he says and ohmygod, I'm gonna lose it.

"I swear to god, Nico, if you don't tell me I'm gonna stab you with this fork."

He throws his hands up in surrender. "Okay! All right! She and I haven't met officially, but last year Monica was dating one of my buddies and she left him for Rose."

"Really? Monica dumped him for Rose?"

"I wouldn't say he was *dumped* . . ." He trails off, and my mouth drops.

"Wait, are you saying Monica . . . *cheated*—with *Rose*?" I say it out loud, but I'm mostly asking myself because I need to deconstruct this new piece of information. I find it really hard to believe that Rose would knowingly hook up with someone who was in a relationship, I mean, Rose is all moral and monogamous and shit! Maybe there's another part of the story I'm missing—

"Is your food okay?" Nico asks. "You've barely touched your

pasta." I return my gaze to my handsome date and resume eating like normal people do on dates. Our table is so small that at one point our knees touch. I scooch forward on my seat and press my legs against his harder.[67]

"So what about you?" I ask him playfully. "Any ex-girlfriends leave you for Rose too?" He rolls the sleeves of his sweater up to his elbows and leans forward on his arms.

"No. There's been no one I wanted to call my *girlfriend*," he whispers over the candle that's dancing between us. "But that may change."

An hour later, we leave the restaurant, just as the moon begins to rise. The night is crisp and clear and even though it's dark and late, I feel very awake. We walk to the water and I can't help but notice that every person we pass stares at Nico like they all have tender chicken for him. Our conversation starts to run dry by the time we reach the harbor, but it doesn't matter because the view is breathtaking. That's something else I forgot, isn't it? I've been in Boston for six months now and this is the first time I've seen the bay. I've never even bothered to explore this new, beautiful city.

And then a cold gust blows in off the water and I remember why I haven't explored this city. Boston is cold. Really really really fucking cold. I shiver and mentally curse Sasha and Lucy for convincing me a miniskirt and thigh-high boots were a smart choice for a date in the dead of winter. I go to

---

67 Tender Chicken Mode has been reactivated.

zip my coat up but the zipper gets caught and Nico notices me struggling.

"Here, let me help you with that." He inches closer and I catch a whiff of his cologne and breathe it in deep. He takes his time zipping up my coat. His fingers travel from my thighs to my neck, slowly and deliberately, like he's mapping the topography of my body. The way he's looking at me sends a rush of heat to my lady parts and suddenly I'm not so cold anymore. A few strands of hair come loose from my bun and fall in front of my face. His fingertips graze my cheek as he tucks my hair behind my ear. His hands linger on the sides of my face and neck.

"So are you gonna kiss me or what?" I say, biting my lower lip in anticipation. He lowers his lips to mine and then it happens. We kiss.

[MUSIC SWELLS]
[FADE TO BLACK]
[END SCENE]

I know what you're thinking. You're thinking that our kiss was the kind that inspires art and poetry, the kind of kiss that shifts and cracks my emotional tectonic plates, resulting in volcanic eruptions of happiness. You could think that, and perhaps in some alternative dimension that's what happens, but not in this dimension I'm sorry to report.

"It was so bad, Luce. *SO BAD*," I tell my roommate the following morning as soon as she gets back from her morning run. "His tongue was all over my face, Lucy, it went every-where except my mouth."

"Oh. *Oh no*," Lucy says as she gets hot water brewing at the coffee and tea station in the back of our room. My roommate is a firm believer that all romantic debriefings require hot tea and baked goods. She serves us tea in matching *Golden Girls* mugs and hands me a tin of chocolate-dipped biscotti as she joins me on my bed. As I pour honey into our mugs, Lucy pulls her phone out of her pocket, fires off a quick text, and then presses me for more details.

"Maybe it was just our height difference or something but one minute he was trying to suction my lips off and the next minute he was lapping my entire ear?!?!" I grimace.

She laughs and asks, "What did you do?"

"I just kinda . . . froze? I mean, I wasn't even mad as it was happening, mostly surprised, and a little bit confused. He totally caught me off guard." I start to tell her more details when Micah walks in our room, balancing an open laptop in one hand. He doesn't bother closing the door and Lucy and I make no effort to get up from our cozy spot.

"So are you going to go out with Nico again?" Micah asks as he takes a seat at my desk. "If he's bad at kissing, he's probably bad at other things too . . ."

"How do you even know *already*?" I look over and Lucy is sporting a sly little grin. "You told him?"

"Of course I did!" she says proudly. "We're both very excited for you."

"Why?" I ask the room. "It was just one date."

"Are you serious?" Micah says. "He's a hot, starting point guard who pays for dinner and wants to get into your panties."

"He's on the basketball team? How do you know that?" I ask, confused because it now seems odd that he never brought that up. *Oh, hey, I spend 70 percent of my time playing sports* is one of those low-hanging trivia facts usually shared on first dates.

Micah flips his laptop around and shows me Nico's Instagram. "Would you please get on Instagram already?"

"I told you, I'm a lurker, and besides, my family is on that shit. I don't want to give them more ways to access me, but hey, click that photo, I want to see his face again." Micah obliges and a bright photo of Nico shirtless on a beach illuminates the screen. The three of us take a minute to just stare at it.

"Damn, he is hot," I say.

"Yes, he is," Micah says slowly while nodding.

"What are y'all looking at?" A deep voice asks and we all turn our heads to see Brad leaning against the doorframe wearing nothing but a blue towel at his waist—his hair and body still dripping with water from the shower.[68]

"Hey, Lucy," he says and she pokes her head out from behind me and waves to him. Brad runs his hands through his hair, sending little droplets of water all over our room.

Micah whistles to Brad. "Boy, either put more on or take more off but either way, you can't stay there, dripping water

---

68 Whoa. How have I never noticed what a tasty little snack Brad is?

everywhere." Brad blushes and runs across the hall to his room and we all return our attention to the photos of Nico.

A fully-clothed Brad re-enters the scene, points at the computer, and asks, "Who is that?"

"Elliot's new fuck boy," Micah says and I smack his arm.

"He is *not* my fuck boy," I say. "Well, not *yet* anyways."

Brad leans in and squints at the screen. "Wow, he's quite the handsome fella," Brad says and for some unknown reason I get so embarrassed.

"Think of how cute your babies would be," Lucy babbles and I bury my face in a pillow.

"What's the verdict, Elliot?" Micah pesters again. "Are you going out with him again or no?"

"I don't know!" I whine into my pillow.

"You do *you*," Micah says like a warning. "But this guy is a bit of a catch and if you don't take him up on the offer, someone else will, and quick. He is easily the best-looking straight guy on campus," he says and then looks over at Brad. "No offense."

Brad holds his hands up. "None taken! Micah's right, Elliot. The man is a ten."

"What's holding you back?" Lucy chimes in.

I peel myself off the pillow. "The kiss," I say. "It was that damn kiss! Everything was going great until that sloppy-ass kiss."

"Are you really going to end a relationship over one bad kiss?" Lucy asks and I immediately freak out. I know I told

Rose I wanted to *date* date Nico, but I can already feel myself backsliding toward old habits.

"*Relationship*? It was just *one* date!"

"Maybe that's the problem. Maybe the kiss was bad because you're overthinking it," Brad suggests, and we all look at him in surprise. Brad the Bro is dropping nuggets of emotional wisdom?? "I get that you're all Netflix and chill instead of Hulu and commit," Brad continues, "so maybe it's been a while for you and you forgot that first dates can be pretty awkward. No doubt he was nervous too."

"Huh," I say thoughtfully as I consider Brad's shockingly insightful feedback. Maybe Brad is right. Maybe I am psyching myself out and the kiss was bad because we were nervous, and not due to a lack of chemistry. I remind myself of the reasons for giving a relationship a try and I start to perk up. "You're right, Brad. I am overthinking it. I should go out with Nico again."

"Yay!" Lucy cheers.

"And just think," Micah starts to say. "If the kiss was that bad, it means it can only go up from there."

"It can't get any worse, right?" I ask.

"Right!" Micah exclaims excitedly. I reach out my hand for a high five but it's Brad who obliges me and slaps it so hard I wince.

"Sorry," he mutters. "I got caught up in the moment."

CHAPTER 16

LET ME TELL YOU ABOUT THE VERY FIRST TIME someone went down on me.[69]

It happened in November of my junior year of high school. My boyfriend—yes, *that* boyfriend, the one who cheated on me—and I had been together about two months and we were at his house after school one afternoon. No one was home and we were making out on the couch in the living room. I can't quite recall what led up to the moment in question, but let's just say one minute I was fiddling with his Jigglypuffs and the next, he was munching on my Squirtle. As it was happening, I was so stupendously nervous that I couldn't steady my breathing and all the muscles in my hands froze. I couldn't bend my fingers—AT ALL. I'm not even exaggerating for comedic effect; I was essentially paralyzed from the elbow out to my fingers. It looked like I was about to do the robot dance but

---

69 I have nothing to add here, I just wanted to call out that this is the sixty-ninth footnote. Heh.

my wiring short-circuited and I powered down mid-dance. Eventually, I had to ask him to help pull my pants back on because my hands were stuck in the same position as Barbie's. Anyhoo, I bring this flashback up because if you compare that experience to what is currently happening, THIS ONE IS SO MUCH WORSE.[70]

It's been a month—that's right, a whole *month*—since my first date with Nico. Recalling what my Love and Eroticism teacher said and on the advice of my friends, I decided that perhaps the loneliness I was experiencing at the tail end of Project Tender Chicken was from a lack of intimacy, not desire. So this time around, I've gone in the opposite direction and done my best to embrace *intimacy*. Nico and I have hung out, nonstop, for an entire birth control blister pack and I feel like I've gotten to know him really, really well. But tonight is a test. It's the first time we will see each other naked . . . and it is NOT going well.

So here I am, lying on my back in Nico's bed on the tenth floor while he goes spelunking in my lady cave. At least I'm not nervous. No robot hands this time, folks—but it's worse than that. You see, what I'm currently experiencing is 100 percent pure, raw, unadulterated boredom. I am so bored I have had complete thoughts about a wide variety of topics in the twenty minutes since he's been rummaging around down there, including, but not limited to:

----

70 Remember at the end of the last chapter I said it couldn't get any worse? Turns out, it *can* get worse. Much worse! Ha!

- We really should have put music on.
- Should I be making more noise? Should he?
- I hate that this is called *eating out*. It sounds so cannibalistic.
- Which movie won last year's Best Picture Oscar?
- Reminder to self: Call Izzy on Sunday. It's her birthday.
- Where should I put my hands? On his head? Behind my head?
- OH GOD, WE MADE EYE CONTACT! NOPE NOPE NOPE
- When was the last time I had to do long division by hand?
- Reminder to self: Pick up face wash the next time I'm at CVS.
- My clitoris is two inches higher than where he thinks it is.
- I still really don't know what to do with my hands right now.
- Is one of his suitemates singing "Let It Go" from *Frozen*?
- Has anyone ever mixed a ramen packet with mac and cheese?
- I'm hungry.

THE ELLIOT MCHUGH INTERACTIVE EXPERIENCE:
THE POST-COITAL EDITION

Which of the following should I do next?

OPTION A: Should I stay, be honest, and tell him I didn't come?

OPTION B: Or should I fake an orgasm and wrap this up?

If you selected option B, please proceed to the next paragraph. If you selected option A, please proceed to the next footnote.[71]

I give it all I've got and put on the performance of a lifetime. And when I've successfully convinced Nico that I have climaxed, he pops his head up from under his blue sheets and gives me this sweet, goofy smile. He shimmies up from under the covers and flops down next to me, tucking his hands behind his head.

---

71 I stop Nico and gently tell him the truth, that he sucks at giving head and I spend the next two hours giving explicit instructions on how to please a woman, but when everything he tries *still* doesn't work, he breaks out a special bottle of lubricant he bought for the occasion and applies a generous amount, but it turns out, I am allergic to the special ingredient and my cooter burns, catches on fire, and the Little Building explodes. The end.

"How was that?" He asks, and I cannot for the life of me understand why some people always want a report card as soon as they're done. I look over at him and he really looks so happy and proud of himself. I don't have the heart to tell him I faked it, so I do what I always do when I'm in an uncomfortable situation: I lie.

"It was great!" *Please don't ask me anymore questions,* I silently beg him. A stiff silence ensues and I don't know what the protocol is for moments like this. What is the polite length of time one must lie there next to the guy who just failed at getting you off? Two minutes? Ten minutes? An hour? The last thing I want to be is rude, so I figure twenty minutes is a decent length of time to convince someone they've just rocked my world.

. . .

Has it been twenty minutes yet?

. . .

Nico isn't saying anything, so I don't say anything, and we both just lie here, not saying anything. I look up and stare at the ceiling and start counting the tiles. Thirty-four. There are thirty-four tiles in Nico's room. I wonder if mine has the same number of tiles? I feel like mine has a lot more since it's bigger than this single.

. . . .

Has it been twenty minutes yet?

. . . .

This is cool. This is totally normal. I think I'll continue to just lie here, not saying anything.

. . . .

Has it been twenty minutes yet?

. . . .

Good god, I can't take this anymore. I gotta get out of here, like, now. I turn to Nico and throw my hands up to my face.

"Ohmygod, I just remembered something![72] I have a script due in the morning and I haven't even started it![73] But this was so much fun, I really had a great time. We should do it again!"[74] Before he has the chance to respond, I whip the covers off my naked body, leap out of bed, and snatch my clothes off the floor. I am pulling my sweatshirt on backward when he calls to me from the bed.

"Yeah, babe, no worries. I think I'm free tomorrow night if you want to go see a movie and—"

"Oh, um, I'd love to, but tomorrow night is laundry night and you know how I love my laundry time, but I'll text you. Okaythanksbyeeee!" I yank jeans over my ass as fast as possible and leap over his gym bag to get to the door. I give him a little wave goodbye as I close the door to his single. I tiptoe out of his suite and escape without waking any of Nico's suitemates. Thank god the hall is empty. I am not at all prepared to deal with prying eyes and judgy looks right now. I lean my back against the wall and take a deep breath as I try to get my shit together.

---

72 Lie.

73 Lie, I finished it a week ago.

74 Lie, lie, lie.

I don't understand what is happening with Nico. Outside the bedroom, there is so much heat and chemistry between us, but as soon as we start doing *anything* sexual, it's the equivalent to the game-over sound effect in Super Mario Bros. We're dating. I even introduced him as my *boyfriend* once! But for fuck's sake, that time that dude Anders almost slipped it into my butt was a hotter experience than this!

And over on the other side of my brain, I find myself thinking, *Sure, Nico can't find my clit with Google Maps and a magnifying glass, but he gave it his all and that has to count for something, right?* So why do I feel so—*blah*—about him? I came to college so amped to get it on and hook up and have a good time but that was unfulfilling and now, when I actually make an effort to be in a real relationship—*that* doesn't work either. Why is nothing working?!? I DON'T UNDERSTAND.

I hear the door to the girl's bathroom swing open and a girl I've never seen before steps out looking like she has an interesting story to tell. I bet, to her, I look the same. We nod to each other but don't say anything—a silent acknowledgment that we are both members of *The Sisterhood of the Walk of Shame*. She disappears around the corner and that's my signal to get the hell out of here and back down to the third circle of hell. I decide to take the stairs because a) I'm lazy and they're closer than the elevators and b) I could use the walk to try to clear my head. The Little Building is tall and the stairs spiral, so it's extremely easy to get dizzy, which is why students rarely take this method of vertical travel between floors—so it's a great place to go when you want to be alone. And since Nico lives on the tenth floor and I'm on the third, you can do the math to figure out exactly how many floors it will take for me to regret my *I'll take the stairs! It'll be so good for me!* decision.

●●●

I am somewhere between the fifth and third floors, resting on the steps while I reevaluate my whole anti-exercise position, when I hear a door open. Someone has entered the stairwell below me. I stay silent, hoping they'll just go on or go away, but I hear no movement. Whoever is in here with me is trying to listen for signs of life too. After a few tense moments of ear-ringing silence, I hear the very faint sound of someone clicking on a vape pen and inhaling. The unmistakable scent of marijuana wafts up and now I know *exactly* what I need in this moment. I don't need mindfulness or head-clearing walks or sex-positive psychotherapy. I need to get high. I step quietly down the stairs so I can see who it is and when I peek over the railing, I see Rose.

Rose, my RA.

Rose, my RA who *always* writes up anyone who vapes inside the building . . . is vaping inside the building. I cannot let a delicious moment like this pass me by. I lean against the railing just above and smugly call down to her. "Well, well, well. What do we have here? I do believe I am witnessing *several* violations of the Emerson student handbook, Ms. Knightley."

Rose coughs out white vapor. "Fuck! Elliot, you scared me."

"Ha! Now you know what it feels like."

To her credit, Rose does put on a show of trying to fan the smell away and hide the pen but she sighs and gives up almost as quickly. I hold my hand down to her. She looks up, her eyes narrowing as she studies me for a moment.

"Ah, fuck it," she says and then hands me the vape pen. I take a deep pull. I exhale as I descend the last few steps and take a seat on the one above her. We pass the pen back and forth a few times and once I start feeling buzzed I notice she's wearing pinstripe bike shorts, a T-shirt that reads ARE CLOTHES MODERN? and six-inch red stilettos.

"Do you ever just wear sweatpants?"

"Never," she says, glancing down at her clothes. "What are you doing here so late?" she asks.

"What if I told you I was up late studying?"

"I'd say you're full of shit."

"Is it still a walk of shame if it's not morning?"

She looks down at her watch. "*Technically*, it's three in the morning."

"Well then, *technically*, you caught me in the midst of a classic walk of shame. And why might *you* be in the stairwell, disobeying the rules?" I take another hit from the pen and pass it back to her.

Rose takes a long drag and as she exhales she says, "Got caught in a long argument with Monica and I needed to blow off some steam." I think about asking if she'd like to talk about this, but I get my answer when she quickly changes the subject. "Plus, I figured since I'm still awake I might as well call my parents."

"At three in the morning?"

"They recently did one of those DNA tests and decided to go on six week vacation exploring 'the origins of their ancestry,'" she says using air quotes. "So far they've been to Scotland, France, and Italy, and the next two weeks they'll be in Tunisia and Greece."

"I did one of those DNA tests and it came back a picture of a loaf of white bread." Rose laughs and it's nice. I like making her laugh. "Well, I'll leave you to it, then. Tell your parents I say hi." I make a move to stand up but she stops me.

"No, please, stay. I'll call them tomorrow." I smile and sit back down. She takes another long drag and asks, "So who had the pleasure of your company this evening?"

"Nico," I tell her and she coughs the vapor out.

"That's still going on?"

"Not after tonight it isn't," I tell her.

"What happened?" she asks.

"I don't get it. He's a nice guy, he's obviously very good-looking, and I'm attracted to him, but every time we do *anything* sexual, it's awful." I reach for the pen again and she hands it to me. "It also doesn't help that he's downright awful at giving head."

Rose laughs. "What makes you so sure it's him?"

"Rose, he is so freaking bad. He's like a bottom feeder trying to suck off microscopic bits of food from my ocean floor." I take one last pull and hand the pen back to her. She turns it off and rests it on her lap.

"Did you say anything to him? Give him instructions?"

"No . . . ," I confess.

"Well then it's not *his* fault!"

"Ugh!!!!!" I throw my hands up in frustration. "It's hard to explain and I don't fully understand why, but I can't seem to fully enjoy sex when I'm emotionally intimate with someone."

"How so?" she asks gently.

I pause and take a moment to gather my words. "Last semester, I hooked up with this girl, Eva. It was her first time with a woman and well, she did *not* know what she was doing. And tonight, Nico went down on me for the first time and *he* did not know what he was doing. But with Eva, I was able to enjoy myself, I had no problem at all giving instructions, telling her exactly what to do to get me off. But when Nico was down there, I couldn't get comfortable! I couldn't come, and I couldn't bring myself to tell him what I needed. How can I have sex with two people who are equally clueless but be comfortable with one and not the other? When I sleep with someone who knows me . . . it's like I'm afraid to be myself." I lean my head back against the wall and look up at the winding stairs above me. "I suck at this shit. I should just go back to casual hook-ups."

"So that's it, huh?" Rose asks. "You're giving up on commitment because you had one bad night?"

"It's not just Nico!" I finally tell her. "I tried this in high school too and it was the same shit. I was dating this guy, pretty seriously actually, and when we finally had sex, I froze. We tried it again a few more times and it never got any better and every time I *didn't* come, the pressure built even more until it wasn't that fun and he ended up cheating on me. It really fucking sucked. I don't ever want to feel that way again."

Rose gives me a sympathetic look. "You got hurt. I know what that feels like."

"It's not just about being hurt." I look away from Rose and down at my hands. "I don't know what it is, but the second I'm with someone and they start trying to open me up, I freak out. It feels like the walls are closing in and I can't escape."

Rose sits up straighter. "Being in a relationship doesn't mean you are shackled and locked down. Commitment is being free but choosing to stay."

"I'm constantly afraid of being a disappointment again," I say quietly.

"Stop letting your past predict your future," Rose demands, and I glance up. "One bad relationship doesn't mean all your relationships will be bad. If you want to spend your life bouncing from person to person, never letting anyone get to know the real you, then do it. There is nothing wrong with that, *if* that's what makes you happy. But it sounds like you tried that—"

"And it left me wanting more," I say.

"Exactly," she says, relaxing her posture again. "And as far as the sex goes, it's just as much about you as it is about the person you're with. You have to choose to open up, no one else will do that for you."

"Ughhhh," I groan loud enough for it to echo above me. "When it comes to sex, I get it, I know what I'm about, I'm horny on main, but romance? When it comes to romance I'm just—what the fuck romance, you know?"

"I thought you didn't like labels?"

"That's a label?!?"

"Yeah," she smiles. "*WTFromantic*, although I believe it's more commonly called *quoiromantic* now." She narrows her eyes at me. "Don't you ever look this stuff up online?"

I slump back against the wall. "I only use the Internet for porn, cat memes, and IMDB trivia."

"*Quoi* comes from the *French* word for *what*—" Rose gets that look in her eye like she's about to go on a long one so I kick her gently with my foot and interrupt.

"Ohhhh my god, Rooooooseeeee. Can you not babesplain for, like, one second? You are killing my high."

"Sorry! Sorry!" She grasps the vape pen in her lap and clicks it on again. She takes a long pull and holds it in for a moment. "Look, when it comes to sex, all I was trying to say earlier was, when you finally get with that someone you are willing to open up to, my god, Elliot . . ."

"That good?" I give her a moment to respond but Rose doesn't say anything. Instead, she gives me a look so sexy that it makes me blush. "Damn . . . All right, maybe I should give Nico another shot, you know? Make more of an effort?"

"What? No!" Rose says, looking surprised.

"I thought that's what all this was about? That whole thing about relationships taking work and shit!"

"They do! But with someone who is right for you! And that is not Nico. I don't want you giving up on relationships just because you have terrible taste."

"Shut up, I do not!" I smack her leg.

"Please!" Rose exclaims. "You know what I'm talking about. I bet you've known you weren't that into Nico since your very first date." I scrunch my face and refuse to say it. I hate being confronted with the truth. She taps my hip with her foot and taunts me. "Come onnnnn, you can admit it."

I flip my hair back and turn my chin up. "I will do no such thing."

"You can do it," she badgers me. "Here, I'll help you. Just say, 'Rose, you were right. Nico was sweet but bored me to death and I should always listen to you because you are *always* right.'"

"I will *never* say that."

"That's okay, you can just tell me I was right, you don't need to say all the extra stuff," she says with a playful, flirty smile. I shake my head and give her a sideways glance.

"God, you're annoying," I say.

"I know." She grins and bites her bottom lip. I reach over and snatch the vape pen out of her lap and take a pull.

"Man, this sucks," I say.

"Yeah . . . dumping someone is never fun."

"Oh, I wasn't talking about that. I was referring to the fact that I hate feeling lonely."

"No one loves being lonely," she says. "But you aren't alone. You've got Lucy and Micah and I'm here for you."

"Thanks," I say, but it doesn't make me feel any less bummed. As I reach down to hand the pen back to her, I take her wrist and look at her watch. "Shit, it's getting early. I should get some sleep." I stand up to leave but Rose stays. "You coming?"

"Nah, I've got some shit of my own I need to sort out," she says and I nod. As I step over her to exit the stairwell, she touches my hand. "Hey, don't tell anyone I smoked in here."

"I wouldn't dream of it," I say to her with a smile. She lets me go and as I open the door to the third floor, I call back to her.

"But this does mean I get to put the fairy lights back up, right?"

"Not a chance, McHugh."

I shrug. "Ah well, had to try."

CHAPTER 17

"SO THAT'S IT THEN? YOU'RE BREAKING UP WITH Nico?" Lucy asks the next afternoon as we catch up between classes. I watch from the bed as she changes into purple Emerson sweatpants and a vintage Dunkin' Donuts sweatshirt.[75]

"Yeah, I sent him a text this morning and blocked his number so he can't call me back."

"Harsh!" Lucy chides.

"Breakups always suck, why prolong the agony? We weren't even together for very long. I prefer to just rip the Band-Aid off and get it over with."

"I dunno, Elliot," Lucy says as she pulls the sweatshirt over her head. "That's pretty cold, even for you."

"Well, whatever. It's too late now." I'm hoping she'll leave it at that but the look she is giving me right now is a little scary.

---

[75] I can't believe I made it this far into a book set in Boston without mentioning Dunkin' Donuts (or *Dunkies* as it is known by the locals). It's a big thing here, but I still don't get it.

"Okay, fine! If I see him in the halls I'll apologize, all right? Man . . . I should have just listened to Rose from the start."

"What do you mean?" Lucy asks as she finishes getting dressed and joins me on my bed.

"Do you remember when I was getting ready for my first date with Nico and I couldn't stop sweating?"

"I think you need to see a doctor about that . . ."

"Well, while Rose was helping me with that whole *pitu*-ation, she made this off-handed comment about Nico being wrong for me."

"Really?" Lucy asks.

"I kinda put it out of my memory, but then I saw her last night and she brought it up again. Don't tell her I told you this, but she was right. I think I just *wanted* Nico to be right for me, but I knew it from that first kiss that I just wasn't feeling it. Rose was right all along."

Lucy freezes in that intense stare she gets whenever she's deep in thought. "Huh."

"What?" I ask her.

She holds her stare for a moment longer and then abruptly returns to Earth. She sits up, crosses her legs, and folds her hands together in her lap as she addresses me. "How often do you hang out with Rose?"

"I dunno." I shrug. "Not that often? And it's usually by accident—why?"

"It just seems like you really care about Rose's opinion. You talk about her *a lot*," Lucy says and I make a face.

"No I don't!"

"Yeah you do! Rose is my RA too, but I think I've only ever spoken to her a handful of times and we've *never* talked about anything other than resident stuff."

I narrow my eyes at Lucy. "What are you trying to get at?"

"Nothing!" Lucy says, relaxing her tone. "Sorry, you're right. She probably hangs out with a lot of her residents. I mean, she *is* really nice. Last semester she helped me with this marketing project on colors in advertising and let me borrow some of her fabrics for a presentation. She has such great style and she's just so . . . *cool*, you know?"

"Yeah, I get it," I reply. "She's so *effortless*."

Lucy tilts her head. "What do you mean?"

"The woman crushed me in Ping-Pong while wearing a tutu. I mean, who does that?" I say. And without really thinking about what I'm saying, I keep going. "I love that she doesn't hold back, you know? She's bossy as hell and I hate that she's always calling me out on my shit, but she's also protective as a motherfucker. I mean, she really had my back that night with Kenton. She's smart and focused and competitive. But she's not always serious. I mean, she knows how to name a mouse and secretly vapes in the stairwell and she'll probably win an Oscar for costume design someday. Plus she looks mega hot in overalls, which is nearly impossible, but to be honest she is such a babe she could wear a trash bag and make it look couture—" AND OH MY GOD DID I JUST SAY ALL THAT OUT LOUD?

I stop talking and glance over at Lucy. She's covering her mouth with both of her hands. She looks like she's about to burst.

"I KNEW IT!" Lucy smacks me in the arm. "I TOTALLY FREAKING KNEW IT!"

Lucy jumps out of bed and starts heating up water at our tea station by the window. When the electric kettle chimes, Lucy pours steaming water into our matching *Golden Girls* mugs and the room is instantly filled with a woody, fresh aroma from this special Armenian mint tea her grandma gave her for Christmas.

"I feel so confused right now," I say.

"First, you need to drink this. My grandma *insists* this will boost our moods, clear our skin and has antioxidants that are good for preventing cancer." She hands me a mug and I take a sip and grimace. It tastes like ass.

"No offense to your grandma, but this tea is bullshit, I don't feel any prettier."

"Oh, shush your mouth and drink it," Lucy scolds. She takes a seat on the bed next to me and takes a sip for herself. She lets the water dribble out of her mouth back into her mug.

"Oh *no*. This is bad," she says.

"*So* bad."

She takes our mugs, sets them aside on her desk, and then gives me that head-tilted, pinched-eyebrow, narrowed-eyed look that means she's about to get all serious on me. "Elliot, I'm about to say something that is going to make you very uncomfortable."

"Oh god—"

She rests her hand on my arm. "Elliot . . . I think you like Rose. As in, *like* like. As in you have genuine feelings for her."

"Shut up, I do not." My cheeks are on fire right now.

Lucy smacks me in the arm. "You do! Ohmygosh, you totally do! Look at you, you're blushing!"

"You cannot diagnose my feelings based on blood flow, Lucy," I retort, glaring at her.

"I can and I did," she says, looking very proud of herself. "I've known you long enough now to recognize something new and this? This is new." Forgetting how nasty the tea is, Lucy reaches for her mug and takes a victory sip and immediately spits it out again. "Oh god! Why do I keep doing that?"

I bury my face in my hands in disbelief. "There is no way I *like* like Rose! The woman drives me crazy! She is always lecturing me and shit, I mean, she literally took my phone and changed my class registration once."

"Yes, but you could have changed your class back just as easily. You could have ignored all those lectures . . . but you didn't. You *chose* to listen to them."

And then it hits me.

HARD.

I have opened up to Rose. I have told her all about my issues with sex and intimacy, she's even seen me and helped me through one of the worst moments of my life. I shudder at the memory of that night.

And yet . . .

. . .

And yet . . .

I don't feel like running away.

In fact, I want to run *toward* her. I can't believe it took me this long to realize it.

I look over at Lucy. Time for the truth. "You're right. I like Rose. I *like* like her, Lucy. I like her *a lot,* a lot."

Lucy gasps and scrunches up her shoulders like she's about to explode but instead she tackles me. "I KNEW IT!" she yelps as she smothers me with love. She bounces on my bed and when that's not enough, she grabs my pillow and starts hitting me in the head with it.

"Woman! Settle down!" I peek out from under her but she keeps whipping the pillow. When Lucy finally gets off me and regains composure, I ask, "What should I do?"

"Tell her!" Lucy says.

"I can't," I whimper.

Lucy immediately deflates. "Aww what? Why not?"

"Oh, I don't know, a MILLION REASONS?" I flail backward on the bed.

"Give me one," she insists.

"Fine. Here's one: She's my RA."

"That's not a real reason, that's an excuse. There are no rules saying students can't date their RAs. Give me a *real* reason."

"Okay, fine! She has a *girlfriend*! There are very few lines I won't cross, but that is one of them." I cover my face with a pillow and scream for a minute. When I've calmed down, I reemerge. "It's just going to be me and my vibrator for the rest of the semester then . . ."

"What? No more casual flings?" Lucy asks, looking surprised.

"One day, sure, but not right now. I dunno, this whole Nico thing and now the Rose thing . . . it's bumming me out. I think I need to be alone for a while." I turn on my side and face her. "But what about you? It's been two months since—" I wince at the thought of saying his name again. "*How* are you feeling about all of it?"

"I miss it, being loved," she says and my heart aches for her. "But I don't miss him. I think it's going to be a good long while until I'm ready to—"

"Dip the wick."

"Ew."

"Bake the potato?"

"No."

"Ride the bony express?"

"Why?"

"Beat that meat. I could keep going—"

"All right, all right. You can stop now," she says while laughing. "At least we can be old, boring, dried-up ladies *together* this semester." She reaches over the top of the covers and takes my hand. I give it a squeeze.

"In time, you'll be ready to put yourself back out there. And when you are, boys will be lined up around the block," I tell her.

She squeezes my hand back. "Do you think you'll ever tell Rose how you feel?"

I sigh. "I think that's a secret I gotta be buried with. Even if she was *available*—and she *isn't*—if I tell her how I feel, I run the risk of it going unreciprocated. I don't even know if she likes me like that. She's so hard to read."

Lucy sits up in bed and looks back at me. "Elliot, the woman sat atop a metal washing machine for two hours and watched *The Matrix* with you. She *likes* you. It's a terrible movie."

I squeak in shock and sit up. "Take that back or I'm breaking up with you right now."

"You can't, you're my wife," she says with a straight face.

"Well then I'd like a divorce. I can't be married to someone who doesn't love *The Matrix*."

She tilts her chin up and crosses her arms in front of her chest. "It's too late. We signed the binding friendship contract when I ate your Cheez-Its. You're stuck with me for life."

"Ugh, why won't *you* just be my girlfriend already?"

"Because I am *way* out of your league."

"True."

"And because you're in *love* with Rose."

"SHUT UP I AM NOT." Lucy looks deeply disappointed, so I shrug her off. "Look, it's fine—I'm fine. Really! It's just a crush, I'll get over it." Lucy gives me one of her patented side hugs and I rest my head on her shoulder.

"Are you sure?" she asks.

"Yeah, I'm sure."

"Unrequited love is such a bitch," she says woefully.

"Yeah," I sigh. "It really fucking is."

CHAPTER 18

AFTER A WEEK OR SO OF WALLOWING OVER MY FEEL-
ings for Rose, I decide to shove that shit wayyyyy deep in the
basement of my mind and focus all my energy on helping Lucy.

I don't know if you remember, but several chapters ago,
Lucy and I mended our friendship right around the same time
I started dating Nico and since I was all caught up with that
nonsense, I kinda failed to see that my roommate was having a
rough time. This whole time I thought she was doing okay with
the whole post-breakup thing—we had that great talk! She
moved back in! I gave her a bunch of sexy romance novels! But
now that I've paid closer attention to her, I'm worried about
her. It's like something inside her cracked and I don't know
how to fix it. I have done everything I can to break my roommate's sad spell—I restrung all the fairy lights Rose made us
take down,[76] we rewatched every season of *The Golden Girls*,

---

[76] Don't tell Rose.

we fed those baby ducks Bostonians are weirdly excited about, and I even baked her cookies![77] But she's still missing that patented Lucy sparkle. I didn't know what to do anymore, and since I'm avoiding Rose like the plague, I had to turn to someone else for advice. Well, *two* someones.

A TELEPHONE CONVERSATION BETWEEN THE THREE MCHUGH SISTERS

Izzy: Why don't you stop trying to fix her and just let her work through her shit at her own pace?

Remy: Don't say *shit*, Izzy.

Elliot: What about a jigsaw puzzle? I haven't tried that yet.

Izzy: Honestly, I don't know why you call me. It's not like you ever take my advice.

Elliot: Maybe I should take her on one of those ghost tours!

Remy: No! That's too scary! What if you got her a Switch? That way I could play *Animal Crossing* with her—

---

77 Okay, so it wasn't cookies, it was PopTarts, but the toaster in the common room is a little tabletop convection oven and I used the Bake setting instead of the Toast setting SO IT TOTALLY COUNTS AS BAKING.

Izzy: Why don't you join a club or something? It'll look good on your resume and—

Elliot: That's a great idea!

Izzy: Dammit, Elliot! I hate it when you do this, you know I'm busy and—wait. What did you just say?

Remy: Don't say *dammit*.

Elliot: I said that's a great idea. *[long pause]* Hello? Izzy? You still there? Remy, is Izzy still there?

Remy: I dunno?

Izzy: Yeah, I'm still here—I'm just trying to think of all the possible ways *you* could turn joining a club into a bad idea. Emerson doesn't have any weirdo clubs, does it? They are all pretty standard?

Elliot: Absolutely, they are totally normal.

ELLIOT MCHUGH PRESENTS: THE LET'S JOIN A CLUB AND CURE LUCY OF THE SADS! SPECIAL

The Breakfast Club

The first club Lucy and I tried was the Breakfast Club. Joining would have granted us early access to the dining hall and we'd get to use the kitchen to cook our own breakfasts together. Sounds amazing, right? Well, we were just shit out of luck because it was shut down right after our first time attending when an overzealous freshman grabbed a hot waffle right from the griddle and slapped his friend in the face with it, leaving a grid-shaped burn mark on his cheek.

The Bread Club

We thought maybe the Bread Club would be a nice substitute for the Breakfast Club, especially since it conveniently met outside Lucy's marketing classroom every Friday morning, but they only eat Wonder Bread. That's it. I thought for sure there'd be at least pastries or doughnuts, but no. No jams, no butter, no nothing. Strictly white Wonder Bread.

Boston Common Squirrel Club

And then, finally! A club Lucy liked! Almost! We had fun feeding raggedy squirrels stale bread for about twenty minutes until a plague of rats showed up and ruined everything. I don't know if you've ever met a Boston city rat, but these were not the country rats I'm used to in Ohio. Boston rats are organized, shameless, aggressive little motherfuckers. Those bastards emerged from a sewer grate and came at us so fast that one jumped—literally, JUMPED!—onto Lucy's back.

After the squirrel disaster, I decided to give up on my whole Joining a Club Will Cure You of The Sads! project. But then Micah came to my rescue.

> **Me:** Sadly no, Squirrel Club did not work. She's still mopey. How can I help Lucy get over K?
>
> **Micah:** . . .
>
> **Micah:** BY GETTING HER *UNDER* SOMEONE NEW!

Me: lol that's good

Micah: im serious. sign her up for the dating auction

Me: wut dating auction?

Micah: the one that all those flyers are about? you've seen those, they're all over campus

Me: Nope, haven't seen em.

Micah: OMG. Just go check the announcement board in the common room.

● ● ●

So Lucy is going to sell her body to the highest bidder.[78]

"Dude, you should totally do this." I hand the brightly colored flyer to Lucy, who is lying face down on her bed in the same clothes she's worn for the past three days. She doesn't take the flyer and it falls to the floor beside her bed. I hand her the flyer again. She looks at it for half a second.

She shrugs and says, "I dunno." I take a deep breath and resist the urge to shake her.

"Come on," I said, giving her a little nudge. "Look! It's for a good cause! I volunteer you as tribute—and besides! Having a bunch of dudes compete for a date with you will be such a confidence boost!"

"Doesn't this seem a little, I dunno, sexist?"

---

78 FOR CHARITY. God, get your mind out of the gutter. The dating auction is raising money for incarcerated LGBTQIA+ youth—a cause worthy enough for some light prostitution.

"Oh, don't worry! Guys are auctioning themselves off too. This will be an equal-opportunity-sexploitation affair." I give her a little wink and oooh, there it is! The beginnings of a smile! Lucy peels herself off the bed and sits up. Her right cheek is wrinkly and covered in drool and her hair looks like it's several hours away from becoming habitable for lice.

She rubs her eyes and asks, "What if no one bids on me and I'm standing up there in silence?"

I am doing my damn best to be patient with her. I can put up with a lot, but what I can't tolerate is my best friend being so hard on herself when it's some asshole guy who's to blame. It's my fault she got with Kenton, and now it's my job to get her over him. I want to slap some common sense back into her but that's not what friends do. Friends don't slap sense into friends, right? At least, not for this.

I stand up in the middle of the room, straighten my back, look her straight in the eye, and use my most capable-sounding voice. "Lucine I-Don't-Know-Your-Middle-Name Garabedian. You can continue to stay in our room until you are ready to come out, which is fine, no one will ever judge you for that. Or you have another choice. You can decide right here and right now that you are *done*. Done wasting your energy on someone who doesn't deserve a second thought. Done crying over some loser who didn't treat you with the respect you deserve. You can pick yourself up, put yourself out there, and let a room full of strangers confirm what *you* already know—that you are one badass babe who isn't going to let some asshole keep her from living her best life. And if no one bids on you, I make a solemn vow to spend every last cent in my bank account to bid on you. And after I win, after we go on that date together, you can finally admit that you're in love with me."

I stop pacing in front of her like a drill sergeant and give her a moment to respond. She doesn't say anything, not at first. But then slowly, ever so slowly, the corners of her mouth tick up and she smiles.

It's small—more like the ghost of a smile—but goddammit I'll take it.

CHAPTER 19

SO HERE WE ARE, BACKSTAGE AT THE STUDENT PER-
formance Center in the basement of the Little Building, preparing my darling roommate Lucy to go out onstage and
prostitute herself.[79] There are supposed to be ten people getting auctioned off tonight, and everyone seems to have rolled
up with a glam squad, so the backstage is crammed as all hell.
I didn't think the auction was going to be a whole *thing*. I just
thought it'd be a minor thing like speed dating or something,
not a whole *production*. It's like a fashion show with lights, a
smog machine, and a freaking DJ.

Sasha is putting the finishing touches on Lucy's makeup
while Micah engulfs her in a cloud of candy-scented hairspray.

Lucy nervously reaches her hand out to me. "Do I look
okay?"

---

79 FOR CHARITY.

"NOBODY MOVE!" Sasha commands and we all stop in our tracks. "I need to very, *very* carefully put these lashes on—and if I make a mistake, we have to start all over."

We all hold our breath as Sasha surgically applies the glue-soaked lashes to Lucy's lids and when she's done, we take a step back and sigh in relief. Lucy looks perfect. I crouch in front of her and hold her hands.

"You look marvelous, dahling, simply *marvelous*," I tell her like a pageant mom. I grab a hand mirror and hold it up for Lucy to see. "Look at you! Now you go out there and show the world what a smart, successful, and talented young woman you are."

"Butt out and boobs to the sky!" Micah chimes in.

"Ooooh!" I wave my arms to get Sasha's attention. "Do you have any shimmery body powder?"

"Of course!" Sasha says. She digs through her suitcase full of makeup and pulls out a big round box and a big fuzzy, pink pouf.

"What's that for?" Lucy asks.

"Your taters. I want to make them *sparkle*." Sasha and I start bedazzling Lucy's killer rack, but she blushes and pushes us aside.

"No, no, no. I don't need any glitter," Lucy says. "I just want to get this over with."

I look around for any sign of the stage manager and when I don't see him, I pull out a tiny bottle of Kentucky bourbon from my leather fanny pack. "Do you want a little liquid courage?" I assume she's going to say no, so I'm shocked when she grabs the bottle out of my hand, unscrews the cap, and tosses it all back in one go. "Damn, girl," I exclaim. "Do you want another?" I take out a little bottle of vodka this time.

"How many of those do you have?" Sasha asks.

"Enough to go around," I tell her and offer one to everyone. Micah and Sasha happily accept theirs, but Lucy shakes her head.

"No, one was good. Thank you." She closes her eyes and takes a deep breath. And then, in extremely slow motion, Lucy transforms before our very eyes. She rolls her shoulders back, slowly stands up, and finally opens her eyes. "You guys should go get seats," she says confidently. "I've got this."

Leaving Lucy backstage, Sasha, Micah, and I take our seats in the front row just as the doors open and a decent crowd rolls in. The theater continues to fill up with students and eventually there isn't a single seat left in the audience. As the lights dim, Micah leans over and whispers in my ear.

"So what's the plan?"

"What do you mean?" I whisper back.

"For Lucy. You would never let her get up there and auction herself off like this without at least *some* kind of plan." I roll my eyes, not because his suggestion is absurd, but because I hate how Micah always knows what I'm up to.

"There's no plan," I lie.

"Girl, please," he says as heavy bass kicks on the speakers. I give him a wink and he shakes his head. The lights dim and the show begins.[80]

●●●

A spotlight shines on the stage curtains. They slide back as the host comes out dressed like an erotic Cupid, but then the curtain moves again, and Rose walks out onstage dressed like Aphrodite. Picture the kind of toga a woman in ancient Greece would wear, two pieces of flowy white fabric draped over her shoulders that cascade down to the floor and cinched together at the waist. The only difference between that image and what Rose is wearing is that it is iridescent—and completely sheer. She's wearing nude underwear but she's completely bare breasted on top. The shimmery, gauzy fabric has a slight blurring effect as she glides across the stage—the effect is absolutely hypnotic. My breath catches in my throat. I haven't seen Rose since that night in the stairwell a few weeks back and seeing her now, seeing her dressed like this . . . *damn*. She is talking into a microphone, something about thanking everyone for coming and something about the charity, but I

---

80 Yes, I have a plan. Of course I have a plan! You think I'd let my emotionally fragile best friend get up onstage without so much as a guarantee of a bidder? Reader, please. I took every last cent from my bank account, the $300 I promised Lucy I would use to bid on her, and gave it to this cute guy named Jesse I met in one of my classes. He's been instructed to bid on her *if* and *only if* no one else does. My plan is foolproof.

honestly can't hear anything because all I can focus on is how sexy she is.

"Fuck," I murmur.

"Damn," Micah mutters too, and I shoot him a look. He shrugs, "What can I say? She looks hot. Even *I* can admit that."

"I didn't know Rose was hosting this," I whisper to Micah.

"Really? Her name was on the flyer, this is *her* club."

Rose exits stage left and I feel her absence acutely. Rose's cohost takes the mic and introduces the first person up for bid. A cute boy with floppy hair and a big smile trots out on stage and introduces himself. "Good evening," he says cheerily into the microphone. "I'm Dylan! I'm a junior, an advertising major, and a Taurus. I like candlelit Italian dinners and working out."

"Show us your abs!" Micah yells out. Dylan blushes innocently and then lifts his shirt to reveal a *how-the-fuck-are-those-real* set of abs. Micah whistles and leans over to whisper in my ear. "I think I just found my next boyfriend." Others in the crowd cheer and whistle too, making Dylan grin so hard that dimples appear on his cute cheeks.

"Let the bidding begin, ladies." Dylan barely gets it out before girls all around the room start yelling out dollar amounts, including Sasha, who, to everyone's surprise, wins a date with Dylan with a bid of one hundred dollars. The energy in this room is infectious as hell. A giddy Sasha runs up to the stage and hands Rose her cash. Dylan escorts her behind the curtain, and she disappears for the rest of the show. I look over at Micah, who is sulking in the chair next to me.

"Don't worry, little buddy," I say to him. "You'll get the next one!"

Rose reemerges from behind the side curtain in a new costume. This time she is wearing a perfectly tailored, black satin tuxedo with no shirt beneath the buttoned jacket. Just cleavage. Somehow this more conservative outfit looks even hotter than the first one. She introduces the next person to be auctioned off and I'm so distracted by Rose that I almost miss her saying Lucy's name. Rose struts off stage and Lucy takes her place and Micah and I jump to our feet and start cheering wildly for our girl. Lucy smiles shyly and waves for us to sit down as she steps up to the microphone. She looks so confident up there. I am so proud of her.

"Hello," Lucy says into the microphone and we all jump up again. She giggles and waves at us to keep it down. "Hello," she starts again. "My name is Lucy Garabedian. I'm a freshman double major in PR and marketing. I'm from Watertown and—"

Lucy is cut off when some guy in the audience yells out, "Fifty dollars!" I look around to see who was so quick on the draw and it is freaking Jesse, the guy I paid to bid on Lucy *only if* no one else bid on her. I silently pray to the gods for someone else to bid on Lucy, and at least one god must be home because someone else shouts, "Sixty dollars!" I look around trying to see who to thank later and it's Brad. *Interesting.* Is this a platonic bid or a romantic bid? I'm still pondering this turn of events when I realize that Jesse is still bidding—with *my* money.

"Seventy-five!" Jesse yells out.

"Ahhhhhh, goddammit," I say through gritted teeth.

"Eighty!" Brad yells.

The crowd whoops and hollers as Lucy stands up there looking positively radiant while these two dudes fight over her. I wave my arms at Jesse, trying to get his attention and stop him from hemorrhaging all *my* money but the idiot has completely forgotten my explicit instructions and keeps bidding higher and higher. "One hundred dollars!" He yells out again and I cringe.

"Two hundred!" Brad counters and the crowd gasps at the price. Brad looks pretty damn pleased with himself right now. I grab my phone and text Jesse, DO NOT BID ON HER ANYMORE. But either Jesse ignores it or doesn't have his phone on him because he stands up. I sink my face into my hands. *Fuuuuuuuck.*

"Three hundred dollars," Jesse announces to the crowd. Everyone. Loses. Their. Damn. Mind.

Rose reappears on the stage and says, "Three hundred going once!" I look at Brad and he can't believe how much Jesse bid on Lucy. No one can. Brad looks genuinely disappointed and shakes his head no. "Three hundred going twice!" Rose says again. "Sold!" she shouts as her cohost appears from behind the curtain and explodes a confetti cannon into the ecstatic crowd. Lucy beams as Jesse bounds up to the stage. He hands Rose the cash, *my motherfucking cash*, and all three exit the stage. I sink back into my seat and try to remind myself that all my money just went to a good cause, even though losing it all *stingggggs*.

The auction continues with Rose appearing every now and then in completely different looks. Micah bids on this guy, Simon, and actually wins, leaving me to go backstage to meet his betrothed. Everyone is having the time of their life, but I seem to have lost all interest now that I'm alone. As the seventh auction starts getting underway, I get up to leave when I hear someone calling my name from the side of the stage. It takes me a minute to realize that it's Rose, trying to get my attention. I crouch-walk down the aisle and work my way over to her.

"What's up?" I ask. She takes my hand and pulls me behind the curtain. She's halfway through changing into her next look, a riff on Cleopatra, and I try my best to not sneak a glance as she slips into another toga, this time a gold silk one that clings to every curve of her body.

"I need you to go on next." She's not asking me. She's telling me.

"Excuse me?"

She grabs gold stiletto gladiators and wraps the strands up and around her calves. "We're supposed to be auctioning off ten people and a girl just canceled on me. Will you please fill in?"

"Are you serious?" I ask in earnest. I wait for her to answer but she doesn't say anything. "Ohmygod. You're serious! Why me? Aren't there a ton of people in your club that can do it instead?"

"They're all running this show with me!" she exclaims as she frantically puts on her wig. "Please, Elliot? You'd be doing me a huge favor." I hesitate but Rose doesn't give me long to consider it. "I need you to decide *now*, Elliot."

"Sure, yeah, okay, jeez," I relent. She wraps her arms around me, completely catching me off guard, and then shuffles me to the side of the stage. Rose takes a quick inventory of herself, adjusts her wig, and then elegantly strides across the stage to introduce me. Oh shit, she meant *now* as in *right fucking now*. In a moment of panic, I realize that I'm not wearing anything remotely sexy like all the other participants. All I'm wearing are black jeans, a T-shirt, and a black leather jacket. I quickly take my jacket and shirt off and thank the gods that I am wearing a real bra and not one of my usual sports bras. I leave the T-shirt off and put the leather jacket back on over my black bra. My boobs aren't my best asset but they're all I have to work with, so fuck it. Let's do this.

When I hear Rose say my name over the mic, I give my hair a quick toss to one side and walk out on stage with my butt out and boobs to the sky. The lights are blinding and it takes a second for my eyes to adjust. I saunter up to the microphone and purr into it.

"Well, hello there. My name is Elliot. I am a freshman, I'm undeclared, but if you bid on me, I'll declare myself all yours." It's cheesy, I know, but it's the only thing I could think of in the three seconds I had to prepare for this moment.

My joke doesn't quite have the effect I hoped for and there's silence from the crowd. My heart starts to race. I squint out into the crowd. I can really only see the first two rows and the front row, the row I was in, is empty. Micah, Sasha, and Lucy are still somewhere backstage. That's fine. I can still do this without their help.

Fine. This is totally, absolutely, 100 percent fine.

I roll my shoulders back which makes my jacket pop open a bit more, showing the audience my bra, a little tease if you will. I grab the mic and take it off the stand so I can strut around a little bit. "Ladies, gentlemen, don't be shy." My voice is low, smooth, honeyed. "Let's start the bidding at twenty-five dollars and, please, keep in mind that right now, I am not wearing any underwear." I bite my lower lip to really sell it.

But no one is buying what I'm selling.

The crowd is silent.

No one is bidding on me.

My initial anxiety, masquerading as worry, grows up, gets married to fear, and settles down as full-blown panic. I can feel liquid heat inching up my neck and I start to sweat, well, pretty much everywhere. Something must not be right—people have been bidding on everyone else all night long. I signal the DJ to play some fucking music and he obliges. I take the mic and strut to the front of the stage to get out of the blinding spotlight. After a moment my eyes adjust and the problem becomes instantly clear. Everyone left in the audience is either not interested or . . . someone I've already hooked up with.

And there are a lot of them.

I might be screwed here. In the fucked kind of way. I recognize the sparkly top of the girl I hooked up with in the bathroom at the first party in Allston back in September. I think her name is Lottie, and I never did get her last name. I see Anders, Yvonne, Tobin, and a few other people I slept with looking particularly salty, and in the third row is Eva, the girl who had her first sapphic experience with me. She won't even look at me.

And then I spot him.

Sitting at a table, alone, in a dark corner in the back is Nico. I can't see his face clearly, he's too far away, so I shoot him a *please, for the love of god, bid on me* look, but he doesn't make a move. I frantically look around for anyone, *anyone* who can save me from this humiliation but there's no one. I am literally living out everyone's worst nightmare. And then from somewhere in the back of the room, I hear someone call out, "Slut!" and it lands like a bomb.

Now I am living out my *own* worst nightmare.

I run back to the stand and try to put the mic back on and it keeps falling off and I'm trying to fix it but then I hear laughter and fuck this fucking situation. I throw the mic on the ground and just as I'm about to jump off the edge of the stage and sprint out the side emergency exit, someone bids on me.

"One hundred dollars!"

I squint and peer across the audience to see who saved me. I look to where Nico is sitting but he's already gone. No one in the audience is standing or making any kind of motion to identify themselves, in fact they are all looking around too. They're just as confused as I am. Did I make up someone bidding on me? I am *dangerously* close to crying in front of everyone. But then I see movement to my left. The curtain is pulled aside and Rose steps out onto the stage holding a crisp one-hundred-dollar bill in her hand for everyone to see.

"What are you doing?" I whisper to her as she approaches me.

"I'm bidding on you," she says while she smiles warmly out to the crowd.

"You can't bid in your own auction!"

"I can and I just did so shut up and let me win a date with you." Rose's cohost reappears on the stage and takes her one hundred dollars. Everyone in the crowd claps politely and the DJ starts playing our exit music. And it's over. My nightmare is over.

Rose takes my hand and we leave the stage together.

● ● ●

There's a date-auction after-party at an apartment in Kenmore Square because of course there is.

As soon as I arrive, I toss back the last three little bottles of booze from my fanny pack, fast tracking me right to Three-Drink Elliot, the appropriate stage for right now, because I am pissed off and bitter about the fact that no one bid on me tonight and I was slut-shamed in front of an audience. I shouldn't be here, I don't feel like partying, but Sasha and Lucy talked me into making an appearance instead of hiding.

So I'm here, I'm not hiding, but I have found a quiet corner in the living room where I can settle into the darkness and watch the party without actively participating in it.

I thought I had reached the bottom at the end of last semester, but apparently my feelings have subterranean levels. What happened with Kenton, Lucy, Micah, my grades— all that was private, but what happened tonight was public. Reader, I think you know by now I'm not shy about telling people embarrassing personal info. But it's different when it's not my choice to tell, when everyone's reveling in my humiliation. To be down here again in this low, miserable place after I was finally turning things around is so defeating. I am in no mood to make small talk tonight and it seems as though most everyone has picked up on that by the way I'm being avoided. But shit, Micah and the guy he bought and paid for are walking toward me. I dig through my fanny pack, hoping to find one last bottle of vodka I may have missed, but I come up empty. Dammit.

"Elliot, I want you to meet Simon," Micah says. The cute, blond, white guy holding Micah's hand comes out from behind him and gives me a smile. I wish I could meet him under different circumstances, but right now I am not in the mood to be charming.

"You must be the guy Micah won during the auction," I say as I shake his hand. "Is this part of the date he won or will you be billing him for this evening's services later?" As soon as it's out of my mouth I regret it.

Micah brushes me off and kisses Simon on the cheek. "Oh, don't pay any attention to the Sour Patch Kid over here, she's just pissed that our RA had to mercy bid on her at the auction because no one else would."

I glare at him. "Thanks for the reminder, dick."

"Bitch, what did you expect? You've hooked up with half the school!"

"Bitch, you are one to talk!" I lob back. Simon takes a cautious step away from us.

"At least my dating pool is wider," Micah says. "I hook up outside the Emerson hemisphere. Your problem is you're too lazy to go looking for ass outside the Little Building."

Simon pretends someone is calling for him and excuses himself. I don't blame him. I'd run away from me too. Micah watches him go and I can see it there, written all over his face. He likes Simon.

"Hey," I reach out and touch Micah's arm. "I'm sorry for that. I am, just, I am in a real shit mood right now. Please apologize to Simon for me. He seems cool."

"He is cool," Micah confirms. "And lady, you don't need to worry about me. I can handle your flavor of salt, especially given the level of humiliation you endured tonight. But I am a little concerned you're not okay. Do I need to worry about you?"

"I am not okay—but I will be," I admit. Micah reaches out and pulls me into a hug. After a minute, he lets me go and I ask, "Do you think the way I ended things with Nico was bad?"

"Well . . . ," he starts but when he doesn't finish, I give him a look. "You didn't exactly *end* things with Nico. You ghosted him."

"Is there a difference?" I ask.

"Yes! Ghosting is so much worse!"

"Oh," I say.

Oh my god.

Oh shit.

Nico isn't the only one I ghosted. I ghosted all of them. I can't even recall the names of half the people I've hooked up with this year. It all makes sense now. No wonder they all looked pissed. I wouldn't have bid on me either.

"You guys dated for what, a few weeks?" Micah asks. "And then after ghosting him, the first time he sees you is up there auctioning yourself off for a date? Lady, I love you and you know I'm all for free love, but the way you handled things with Nico was—"

"Shitty," I say. "You're right. I was being shitty. Thanks for being real with me."

"Anytime, but you shouldn't be talking to me about it. You should talk to him." Micah steps aside and nods toward the door where I see Nico step outside the apartment. And just then, the memory flashes before me. The look on Nico's face when he saw me standing up there . . . I can't get the image out of my head. It makes me want to curl up and die a little. He looked hurt, really fucking hurt. And I'm the one who hurt him. To me, what we had was never truly serious, but by the way Nico looked at me up on that stage tonight, it's clear it meant much more to him. Micah's right. I shouldn't be having this conversation with him.

"Thanks, Micah," I say as I take off after Nico.

I find him sitting on the stoop outside the apartment building, smoking a cigarette. A real one, an old-school hand-rolled one. He hears me approach and spins around. I try to read his face, but he is stone cold. I expect him to tell me to go away or flee at the sight of me, but he just sits there on the stoop blowing smoke rings.

"Since when do you smoke cigarettes?" I ask as I take a seat next to him.

He takes another drag. "Since you stopped texting me back." *Ouch*.

"I'm sorry about that." I pull my legs up and rest my head on my knees, looking down at the cracked sidewalk below me. "I'm learning this year that I can be a real asshole."

"Yeah, you are," Nico says and I wince. He flicks the cigarette butt onto the wet grass and we remain in silence. I can hear muffled voices and thumping bass from the party above us, and it makes me wonder if Boston has actual, real residents or if the entire population is made up of drunk college students. He pulls out another cigarette and offers it to me but I decline. He lights up and inhales as he leans back on his elbows. After a minute, he starts talking to me again.

"Can I ask you something?"

I already know what he's going to ask. "Why did I ghost you?"

He nods. "Yeah . . ."

"Ohhhhh, who the hell knows," I start to make a joke but stop myself. I dicked Nico over. I owe him a real answer, real closure. "This doesn't excuse the way I treated you, but I think I wasn't ready for you. I wanted it to work out with you, truly, I did, but the idea of a *real* relationship and commitment scared me and I bolted. I've got a lot of weird issues." I lean back too and bump my knees against his. "Or it could have been the fact that you suck at giving head," I tease.

Nico chokes on the cigarette. "WHAT?!?! No! You totally came that night!"

"I'm sorry to inform you, but that's not true."

He waves his hands dramatically. "No, no way. I'm not buying it. I have a perfect record with the ladies, including *you*."

"Are you familiar with the diner scene in the movie *When Harry Met Sally*?"

"No," he says.

"Well, let's just say if I wanted to, I could finally declare a major . . . in acting."

He stares at me, shock written all over his handsome face. "You have *got* to be kidding me."

"Afraid not." He stares out into the darkness for a moment, no doubt replaying every sexual experience he's ever had to figure out if the ladies were faking it or not. He brings the cigarette to his lips and takes a very lonnnnngggg breath.

"Shit, Elliot," he says. "Why didn't you say anything? I would have tried to do it better, you know."

"I know, I know. That's on me, not you. I built up so much pressure in my head that it became impossible to relax and I could never get past that. I could never be myself around you and I never knew how to tell you." I nudge him again. I want to look him in the eyes as I apologize. "I'm sorry for the way I treated you. You deserve better than that. You are a solid dude and any girl would be lucky to have you."

"I know," he says but it doesn't come out cocky. "You missed out on all *this*," he says, showing off his whole body and I laugh because it's true. I am missing out on all that. He finishes his cigarette and stands, brushing the ashes off his pants. "You coming back in?" he asks but I shake my head.

"Nah, I think I'm gonna hang out for a little while longer, but you go on ahead."

"See you around, Elliot," he says and he gives me a small, bittersweet smile as he heads back inside.

Maybe Three-Drink Elliot has burned off a little alcohol and I'm back down to One- or Two-Drink Elliot because I actually feel, like, 5 percent better. Don't get me wrong, it's only 5 percent; I'm still way deep down in the muck of my own making, but it's something.

CHAPTER 20

"SO WHEN ARE YOU GOING ON YOUR *DATE* WITH Rose?" Lucy asks as we cross over the Boston Public Garden bridge. It's been a week since the auction, seven days since I was slut-shamed and publicly humiliated and Lucy's solution to help me process this emotional blow is to run through the Boston Common. Run. As in, move at a speed faster than a walk. Why the hell did I agree to this? This is worse than the auction—wait, that's a lie—no, I was correct the first time— this *is* worse than the auction. My face is so cold, my butt is sweaty, and my teeth, knees, back, and brain hurt so bad and *oooooohmygod, I want to die.*

"She has a *girlfriend,* remember?!" I wheeze in between each word as I struggle to keep up with Lucy.

"Well, if that's still true, then what the heck was she doing by bidding on you at the auction?"

"It was just a mercy bid! It meant nothing! I think she felt obligated to because the only other option was to push me out to sea on a tiny wood boat and shoot a flaming arrow at my head." I barely get the joke out due to all the panting. I stop trying to keep up with Lucy and fall onto a bench in the middle of the park. It takes Lucy several yards to realize I abandoned her, and she doubles back and starts doing that thing runners do where they jog in place and check their heart rate.

"What are you gonna do?" Lucy asks without wheezing once.

"I just need to get through the last two months of school and then I can forget all about Rose, but let's not talk about me anymore. New subject please!"

Lucy gives me a pitying look but obliges. "I went to Pho Pasteur for lunch today with Micah and Simon," she says as she swings her right leg up on the bench and starts stretching. "I sat across from those two lovebirds for two hours and listened as they finished each other's sentences. It was so cute."

"I can't believe they already declared their relationship on Instagram. I mean, the auction was only a week ago," I say but catch myself. "Sorry, I'm trying to be less cynical these days. I guess when you know, you know. You know? I mean, how long did it take for you and Kenton to call each other boyfriend and—" I stop myself as soon as I realize my error. "Shit. Sorry Luce, I didn't mean to bring *him* up." I wait for her to react, to swell up and cry and go numb like she has done so many other times this semester, but she doesn't. She keeps on stretching. This girl is strong as hell.

"Don't worry about it," she says like it's no big deal. "And speaking of the auction, I've been meaning to thank you." She stops stretching and joins me on the bench.

"For what?"

"I know what you did." She nudges me with her elbow. "I know you gave Jesse the $300 to bid on me."

I don't even bother to pretend I'm innocent. "What?! No! How the hell did you find out?!"

"Well, for starters, he told me, like, the second we got backstage." *Fucking Jesse.* "And then there's the fact that you made us all stop at the lobby ATM before heading down to the theater." She gives me a look. "I saw you take the exact same amount out."

"So much for my foolproof plan," I lament. "I'm sorry if you're insulted or anything; I didn't want you to live out the horror of not being bid on—which of course, as you may have heard, I now have firsthand experience with. You only did the auction because of me and I wanted to make sure you felt good about yourself."

"And I appreciate that!" Lucy dips her head and rests it on my shoulder. I lean my head on hers. "But my decision to do the auction had nothing to do with you. Sure, you were the one to tell me about it, but I *chose* to do it because I was ready to put myself back out there again."

"I'm glad because for a while there I was worried you'd never be ready. I was *this* close to calling your mom." She pulls away and looks at me in horror.

"You almost called Carol?"

"My god, Lucy, you skipped some classes! YOU! SKIPPED CLASSES!"

"What are you talking about? I never skipped any classes." Lucy looks at me confused. And I look at her confused and then we look at each other confused.

"Your Tuesday and Thursday schedules are doubled because of your marketing classes. But you were always back in the room when you should have been in class!" I tell her, and then her face floods with relief and understanding.

"Ohmygod! Elliot, I didn't skip classes. At the start of this semester I *dropped* my second major down to a minor."

"But on the stage at the auction, I could have sworn I heard you say you were still double majoring."

"The first rule of marketing is to know your audience and the second rule is to make your product or service sound better than it actually is."

Now it's my turn to give her a look. "Is that really a rule?"

"No, but it should be. It worked, didn't it?"

"Yeah it did, the dudes were all over your junk that night! Did you hear how much Brad bid on you?! I had no idea he was even into you like that."

"I didn't either," she says and then a coy smile appears. "But I'm glad he did."

I slam my fist down on the bench. "TELL ME EVERYTHING."

• • •

OH.

MY.

GOD.

Lucy has had tender chicken for Brad since chapter 4 and I completely forgot about it until a sentence ago. Here's how this crush has developed off-page: Lucy may have put her Brad Feels on the back burner when she was with *[insert your favorite insult here]*, but ever since Brad and I started hanging out after our screenwriting class this semester, he's been much more present in our lives, and slowly but surely, he made his way to Lucy's front burner.[81] And since Brad was willing to drop major dough on our dear Lucy at the auction, I am willing to bet he has tender chicken for her too. However! It appears as though neither of our lovebirds has admitted this to the other yet, so . . .

I think you know what's about to happen.

I cashed in every favor, used every connection, begged, pleaded, and bribed my way into convincing Micah to throw a party. This is how it went down:

[Elliot approaches Micah while he is working out at the Emerson fitness center]

ELLIOT (ME)

Hey, Micah.

---

81 Did this metaphor work? I can't tell, but you get where this is going because of course you do, you brilliant reader, you.

                    MICAH

          Hey, Elliot.

                    ELLIOT

          Whoa, this place is
          cool!

                    MICAH

          Is this your first time
          at the school gym?

                    ELLIOT

          Yes?

                    MICAH

          judging sigh Why am I
          not surprised?

                    ELLIOT

          So do you know anyone
          who'd be down to throw a
          party on Saturday?

                    MICAH

          Sure, Simon lives off
          campus and he loves
          hosting parties.

```
                    ELLIOT
          Cool. Have a good
          workout.


                    MICAH
          See ya.
```

[End scene]

PROJECT
TENDER CHICKEN:
ROOMMATE EDITION

Step 1: Ignore Your Own Unrequited Feelings and Focus All Your Energy on Your Roommate's Love Life

Step 1 has been accomplished! Let's proceed to step 2.

Step 2: Help Your Roommate Pick Out a Costume (and Try Not to Hit on Her Too Much)

As it turns out, Simon does indeed throw parties, but Simon's parties are *always* costume parties. Simon's philosophy, and therefore true of all costume majors based on my interactions with only two of them, is to treat every day like it's your last day—and your last day just so happens to be Halloween. I bought the cheapest, most flammable tuxedo I could find at The Garment District, a vintage store in Cambridge, slicked my hair back into a tight bun, and accessorized with a plastic squirt gun filled with vodka to complete the James Bond look.[82] Lucy decided to go with a Victorian Gothic look, which at first I was all like *noooooo, that's not hot* but at the vintage store she found this floor-length black dress with long, billowy sleeves and a sweetheart neckline that dips dangerously low and the outfit, on her, is most definitely hot.

"Your boobies look amazing in that dress," I told her as we finished getting ready in our room.

Lucy reached in and fluffed her boobs. "I know, right? It's this new bra I got at the Prudential Center." I have been providing in-depth commentary on her boobs all year and I think this was the first time she fully embraced one of my compliments.

"Lady, that is no magic bra. That is all you," I told her.

Step 3: Convince Your Roommate's Crush to Wear a Matching Costume

Not to say that my whole plan rests entirely on outfits and costumes, but they do play an integral role. You see, once I knew what Lucy was wearing, I had to get Brad on board, so a week ago I ambushed Brad outside the bathrooms while he was in between classes.

"Brad! Who are you going as to the party on Saturday?" He looked sleepy and not at all prepared to handle the energy

---

82 I was originally planning to go as Lara Croft from *Tomb Raider* (the Angelina Jolie version, obviously) but bouncing around with water balloons stuffed in my bra would have made dancing more difficult.

I was throwing at him. Too bad. I waved in his face. "Hello? Brad? Hi! What costume are you wearing to Simon's party?"

"Uhh, I don't know," he shrugged. "I think I was just going to go as Steve Jobs?"

"STEVE JOBS?" I yelled/said at him. "That's the most boring costume ever! All you need is a damn turtleneck!"

"Uh, yeah, that was kind of the point," he said.

"What if I told you I know who *someone special* is going as and gave you the chance to surprise them with a matching outfit?" I used lots of hand gestures and vocal inflection to really sell the intrigue of it all.

"Uh, sure, I guess. Who are they going as?"

I had to think about it for a sec. How could I succinctly describe what a Victorian goth babe looks like to someone like Brad in a way that he would understand and also get excited about?

"Think *Dracula* meets *The Phantom of the Opera* meets—" I started to say but he stopped me short.

"Say no more," he said with a level of enthusiasm I was not expecting based on his first costume choice but who cares, I'll take it! This plan is perfect! And now, back to the present tense!

Step 4: Get Your Roommate and Her Crush in the Same Room and Watch the Sparks Fly

"Are you sure this is the right place? This is way too nice for an undergrad," Lucy asks me as we ring the doorbell to Simon's apartment in the ultra-fancy Beacon Hill neighborhood. The door bursts open and Micah greets us.

"Ladies, you made it! Welcome to the *mans*." Micah is wearing tight acid-wash jeans, a white tank top, and a studded bracelet around his bicep. He's slicked back his hair and either grew a mustache or pasted one on for the occasion but either way, he is *owning* this look.

"Who are you supposed to be?" Lucy asks.

"Freddie Mercury!" Micah and I yell at her in unison. It's an extremely obvious reference. Even Lucy should have gotten that one.

"Hiiii!" Simon singsongs as he appears in the doorway behind Micah. I don't know why I'm surprised by his costume, but I am blown away, actually, because Simon is dressed as David Bowie as Ziggy Stardust. He is wearing a red-and-gray-striped onesie with shoulder pads and a red mullet wig, and he's painted a lightning bolt over half his face. Micah grins at us and then leans back to kiss Simon. They match in their 1970s rock god outfits and ahhhh, I wanna die at how freaking cute they are together!

Simon invites us in and *damn*. This place is HUGE. As he gives us the grand tour, Simon tells us about how he inherited the infamous Emerson hand-me-down, a beautiful three-bedroom brownstone with a backyard that's rent controlled. An anonymous alumnus from Emerson's past bought the place in the 1980s and has rented it at a reduced rate exclusively to

Emerson students ever since. Simon was the lucky one to get the call from the mysterious benefactor this year.

"Ten bucks says Micah finds out who owns this place by the end of the night and gets on the shortlist to inherit it next year," I whisper to Lucy.

"Fifty says he already knows," she whispers back and I make a mental note to pester Micah for the details later.

But it's not just the apartment that is impressive, the party decor is so fancy, I legitimately feel like I'm at a ball. The whole house is lit entirely by the same tiny string lights Rose keeps making us take down and instead of sticky Solo cups filled with sweet mystery liquid, people are drinking red wine from vintage crystal glasses. In the kitchen, I am offered a goblet of wine by someone in a Sailor Moon costume, but I wave them off and stick to water. Tonight is about matchmaking, not keeping track of where I am on the Elliot Drink Scale. Within an hour, the place fills up and I see a lot of familiar faces, but it's hard to tell who is who because it's so dimly lit and everyone is in costume, so it takes me a second to recognize Brad and Sasha in the dining room by a chocolate fountain.

"Hey, guys!" I say to them as I approach, but I come to a literal skidding halt when I see Brad more clearly. Ohhhh myyyyy godddddddd. I thought my suggestion of *Dracula* meets *The Phantom of the Opera* meant he'd just dress up as a handsome, gothic king, but he *literally* dressed up as Dracula AND the Phantom of the Opera. He's wearing a cape and a white paper plate to cover half his face like the Phantom, but he's also wearing fake fangs and has fake blood all over his mouth. OHMYGOD BRAD, YOU SWEET, BEAUTIFUL HIMBO. I LOVE YOU. Lucy trails behind me and when Brad sees her costume and figures it out that *she* was the *special someone* I was referring to, he breaks out in the biggest smile. He sets his drink down and I step back as he goes to her.

"Lucy, you look so beautiful," he says sweetly, and Lucy can't hide the blush that's warming up her face.

"I love your costume too!" she says, but it's like he doesn't even hear her because he can't take his eyes off her. He looks positively dazzled. She is smitten. They're both smitten and my heart is soaring just looking at them.

Step 5: . . .

Well, shit. That was easier than I thought. In fact, I don't think I actually did anything. This all seemed to happen on its own. So I guess step 5 is quit giving yourself credit for doing nothing at all and go dance your ass off.

I grab my friends and lead them into the living room just as the song changes and it's some dance remix to Queen's "Another One Bites the Dust." Micah must have put this one on the playlist because when the iconic bass line comes on over the speakers, he jumps up on the couch and starts singing while Sasha, Lucy, Brad, and I cheer him on and Simon tries to get him off the fancy furniture. It's easier to let go when you're surrounded by friends, so to honor them, I start dancing around them like a maniac and shoot vodka at them from my squirt gun. When my squirt guns run low on ammo, I moonwalk back into the kitchen for a refill, but when I return, I see Rose dancing in the crowd. And she's dressed in a black, shiny one-piece latex suit—exactly like the one the character Trinity wears in *The Matrix*. Seeing her like this . . . it's too much. I can't take it. It doesn't matter how hard I ignore my feelings for Rose because they are right there, on the surface, demanding I pay attention.

I don't want her to see me so I slip back into the kitchen and out into the tiny backyard for some air.

●●●

It's an hour before I hear the back door swing open behind me, and when I turn around, it's not anyone I was expecting. Simon finds me on the stoop, alone. He skips down the steps and sits next to me.

"Contemplating life?" he asks.

"More like hiding from it."

"I know that game well," he says.

"If that's true, why host parties?"

"I love putting on a show but I don't necessarily need to be the star. I like being the *host*, not a *guest*."

"You're like a modern-day Gatsby," I flatter him.

"Does that mean you approve?"

"Micah isn't one to need anyone's approval—for anything—

but for what it's worth, I wholeheartedly approve." He smiles and dimples form on either side of his cheeks.

"What brings you out here while everyone else is inside?" he asks.

"Lady troubles."

He starts to get up. "Do you need a tampon? Because I have a nice selection in the guest bathroom upstairs—"

"No, no," I laugh and pull him back down. "Not *that* lady problem, a different kind of lady problem. A romantical lady problem."

"Do tell."

I take a deep breath and rub the back of my neck. "I've been content spending the majority of my life in casual relationships. I've never been bothered by the fact that in most friend-group situations, I was flying solo. It's easy to play that role when you don't take relationships, or anything really, all that seriously."

"And you are content to play that role?" Simon asks.

"Yeah, I am." I pause to think about it for a second. "Or at least, I was."

"And now?"

"Now? Now I want something more, and of course I want something more with my RA who isn't even available, and all this unrequited wanting has left me feeling so fucking lonely. I mean, I am constantly surrounded by people and yet I've never felt more—"

Simon reaches out and touches my arm. "Wait, did you just say you like your RA?"

"Yeah, why?"

"Isn't your RA Rose?"

"Again . . . yeah. Dude, what is it? You are freaking me out!"

Simon drops his head in his hands and laughs. "Wow, ummm, I can't believe you haven't heard this yet, but Rose broke up with Monica."

I think my heart just stopped.

I think I may be deceased.

"What??!?!"

"Yeah, she broke up with Monica, like, two or three months ago."

My hands fly up to my mouth. "Are you fucking serious?! *How* do you know this?"

"Rose and I are in a lot of classes together since we're both costume tech majors, so we're pretty close," he says and my face melts off.

"When did she tell you this?"

"I don't know the specific day they broke up, but she told me about it two weeks ago when we were setting up the auction. She even said something about having feelings for someone else, but I don't remember the details. I'm sorry, it was a busy night." I want to scream at Simon to TELL ME EVERYTHING!!!!!!!!!!!!!!!!!!!!!!! But instead I keep my mouth shut and concentrate all my efforts on keeping my face as chill as possible instead of exploding all over his nice backyard.

Please excuse me while I process this new information on the next page.

ROSE. IS. SINGLE.

ROSE. HAS. NO. GIRLFRIEND.

ROSE. IS. SINGLE.

ROSE WAS SINGLE WHEN SHE BID ON ME.

SHE HAS FEELINGS FOR SOMEONE ELSE.

WAS SHE *FOR REAL* BIDDING ON ME?!

AM I THAT SOMEONE ELSE?????

WHAT. THE. FUCK.

WHAT DOES THIS MEAN?!?

ROSE. IS. SINGLE.

ROSE.

IS.

SINGLE.

;ADJHF;LA;ALGKFJ

Hold up.

Wait.

Even if this news is true,

a) it doesn't prove I'm the person Rose has feelings for,

b) it doesn't mean I deserve to be with her,

c) even if she does have feelings for me and I felt worthy of those feelings . . . even if this were all true—WHICH WE DON'T FUCKING KNOW—it still wouldn't mean our relationship would work. Rose is disciplined and focused and constantly trying to help me bring a better version of myself to the surface, while I am scattered and impulsive and hate being told what to do. How could this ever work? The answer is: It could never work. She's my RA, she just got out of a serious relationship, I'm a mess, and on top of all that, there's only a little over one month left in the school year. These are facts I simply cannot ignore. Maybe if I had recognized my feelings earlier, maybe if I had listened to her sooner, maybe if I hadn't screwed up my grades, maybe if Kenton and the auction hadn't decimated my self-worth, maybe, maybe, *maybe* then I could be someone worthy of a woman like Rose. But those things *did* happen and my confidence is shaken, so she shouldn't be with me until I find a way back to myself first.

"What are you going to do?" Simon asks after I've been quiet for a long time. And man, I feel bad for this guy. We barely know each other and our longest interaction to date has been him watching me go through a rapid-fire display of emotions from,

WTF?!?!

⬇

!!!!!!!!!! Chaotic Good !!!!!!!!!!

⬇

Sweet, Sweet Hope

⬇

THE DEVIL IS IN THE DETAIL

⬇

Existential Crisis

⬇

I Still Suck But At Least I Accept That Now

"I don't know what to do," I say at last.

"Come on." Simon stands and reaches out to me. I take his hand and he pulls me up. "Let's go inside," he says.

"I thought we were gonna be hide-out-on-the-stoop pals?"

"We are," he says, holding the door open to his apartment for me. "But I think you gotta talk to Rose." And he's right. Simon isn't the one who needs to hear this. Rose is the one.

● ● ●

Back inside, everyone is still dancing, although Micah has gotten off the couch. I look for Rose but there is no sign of her. I breathe a little sigh of relief that I don't have to have do this right now. I want to talk with her, but I'm still unsure of what to say. My feelings are a mess.

I work my way into the group and start rubbing my butt all up on Lucy and Brad, and I'm starting to relax and settle into the party vibes when the song ends and a sultry, hypnotic song comes on, slowing the room down. It's like this song was engineered to turn people on, and I only need to look around for proof. Everyone couples up almost instantly and Sasha and I sway together like we're at a middle school dance because we're both still single.

As we slowly shuffle around, a couple next to us dressed like avocados leaves and that's when I see Rose over there in the corner—dancing with someone else. I squint to see and realize it's Eva, one of the girls I hooked up with last semester. I didn't even know she was here.

I hide behind Sasha so Rose doesn't catch me watching her. Eva moves closer and presses her hips into Rose's. I watch Rose slip her hand around Eva's waist, to the small of her back, and pull her in tighter. I watch as Eva leans forward, her lips dangerously close to kissing Rose's neck. And then I cannot watch anymore. I guess that's it then. Eva is the someone else Rose has feelings for.

I thank Sasha for the dance and excuse myself. All the momentum I had going into this party evaporates. I want to be here for my friends, to celebrate Brad and Lucy, but right now I need to go home. I don't want to do the whole song and dance that's customary when leaving a party before it ends, so I don't say goodbye to anyone, but I text Lucy that I have a headache and that I called a Lyft back to the LB. I grab my coat from the pile on the floor in the dining room and go home.

CHAPTER 21

THE LAST SIX WEEKS OF MY FRESHMAN YEAR OF college are so similar to high school—in that they go by sloooooooooooooowly. Every day feels like a week, every week feels like a month, and what a year this month has been.

Seeing Rose with Eva at Simon's party was the harsh dose of reality I needed. Rose and I will not be together. I knew the only way I was ever going to accept it and move on was to avoid Rose, so that is exactly what I did. I started eating most of my meals off campus and Micah got hold of her class schedule somehow, so I was able to avoid seeing her in between classes.

But Emerson is a small school, and we live on the same floor, so running into her was bound to happen. And it finally occurred when I went to pee once. I left my room and started walking toward the bathrooms and saw Rose coming from the other direction toward the bathrooms too. Our eyes locked for just a second before I turned around and ran back into my room. I ended up peeing into an empty Gatorade bottle

I found under my bed. Ever since then, I've been peeing and showering on the fourth floor, just to be safe.

But the past month wasn't all frantic whiz trips to the upper floors—I did other shit too. I started talking to a counselor to help process the trauma with Kenton, I filmed a series of short videos with Brad and Sasha for Lucy's mom to advertise her B&B, I rewatched all my favorite TV shows, Micah and I volunteered to help students register to vote, and then, there was finals. I studied my motherfucking ass off, worked harder than I ever have worked in my life, and managed to pull out three solid B+s and even my first college A.

And I finally declared my major: business of creative enterprises.

Here's the thing I've learned most about myself this semester. I love movies and TV and theater and books and music . . . I love all of it. I love pop culture. And I don't know if you've picked up on it this year, but I also kinda love making things happen, which, I learned from my media arts class this semester, is a good skill to have if you want to be a producer. So I met with an academic adviser and we talked it over and that's when I learned that the Business of Creative Enterprises program is one big dish that has sourced ingredients from all the other departments, like Marketing, Writing, Literature & Publishing, Visual & Media Arts, Performing Arts, etc., etc., etc. According to my adviser, Mr. Tesmond, my whole "take a bunch of random courses" approach this year wasn't a complete waste of time. In fact, several courses have already put me on the path toward the BCE degree.[83] I can't believe I'm going to say this but I'm excited to sign up for classes next year, I might even take some over the summer too. I finally feel like I'm on the right path and I can't fucking wait to see where it takes me. It turns out, if you put in the work to make yourself a less shitty person . . . you become a less shitty person.

Somehow, I managed to do it. I started and finished my freshman year of college. I made it to the end *mostly* unscathed. And now, all there's left to do is pack up my life and say goodbye to the Little Building, to the place I now call home.

So here I am, the last one to leave the third floor. Everyone, including Lucy, left this morning. Lucy and I didn't say goodbye—that's not our thing. We agreed that formal goodbyes were unnecessary given the terms of our friendship contract, which was expanded to include once-a-day video chats until we are reunited in the fall.[84] Micah promised to visit me over the summer when he goes on a trip to visit his brother who just got a job in Chicago, and I reminded him that I'm from Cincinnati, not Chicago, so now I too have a trip planned to visit his brother in Chicago. Sasha, Brad, Nico, Rose, and every other side character I've randomly mentioned in this story have all left for home too. I didn't bother saying goodbye to Rose. There's too much I want to say to her, but nothing I will. Micah found out she is doing the abroad program at the Emerson castle in the Netherlands

---

83 Ha! Who fucking knew?!

84 I did, however, manage to hide a box of Cheez-Its in one of her suitcases as a little surprise for when she gets home.

next fall, so that's that. I doubt I'll ever see her again. And you know what? I'm okay with this. It's better this way.

When I first arrived, I did not bring much, only the essentials: clothes, laptop, bedding, laundry supplies. And yet, I have somehow managed to accumulate *things*, things I would have scoffed at nine months ago but now can't imagine living without. Hand-me-down clothes from Sasha, a vintage edition of *The Princess Bride* book from Brad, throw pillows and tea cups from Lucy, assless chaps from Micah. It would be so much easier to donate all this stuff than haul it back to Ohio, but I've attached memories and meaning to these objects.[85] These people who were once strangers have become part of me. They've become my family.

I'm alone in the dorms again, without my mouse friends this time, and I have nothing to do but reflect on my first year away from home . . . and do one last load of laundry. I'm on the phone with Remy as I gather the clothes I had accumulated from my temporary laundry hiatus during the Avoid Rose at All Costs phase of my life.

"Wait, so why aren't you coming home until Sunday?" Remy asks. "I thought your dorm closed today?"

"Izzy's driving up from New York and we're road tripping home together, but her med school lets out a day later than Emerson. So she'll be here tomorrow."

"How come you're allowed to stay then?"

---

85 Plus, I doubt Goodwill accepts assless chaps.

"I had to get the resident director to approve a one-day extension to my stay. He had to hang back anyway to oversee the cleaning crews."

"Cool, so how was it?" Remy asks, showing off her lightning quick ability to change topics.

"How was what?"

"Your first year?"

"Oh, that? Piece of cake, no problem, a walk in the park," I say as I look under the bed and find the missing bra I've been looking for since September.

"Do you have any advice for me? I can't wait to go to college."

"Advice? No, I have no advice for you, except for shaving— if you want to shave, do it in the sink. Oh, and bring double the amount of underwear you think you'll need. And if you go to a school that has a cereal bar, go nuts but only, like, moderately nuts."

"Is that it? Just shaving, undies, and cereal?" Remy asks.

"Ummm, let's see. Don't date anyone on your floor, you're just asking for drama. Guard your laundry and supplies at all times—oh, and keep a pair of shoes by the door so when someone sets off the fire alarm, you don't have to stand outside in your roommate's boots. And don't get shitty grades your first semester, you'll be digging your GPA out of the gutter for the rest of your life. And, I guess, know that it's okay if you don't know what you want to study or what you want to do with your life, you'll figure it out." I stop and wait for Remy to ask me more questions, but I don't hear anything. I pull the phone away from my face and check to see if the call is still connected or if I just gave a great monologue to a piece of plastic. "Hello? Remy? Are you still there?"

"Yeah, I'm here," she says. "I was trying to write down everything you said so I won't forget it when I go to college in a few years." Ahhh goddammit I love my little sister so much.

"You don't have to worry about remembering it, Remy. I'll write it all down for you. Maybe I'll even turn it into a book one day."[86] I gather the last of my clothes that need to be washed and head to the laundry room, but as soon as I get my clothes loaded into the machine, I realize I'm completely out of detergent.

"Shit!" I say.

"Don't say *shit*," Remy says.

"Hey Rem? I gotta run but I'll see you in a couple of days, okay?"

"Okay!" she squeals into the phone. "I can't wait!"

I hang up and look around the room for any abandoned supplies and over on the window ledge there's a box of detergent—and it just so happens to be the exact same kind I use. Someone must have bought it recently and decided not to lug it home. *Sweet!* I think as I go to grab it but I stop myself short. This is definitely public property now, everyone has left, but it still feels wrong to take what is clearly someone else's stuff. But . . . I still need to wash all these stanky-ass clothes.

---

86 *wink* *wink*

As much as it pains me to even consider stealing, I have a choice to make. Well, actually, *you* have a choice to make.

THE ELLIOT MCHUGH INTERACTIVE EXPERIENCE: THE LAUNDRY EDITION

Which of the following should I do next?

OPTION A: Should I embrace being a total hypocrite and "borrow" some detergent from this fresh, unattended stash?

OPTION B: Or should I take the high road, march over to that ancient-looking detergent dispenser, and cough up four times the normal price per pound for a single packet of liquid blue sludge that will definitely make my skin break out later?

If you selected option A, please proceed to the next paragraph. If you selected option B, please proceed to the next footnote.[87]

---

87 [Movie trailer narrator voice] Elliot McHugh was not a hypocrite. She made the ethical choice and purchased a packet of cheap, liquid detergent. What Elliot did not know was that the detergent had expired. Elliot had an unfortunate reaction to the toxic chemicals and suffered a slow, painful death. The end. Please proceed to the credits. This book has ended for you.

Before I break open the box, I tiptoe to the door and peek up and down the hall, listening for any kind of movement, straining for the sound of someone who might witness my thievery. But I hear nothing so, fuck it. Let's do this. Hypocrisy be damned! I've got undies that need to be washed and I am *not* going inside-outsies again. I reach for the box and open it up.

Hold up.

. . . .

. . . .

What the—

. . . .

. . . .

There's a note inside.

. . . .

. . . .

I unfold the yellow piece of paper that was carefully placed inside the box and this is what it says:

> To the girl who called me an asshole nine months ago,
> I'm sorry I used your detergent. To make it up to you,
> here is a replacement. But the fact that you opened
> this means you are a total hypocrite because you didn't
> know this was for you and yet you opened it anyway.
> I'm glad to see you've *finally* taken my advice.
>   *Love,*
>   *Rose*

A;dlkgfhjfa;dsfjhsdkfjhaergkjba;skdjghad;fjhsalskdjfhsl

I don't.

I just.

I mean.

I can't even.

And that's when I hear a knock on the laundry room door.

CHAPTER 22

SHE'S STILL HERE. ROSE IS STILL HERE. WHO, WHAT, why, when, how is she still here?!?!?

"Rose! What are you—how are you—why are you here?" I ask gracefully as I open the laundry room door for her. This is the first time we've spoken in six weeks. "I thought you left?"

She bounces on her toes and leans against the door frame. "The resident director told me you were staying an extra night so I volunteered to stay back too and keep you company."

"Oh, that's so great!" *FUCK FUCK FUCK FUCK.*

"Are you all packed?"

"Mostly," I say and nod to the washing machine. "One last load to go."

"Do you mind helping me pack? I could use an extra hand."

"Uh, sure, yeah. Just give me a minute and I'll meet you down there," I tell her. She smiles and takes off down the hall toward her room. As soon as she's out of earshot I sprint to my room and text Lucy.

Elliot: HALP! ROSE STILL HERE. SHE NEEDS PACKING HELP. WHAT DO?

Lucy: all you have to do is help her pack. that's it!

Elliot: BUT WHAT IF SHE PACKS THE BOXES ALL SEXILY?

Lucy: keep the convo casual, you only have to get through tonight

Lucy: you can do this!!!!!!!!

I shuffle down the hall to Rose's room and steady myself before knocking. "Come in!" she calls from inside and I push the door open.

This is the second time I've been in Rose's room and it appears as though she has acquired even more stuff. She hasn't packed any of it. Good. That means more packing, more distraction. Mellow, deep house music plays through a pair of speakers, and Rose has switched on two colored table lamps that bathe the room in an amber, moody glow. This room is pure Rose—warm, wild, sexy.

Ahhh god, what the fuck am I doing? I shouldn't be in here.

While Rose packs away her sewing machine at her desk in the back, I take a seat on the soft, tufted area rug on her floor, and start packing her books. I try not to, but I can't help but sneak a few glances at her when she isn't looking. For once, Rose isn't wearing some elaborate outfit. Her hair is unwashed and held together in a messy bun and she's wearing loose-fitting harem pants and a big, hand-knit sweater. Not an inch of her body is showing and yet it is the sexiest look I've seen.

She zips the case around her sewing machine and moves on to clearing out her desk. She opens a drawer and yelps. "Oh! I forgot I had these! Oh, this will be perfect!" She pulls out a few boxes of incense sticks and shakes them. "I like to create an atmosphere, so I need you to pick a scent. And choose wisely because I *will* judge you based on the scent you choose." She arches just one eyebrow, a challenge. I get up from the floor and approach her slowly. I don't know what she's doing, what this is, so I just pick one at random.

"No, no, no," she says. "You have to smell them first. Close your eyes," she says so softly it's almost a whisper.

"What?" My heart beats a little faster.

She takes a step closer to me. "Close your eyes. You need to smell the incense without knowing what they are. It's the only way to make an unbiased decision."

"How can one be *biased* about incense?"

"Shut up and close your eyes already." She takes another step closer and this time I obey. I close my eyes and a second later, I smell something cloyingly sweet and floral, like someone tried to recreate the scent of jasmine in a lab but got it all wrong. "Thoughts?" she asks. I keep my eyes shut.

"No, not that one. Too powdery." I don't know why I'm whispering, it just comes out like that.

"What about this?" she asks. The flower scent is replaced

with something that smells smokey, almost tobacco-like, which of course makes me think of Nico and his cigarettes.

"No, not that one," I say.

"Okay, last one." The smokey scent disappears and a new fragrance takes its place. I can't put my finger on any one note. With my eyes still closed, I reach for her hand and bring it closer to my face so I can smell the incense more closely. I inhale deeply. It smells like wet, dirty roses mixed with sandalwood, cedar, and amber. It's spicy, lush, seductive. I don't know what it is, but what I do know is I want to drink this scent. I want to bathe in it.

"This one," I whisper. I open my eyes and look for the box to see what brand makes it, but it's just a plain black box, no logo or labels or anything. "Where did you get this?" I grab the box from her and sniff it again.

Rose smiles at me. Apparently I've chosen correctly.

"It's custom made, actually, by me. There's this little shop on Newbury Street where you can make your own perfumes. It's me, or at least the olfactory version of me." Rose takes a stick from the box, lights it, and places it in a metal holder on her desk. The smoke spirals into the air and slowly fills the room with the intoxicating fragrance. I stand there, frozen, unable to do anything but breathe in Rose.

"Are you hungry?" Rose asks, shaking me out of my trance. "I just ordered some hot noods."

I nearly choke. "Excuse me?"

"Hot noods, as in spicy noodle soup from Pho Pasteur. It should be here soon in case you want some."

"Uh yeah, sure, sounds good."

As we wait for our dinner, I dip out and go to the bathroom. "Get a grip, McHugh," I tell mirror me after I splash cold water on my face. She's not supposed to be here. I was this close to making a clean break. I've spent the last six weeks trying to forget about Rose and now, in the span of twenty minutes, all my feelings for her are threatening to resurface. I splash my face a few more times and wait until I've calmed down enough to return. I give myself one last pep talk before I leave, "Keep it casual, keep it neutral, keep it in your pants."

By the time I get back to her room, the food has arrived and Rose made us a little picnic spread on the floor. I take a seat on a pillow across from her and start slurping noodles and eventually, we even start talking.

"So, I haven't seen you much since the auction. I was hoping we could talk about it," she says in between slurps of soup.

"Do we have to?"

"No," Rose says and I breathe a sigh of relief, but then she adds, "I want to make sure you're okay, though. You seemed upset by what happened up there."

"I have a pretty broad definition of what *fun* means, but getting publicly slut-shamed doesn't exactly fall under the traditional definition of *fun*." I try to play it off as though I don't care, but Rose has this annoying ability to see right through me. She stops eating and looks me straight in the eyes.

"When that person called you a slut, did it upset you because it forced you to confront something you already think about yourself or did it upset you because it made you doubt yourself—made you doubt a part of yourself that you had already accepted and even celebrated?"

I don't hesitate, I know the answer to that question easily. "I don't think I'm a slut."

"Good," she says and goes back to eating. And then in a louder, fiery tone she adds, "I swear, Elliot, instead of bidding on you, I was *this close* to jumping offstage and smacking the shit out of whoever said that. I couldn't believe no one was bidding, I mean what the fuck is wrong with people—"

"Sorry, but I gotta stop you right there," I tell her. "I mean, it's sweet that you'd get all slappy on my behalf, but I don't deserve to be defended. Yeah, it was a real kick in the nuts to stand up there and be humiliated, but it was only my ego that was bruised. It was my own fault, really. When I was up there, I saw all these people I had slept with and then ghosted, so I don't blame them for leaving me up there high and dry, and you shouldn't either." I think, for a second, that maybe I should say something more on it, try to show her more ways that I've grown up this year, but why bother? It's too late now. We go back to eating in silence, until Rose changes the subject.

"Did you end up declaring a major?" she asks.

"Yeah, actually—business of creative enterprises," I say with pride.

"Elliot! That is so awesome!" She looks happy. She too should be proud—of herself. If it wasn't for her, I'd still have no clue what I want to do with the rest of my life. I may have done the work, but she's the one who got me started.

"Thanks," I say informally, but mean most sincerely.

"I need to introduce you to Eva Grey," she continues. "She's in that program too and really loves it. She is such a sweetheart."

At the mention of Eva's name, the memory of her and Rose all over each other at the costume party flashes before my eyes. I do everything I can to keep my face neutral, to prevent my expression from laying my feelings bare. I don't say anything, opting for a simple nod instead as I shovel a huge bite of noodles into my mouth and accidentally choke.

"You okay over there?" she asks as I cough the noodles up.

"Yeah, wrong tube," I wheeze as I wipe soup from my chin. "Could you hand me a napkin, please?" Reaching over our picnic spread to hand me a napkin, Rose fumbles and drops the bowl of scalding hot noodle soup in her lap. The steamy liquid splashes all over her legs and soaks through her pants.

"FUCK!" Rose jumps up and dabs at the mess but the thin napkin is futile. I spring into action and grab one of the many fabric skeins stacked in her wardrobe and rush to help soak up the rest but she stops me. "You can't use that! That's waxed cotton!"

"And?!"

"It's waterproof!"

"Well, shit, how was I supposed to know that?!?" I panic and throw the skein back at her closet. "Do you have any towels?"

She squeezes her eyes shut in pain and points to a small chest in the corner of her room and I run to it. I grab all the towels, you know, just in case she needs all six of them. I turn around and all the towels slip out of my hands and tumble to the floor in a heap. Rose has taken her pants off. I just stare at her. I stare at her standing a few feet from me wearing nothing but thick wool socks, bare legs, and a big cashmere sweater that only slightly covers her white panties. *Fuck.* I clear my throat as I force myself to look away and give her some privacy. I pick up one of the towels from the floor and blindly toss it to her. I don't dare move any closer.

"Ahh, that's so much better. Hey, would you mind fetching some ice from the common room?" she asks and at first I don't hear her because all I can think is *don't look don't look don't look.* "Elliot?" she asks again.

"Ice, yeah, sure, right. On it!" I dart out and jog down the hall to the common room. I reach for a plastic cup from the side of the ice machine but they're all gone. They must have cleaned everything out today. I look for anything I can use to carry the ice back but there's nothing. "Ahh shit," I say when I realize my only available solution. I take off my thin, ratty T-shirt, exposing my black sports bra. *This is fine*, I think. It just looks like I'm going to a yoga class now. I go to the machine and fill up my T-shirt with ice and carry it down the hall. Before

I reenter Rose's room, I take a deep, not-at-all-calming breath and push the door open. Rose is sitting on the edge of her bed, still pantsless I might add, and rubbing some kind of sweet-smelling balm on her burned skin.

"What's that?" I ask as I set my shirt ice bag on the bed next to her.

"It's manuka honey." She scoops a bit more out of a clear tub and rubs it on her thighs.

"Honey? You can use honey on burns?" I ask, trying not to think about how that honey might taste on her skin.

"You can use it for all kinds of medicinal purposes. My mom is really into homeopathic remedies," she says as she applies another layer of honey. "This should be enough though. Hey, can you help me with the ice? I don't want to get any stickiness on your shirt." She holds up her hands and I fight the urge to reach out and lick the honey right off her fingers.

"Don't worry about it," I tell her as I take a tentative step back from her, hoping that a change in proximity will help. "It's an old shirt anyways, I can just throw it out or whatever."

"Or you could just wash it," she suggests with a small smile.

"Oh right, I guess I could do that too." Rose takes my shirt full of ice and gently places it on her thighs. She holds back a yelp as the cold fabric touches her hot skin. A water droplet forms on the edge of my shirt and I watch as it builds up until it becomes too heavy and trickles down the inside of her thigh and turns inward. Rose doesn't wipe it away. I want to trace that water droplet with my tongue.

"Sorry about all this." She waves to the mess. "I was kind of hoping we could talk over dinner."

"Talk?" I swallow. "About what?" Blood is pumping in my ears, my heart is pounding.

"Monica and I broke up," she says and my heart stops. She has my full attention. She sets the ice aside, tilts her chin up and we lock eyes. Her gaze is intense but unreadable. "I left her, for many reasons, but—"

"Why are you telling me this?" I interrupt.

"Well, for starters, I wanted to apologize for giving you shit for dating Nico. I've spent this whole year lecturing you on who to be and how to love and the truth is, I wasn't even taking my own advice. Since the moment we met, you have been unapologetically *you*. You've let me see you at your best and your worst, and I've been an unfair friend because I have kept so much of myself hidden from you. I want you to see me, all of me, and for that to happen, you need to see my ugly side too."

"Rose, you don't owe me anything."

"Yes, I do, so here it goes," she says, and as much as I want to try to stop her again, I let her keep going. "I fucked up with Monica. When she and I first got together, I had no idea she was dating someone else already. I didn't find out until last summer, just before the school year started. Her lie caused a rift between us, but we worked through it and made a commitment to try and make it work. But then I started having feelings for someone else, strong feelings from the second

I met her. I should have left Monica right then, but I didn't because we had decided to commit. I know rumors about me being a homewrecker have been flying around since last year and I guess I was scared that if I left her for someone else, I would always be seen that way. So not only was I lying to myself this whole time, but I was lying to her as well," she says, her voice starting to crack a little. She stops to take a breath. "But I wanted you to know that I finally listened to my heart and I left Monica."

I have to stop this. I know where this is going. She's going to tell me about how she's with Eva now and how wonderful it is to be with someone who is right for you and how she hopes that I find that *special someone* in the future and blah blah fucking blah.

I break eye contact and stare down at my feet. "I can't do this," I say. It comes out quiet and small.

"Can't do what?"

I reach for something, anything but the truth. "I can't—I can't help you pack anymore."

"Why not?" she asks calmly.

"Because," I say, feeling increasingly agitated.

"Because why?" she says right away, pushing me harder for the truth. I run my hands through my hair and pace in front of her. "Elliot—" She starts to get up from the bed to come to me, so I stop pacing and hold my hand up to stop her.

"Stop, Rose," I say. "Just stop. I already know all of this, okay?"

"You do?" Rose asks. "How?"

I let my arm fall in defeat. "Simon told me at the costume party."

"You've known all this time?" At first her expression is lit with surprise, but then her face falls into sadness. "Is *that* why you've been avoiding me?"

"Yes." I wait for her to say something, anything, but she doesn't speak. She doesn't move. She just looks at me with disbelief, like maybe I cracked her soul, but I don't know why. I'm the one whose heart is broken. "I'm sorry for avoiding you, but I didn't know—"

"I'm sorry, I shouldn't have said anything," she says, her voice cold and distant. Her face goes red as she wipes her eyes, which had started tearing up. "It's my fault for not telling you sooner."

I back up until I get to her door. "Look, I need to get going. I have to wash my clothes and finish boxing up my room anyways, so yeah, thanks for dinner and keep the shirt or whatever—I don't need it. I'll see you next year, Rose, have a great summer."

I back out of her room and close the door behind me. I don't know what to do right now—my mind is scratchy and jagged, so I run to the laundry room. It's the only thing I know to do in this moment that will calm me down. I rip the wet clothes out of the washer and shove them into the dryer, turning the dial to whatever setting it lands on. It is only when the machine starts to rumble that I feel like I can finally breathe.

I lean forward on the washer, placing my elbows on the metal top, and rest my head in my hands.

What the fuck is wrong with me? I never should have agreed to help her pack. The second she showed up at my door, I should have hopped in a cab and gone straight to Lucy's. I cannot be near Rose. I cannot trust my instincts when I'm around her. I have wanted Rose so acutely that I misinterpreted all those flirty moments and playful banter as proof she has feelings for me too, but she wasn't flirting with me in particular. That's just who she is. Rose and I will not be together. And the worst part is *I fucking knew this* six weeks ago. So why the fuck does it hurt so much worse now?!

I slam my fists on top of the dryer and release the guttural cry that has been coursing through me. I take a deep breath in and as I let it out, I let go of the frustration, the embarrassment, the disappointment. Those are feelings I have no use for, so I shove them down deep, locking them away in that old familiar vault.

There's a shuffling noise coming from down the hall and I hear Rose open the door to the laundry room. She stays there, in the doorway behind me, but I don't turn around. I can't face her. "Please go away, Rose," I say firmly.

I hear her take another step toward me. "I'm sorry, Elliot. I know you don't want to talk about it but if I don't get this off my chest right now it's going to haunt me forever," she begs.

I say nothing.

I do nothing.

I want her to go, I *will* her to go, but she doesn't. Instead she takes another step toward me. She's close enough behind me now, close enough that I can feel the heat coming off her body. I refuse to turn around. Why won't she just leave me alone? This is mortifying as it is, I don't need to *talk through it*. I don't need to hear any of it. She takes another small step and rests a hand on my shoulder. "Elliot—" she says and that does it. I asked her nicely to leave me alone and clearly that didn't work. Everything I'm feeling boils over and now I'm just pissed off.

I spin around and face her with fire in my eyes. "What, Rose?! What do you want?!"

"You. I want *you*," she says and the world stops spinning. "You are stubborn and frustrating and you know exactly how to push my buttons but whenever we're together all I can think about is what it would be like to kiss you, to touch you, to taste you." She throws her hands behind her head, her voice overcome with emotion as she goes on. "I knew the moment I met you I was in trouble, so I tried to keep my distance, I tried to push you away. I scolded you and I lectured you and I even made you take those string lights down—which were not a fire hazard, by the way—but nothing worked. And I know I shouldn't be telling you any of this, I know you don't feel the same way and the last thing I want to do is burden you with a one-way love, but I had to say it, out loud, just this once. I want you beyond reason and with my whole heart."

Rose finally stops talking.

She is out of breath and out of words.

But I, on the other hand, know exactly what needs to be said.

"Are you serious?" I pause. I look at her in disbelief. And then I take a careful, slow step toward her. "You mean to tell me, right here and right now, that I could have kept the fairy lights up this *whole time*?"

"What?" Rose cries out. She looks desperate and worried. "No—I mean, yes, I mean—UGH!—What I mean is—"

And then, I close the distance between us. I press my body into hers, our lips touch and it is heaven and earth and everything in between. I kiss her hard and deep. She pushes me back up against the vibrating washer, her hands tug on my hair and I wrap my arms around the small of her back as I pull her into to me.

After a moment we part, her lips swollen and wet as she asks, "Are you sure?" I cradle her face in my hands and trace the tip of my thumb along her jawline and over her bottom lip.

"I'm sure," I whisper. And I am.

● ● ●

I know you are dying to find out what happens next. You're probably all *Rose is going to be in New York all summer! She's studying abroad next semester! What are you gonna do!?!?!* And the truth is, I don't know what's going to happen but I do know this: I did not go through all the shit this year just so I can fuck it all up over summer break. I'm done winging it. I'm done half-assing things. As of today, I am officially no longer a freshman. It's time to start full-assing things. So, here's what Rose and I did on our last day together:

1   I immediately called Izzy and got her to delay picking me up so I could have a few extra hours with my girlfriend.[88]

2   We made out on every single floor of the Little Building.

3   We searched for summer movie production internships in New York and created a list of all the ones I'm going to apply for in the next few days.

4   Since I missed the deadline to apply to study abroad, Rose called the director of the Kasteel Well program and switched it so she'll be spending her spring semester next year in the Netherlands. Now we get to spend next fall together.

5   We made two PowerPoint presentations for my parents on why they should let me

---

88 THAT'S RIGHT. I SAID **GIRLFRIEND**.

spend part of my summer in New York. One presentation is in case I get accepted for an internship and I need to convince them to let me take it. And the other presentation is in case I don't get an internship. It's just a bunch of old memes and a shameless video slide of me begging them to let me visit Rose for a week . . . or two or three or four.

6   We continued to pack all of Rose's crap but she has so much stuff, I gave up and instead made her a PowerPoint presentation on why she should own less shit. But then she pulled out her Trinity costume from *The Matrix* and I concluded the presentation by taking back everything I had just said.

7   We said goodbye to each other in the most epic way possible but I'm not gonna tell you about that. Some things are between me and my girlfriend.[89]

---

89 My girlfriend. *My girlfriend.*

EPILOGUE

THE NEXT DAY, IZZY PICKS ME UP IN BOSTON AND WE
set out on the twelve-hour drive back to Cincinnati. My phone
vibrates when we're somewhere in the middle of Nowhere, Fly
Over State and I get a text from Lucy.

> **Lucy:** What happened? Did you survive the night?
>
> **Me:** 😌
>
> **Lucy:** WHAT DOES THAT MEAN? WHAT DOES
> THAT MEAN?!??!?!?!

My phone buzzes again and I think it's Lucy pleading for
more details about my night, but when I look down, it's a text
from Rose.

> **Rose:** Did you get off okay?
>
> **Me:** Which time? Last night or this morning? 😌
>
> **Rose:** Stop! You're going to give me tender
> turkey again.
>
> **Me:** It's chicken, Rose. Tender CHICKEN. 🐓
>
> **Rose:** You're so weird.

Me: Fuck, I miss you already. How is that possible?

Rose: I'm just that good.

Me: Yeah you are.

Rose: Call me when you get home?

Me: Definitely.

Rose: xxxxxxxxxxx

Me: 🐓💗🐓💗🐓💗🐓💗🐓💗🐓💗🐓[90]

---

90 The end.

CREDITS

First and foremost, to my personal chef, Sean: thank you for feeding me. I lur you.

I will be forever grateful to Joanna Volpe for believing I could do this, even when all I had to show her at our first meeting was one very raunchy chapter. Jo and the New Leaf team have been in my corner since day one, and I am incredibly lucky to be working with them.

If you finished reading this book and you have had the thought, *wow, that was a good book*, you have Maggie Lehrman to thank for that. She's the editor who uncovered all the hidden depths I didn't know this story had. I am a better writer today because of her.

The tricky thing with acknowledgments is there's going to be people you'll forget or people you'll meet along the road to publication who support you in ways that are absolutely deserving of recognition but you already submitted your acknowledgments and it's too late to add them. Therefore, to all those I forgot to include because I'm writing this at 2 A.M. and all those I haven't met yet who are future champions of *Fresh*: I will find a way to thank each and every one of you personally. You know who you are. I love you all!

THE INCREDIBLE CREW
BEHIND FRESH

Agent	Joanna Volpe
Editor	Maggie Lehrman
Editorial Assistance	Emily Daluga
Publisher	Andrew Smith
Cover Design & Art	Hana Anouk Nakamura & Noah Camp
Production	Erin Vandeveer, Kathy Lovisolo
Managing Editorial	Marie Oishi, Shasta Clinch, Sara Brady, Margo Winton Parodi
Marketing & Publicity	Kim Lauber, Patricia McNamara O'Neill, Megan Evans, Mary Marolla, Jenny Choy
Sales	Elisa Garcia & her team!
The New Leaf Team	Jordan Hill, Veronica Grijalva, Victoria Hendersen, Pouya Shahbazian, Katherine Curtis, Hilary Pecheone, Kate Sullivan, Meredith Barnes, Abbie Donoghue, Jenniea Carter, Suzie Townsend, Madhuri Venkata, Patrice Caldwell

FRIENDS & FAMILY TO WHOM
I OWE MANY FAVORS

Favorite Person	Sean
Best Dog (sometimes)	Olive
Seestors	Val, Smeek Master 2000
Daily Source of Entertainment	Eric & Baby Leo
My Soulmates	Alien #3, Jamie, Rebecca, Sarah
Forever Work Wives	Aubry PF & Emily Butler
NYC & PDX Squads	Maggie, Meaghan, Lizard, Ku, Reb, Jess, Kristen, Ali, Monica
Emerson Mafia (Friend Edition!)	Maggie, Adam, Dylan, Claire, Sylve, Brendan, Jesse, Savasti, Sa'iyda, Kathryn
The Person Who Introduced Me To YA	Kristan
My Aunties	Andrea, Carrie, McCrystle, Alice
Families Who ~~Tolerate~~ Support Me	Wood, Willis, Kotchka & Tesmond
To Whom I Owe My Good Looks	Mom, Nana, Papa, Pappy, Mimi
The Seven Hills Crew	Maggio, Emily, Ashleigh, Meg, Susie, Sarah & Ms. O'Brien.
Person I Miss Most But Am Glad Is Not Around to Read Those Sex Scenes	Dad

FRIENDS & COLLEAGUES TO WHOM I OWE MANY DRINKS

The Brave Ones Who Read *Fresh* First
: Gayle Forman, Veronica Roth, Danielle Paige, Abigail Hing Wen, Sara Farizan, Adam Silvera

Author Cheer Squad
: Elissa Sussman, Preeti Chhibber, Eric Smith, Sara Raasch, Sarah Enni, David Arnold, Kim Liggett, Kami Garcia, Z Brewer, Farrah Penn, Dahlia Adler, Ayana Gray, Kosoko Jackson, Robbie Couch

Emerson Mafia (Author Edition!)
: Katie Cotugno, Taylor Jenkins Reid, Maureen Goo, Sasha Alsberg

Publishing People I Love
: Matthew Sciarappa, Dulce Rosales, DJ DeSmyter, Melissa Lee, Rachel Strolle, Pam Pho, Gaby Salpeter, Kat Salazar & everyone at Oni Press!

Team Epic Reads
: Alex, Colleen, Shazmin, Nina, Emily, Kate, Martha, Natalie, Meghan, Michael

Special Shout Outs
: Lottie! Liv! Sophia! Fizza! Rihna! Javi!

And finally . . . to the best community in the world:

There are so many bloggers, bookstagrammers, booktubers, booksellers, booktokkers, and book nerds in the YA community who have supported me since the early days of Epic Reads. Thank you for book shimmying with me all these years!

This one is for you.

Holy shit! You're reading this? Not only did you finish the story and read the acknowledgments, you also flipped the page hoping, against all odds, that there would be something else for you to read. Maybe you had so much fun reading this that you aren't quite ready to move on? That's okay, I know the feeling, but I'm sorry to say that it's time for us to part ways! It's time for you to start reading another book because if you don't, you'll get a book hangover, and we all know how annoying book hangovers are. So, go on! Get out of here! And don't worry, if in a few days or weeks or years you want to come back and read me again, I'll be here, waiting. Until next time . . .

Ha!

I knew you'd flip the page to see what else would be here.

The book is over!

For real this time!